IN THE COLD SHADOW

IN THE COLD SHADOW

ARTHUR WEIGOLD

For my brother Bobby, who lived the hard truths of New York's cold shadows

1

LAS VEGAS BY THE SEA

A falling body's acceleration to terminal velocity is calculated at thirty-two feet per second squared, depending on the drag of air density and wind resistance against loose clothing. The body falling on this particular night, accelerating through the thick summer air of Manhattan, was dressed in a white shirt, Italian loafers, and pale linen slacks that rippled in the wind as the limp figure plummeted earthward.

The body landed on the roof of a black limousine idling by the curb outside The Polo Bar, blowing out the car's windows and snapping the neck of its Russian immigrant driver as he sat waiting for his clients in the air conditioning, listening to the Yankee game. He had been in America less than six months; it was his second week on the job.

The old man's hands trembled slightly as he unfolded the small paper packet to reveal a sparkling diamond. The stone dazzled as Murray delicately picked it up with a pair of tweezers and held it under the intense white light of the LED lamp that stood on the glass display case. Its brilliant fire refracted the light, fragmenting the rainbow like a laser light show and producing for Murray the effect he desired. It was Murray's performance, one he had perfected over many years, and Michael was suitably impressed, though he did his best to hide it, trying to stay ahead of the wily merchant.

"Nice," Mike said, at something of a rare loss for words. "How much?"

Murray glanced at his customer with a knowing smile. "It took God ten million years to make it, machinery as big as this building to dig it up, and hundreds of hours of cutting and polishing to bring out its brilliance, and all you gotta say is 'nice'? It's not just 'nice,' Michael. It's more than nice, it's stunning," Murray said in a heavy Yiddish accent, never at a loss for words.

"Okay, yes . . . it is," Mike stammered, feeling a little outmaneuvered. "How much?"

"Michael, money in these things doesn't matter. When she sees this her eyes will open wide, and her heart will open too. It's a symbol of your love for her. She's the greatest woman in the world, no?" Murray smiled as he adjusted the yarmulke on his mostly bald pate. "You never want to risk her saying no. She could, ya know," said

Murray, now in rare form. "Nothing is for certain with women."

"She could have another guy after her," he continued. "It's possible. What if his is bigger than yours—I'm talking about the diamond, that is," Murray said with a wink and perfect stand-up timing. "Whaddya got then?"

"Yeah, Murray, you're right. Nothing is certain with women. But I have no doubts about Courtney—she loves me. That I know. She's not saying no. How much?"

Murray rubbed his scraggly gray beard. "For this kind of stone? Three carats plus. Perfect cut and color. No flaws, and all God's good work. I'll give you a deal, because I like you and you've sent me some nice people from that firm of yours. For you, forty-five thousand."

"Murray, come on, you could do better than that. Fifteen thousand a carat? Rubenstein is talking ten to twelve thousand per." Mike shrugged his shoulders and delivered his best what-can-you-do for-me look.

"Michael, forgive me, but please don't be a schmuck. Inferior goods—schlock, that's what he is selling. Not this quality. I defy you to match this kind of stone for any less. Go ahead, I trust you. Take this stone to any counter here and ask them what it's worth. Not a penny less than fifty thousand. Guaranteed. Don't listen to that schmendrick Rubenstein."

"All right, I'll give you forty," Mike said, enjoying the challenge of the exchange.

"Oy vey, at forty I'm losing money. Michael, in life it's important that you're not a guy who knows the price of everything but the value of nothing." Murray stared at Mike for a long time. "Give me forty-three, no taxes. I'll even throw in the setting. I got a hundred of them here."

Without waiting for an answer, Murray reached into the display case and brought out a black velvet tray of stoneless engagement rings, their empty prongs reaching up like so many crab claws. "Here, take your pick. We got platinum, eighteen-carat white gold. Nobody uses yellow gold anymore. We can have it set for you by this afternoon."

Mike stood for a minute examining the settings, missing Murray's classic sales misdirection of not waiting for a yes but changing the subject to the settings and moving right into closing the sale.

"Here's one of our most popular," Murray said, as he saw the close at hand.

"Yeah, I like that one. Simple, clean, and classic, like her." Mike thought briefly about Courtney and her arresting good looks, her long legs and blonde hair. "Yeah, Murray, that's beautiful. I'll take it. Is that platinum?"

"Yes, of course. Only the best for you, Michael."

"Can I give you a check?"

"Why, you like maybe I should pay more taxes?" Murray said with a comic flourish. "We don't accept personal checks, only certified or cash, but, for you, make it out to cash, no problem. You want it today?"

"No, that's okay." Mike reached into an inside pocket for his checkbook. "I'll pick it up tomorrow. Not popping the question for a while yet—our anniversary—but I want to be ready."

"Mazel tov. We'll have it all polished and set for you."

As he was writing, Mike's cell rang. "See you tomorrow," he said to Murray as he tore off the check and started walking. He clicked into the call.

"Hello," he said, straining to hear.

"Mike, dude, where are you?" It was Joey D'Antonio, his best friend and coworker. "We gotta get together and talk about the Sandoval deal. Those guys are coming in tomorrow, and we got to get straight with our numbers. We got a lot of homework to do."

"Joey, relax. I know, it's under control. I had Lara run a spreadsheet for us. I gave her numbers this morning. It's probably done by now. I'm over on Forty-Seventh Street getting the ring. I'll be back in fifteen. We got this, amigo, no problemo."

"Well, shit. Get yer ass over here, baby. I don't know whether to kiss ya or shoot ya, but this is cutting it close. Do I need to remind you this is our biggest deal yet and I'm not ready? No fucking around. These guys are close and asking serious questions," Joey said.

"You're covered, mi amigo. See ya—I mean, adios." Mike clicked off and headed into the maelstrom of midtown Manhattan. His mind was picking through a thicket of issues surrounding his biggest deal to date and polishing his closing pitch. But, at the moment, his pending engagement was most prominent. Without losing a step on the crowded street, he dialed the St. Regis and asked for the banquet manager.

"Hello, this is Molly," a perky voice answered.

"Molly, hi. This is Mike McGowan. I'm only a few blocks away and I think I've got to see the room again. Have you got time for me today?"

"Oh, yes, Mr. McGowan. Come on over. I'm free right now."

"Great and, ah, call me Mike. I'll be there in five minutes."

He turned up 5th Avenue and half-ran the few blocks to 55th Street. Though he was in good physical shape, Mike was puffing by the time he arrived. He was greeted by a professional looking Molly, with her tailored skirt, white blouse, and smiling Irish eyes. She took him to the ballroom on the top floor.

"How many guests are you thinking of having, Mr. McGowan—er, Mike?"

"If it were completely up to me, I'd say fifteen, maybe twenty, no more. This room would probably be a little too big. Probably the back room of McSorley's would be fine," he said with a laugh. "But with big Irish-Scottish families on both sides, friends, associates, businesspeople, and assorted hangers-on, I'd say more like two hundred and fifteen."

"Well, that would be about the limit for this room, but we could certainly accommodate your guests, and we'd be happy to help you in any way we can. I know we can create a beautiful event for you," Molly said, smiling.

Mike looked around at the gilded chandeliers, the hand-painted ceiling, and the silk curtains. It seemed like a scene out of some period movie about Versailles. He pictured his friends drinking at the bar in black tie. *Even some of the rowdy boys would be on their best behavior*, he thought. Everyone would be impressed with the grandeur of the setting. It fit into his image of his new station in life. He was on the verge of making his first really big deal. And he believed everything in his life from this day forward was about to take a quantum leap upscale. Not that by any standard measure he wasn't doing well right now. But since moving over from Citi to Morgan he'd gone into another gear, and it all was coming together. The Sandoval deal would put him on the map.

"Has your fiancée seen the ballroom yet?" asked Molly, shaking him out of his reverie.

"No, not yet." He looked at Molly and smiled. "But we've talked about this place for a long time. It holds a special meaning to her, almost like a fairy tale."

"And she's not my fiancée yet," he continued. "In a few weeks hopefully, and you'll be on the top of my call list if she says yes."

"Well, I'm sure you'll get your 'yes.' I'll be pulling for you. But, please, call me whenever you like. We'll make it a wonderful wedding for you both," said Molly. She handed Mike her business card.

Mike looked at his Rolex. "Oh, shi—I gotta go." As he headed down the hall his cell buzzed. He picked it up as he pressed the button for the elevator.

"Joey? Joey, I'm on my way. Had one quick stop, dude. Coming now. Gonna lose you in the elevator." He clicked off as the gilded doors closed.

As he got off at the lobby he looked toward the back room. The King Cole Bar. He couldn't resist having just one scotch to calm his frazzled nerves. He stared at the Maxfield Parrish mural with its smiling king, ordered a Macallan neat, and thought about his future. He got back to the office thirty minutes later.

"Man, where the hell have you been? I'm dying here," Joey said in a high voice that he often used when stressed. He waved a red folder. "Where the fuck did you get these numbers?"

"Okay, dude, chill. Step into my office and I'll get you up to speed." Mike loosened his silk tie and opened the collar on his white Oxford shirt. He pulled a leather-covered chair from the corner and motioned to a red-faced Joey to sit.

"Joey, these are our projections. They're based on our estimates of revenues in the first three years of operation. There are a lot of assumptions in there, but I can justify them—mostly. I know it may seem a little over the top, but honestly if things go right those numbers may be low. We could do much better than what I'm projecting."

"I know they're projections, but to do these numbers, these hotels would have to be some of the most successful casinos in the world," Joey said.

"Exactly. That's what we're selling them. They will be.

You gotta believe that. If we don't believe it, they won't, and investors won't. None of it will fly," Mike said.

"They've never run casinos before. How the fuck—"

"Stop right there. Don't let that doubt slip in, no way. You can't let them feel any of that. They want to believe. They really do. It's our job to help them believe. Show them the way. Mexico has never had casinos on this scale before. Now they think the government is ready, that it could work. And it can. Why not? Think about three thousand rooms on the beach. A first-rate hotel with a 3500 square-foot casino—like seven football fields. A dozen pools, cabanas, a huge spa, white sand, blue water. And that's just the beginning. In the future, maybe a Disney or a golf course right next door. They have the option on the land right now." Mike took a breath. "What's the one thing missing in Las Vegas?"

Joey, who had heard it all before, tried to answer, but Mike didn't wait. "Water! Big water—the ocean. They got the desert. We got the ocean. I don't care how big their pool is, ours is bigger." Mike took a long drink of Fiji Water as Joey smiled at the familiar refrain.

"If they did it in China, we can do it in Cancún," he continued. "All of North and South America will be flying to the Mexican Riviera to gamble, with lots of attractions for the kids too. Four hours from New York. Two hours from Miami. Sixty minutes from Dallas. No more spring breakers. The high rollers will be hitting town, baby. Sun, sand, and craps. Las Vegas by the sea, only better. It can't miss." Mike spread out his arms and turned his palms upward. The gesture seemed vaguely religious, and classic Mike McGowan. Like all great salesmen, he believed every word. He was his own best customer.

Joey sat in amazement. Mike's belief and his excitement were irresistible. The deep-set blue eyes and strong jaw inspired confidence and somehow managed to wipe away all doubt. His pitch flowed and sunk in. Mike believed and made Joey believe too. That's why they were partners.

Joey smiled and looked down with a sly grin. "I gotta get myself a little more familiar with the numbers you're proposing. Ya know, if you can keep a straight face so can I, but please don't oversell it. I'll check out these calculations, make sure there are no gaps in your projections. You . . . you just keep selling. This shit just may work. I'll take this home with me and look it over. I'll be ready for the morning."

"Beautiful, baby. Beautiful," Mike said.

As Joey got up, shaking his head, Mike grabbed Joey by the shoulders, stopping him in his tracks.

"Joey, Joey—no doubts. None. Remember, keep it all positive. You gotta believe. Come on, dude . . . we're there."

Joey, with a half-grin and now nodding, closed the door behind him.

Mike leaned back in his leather chair and let his mind drift for a moment. *This can really work*, he thought.

"Sort of amazing that this has never been done before," he said to himself as he checked the time. The gleaming stainless watch was a birthday gift from Courtney, and it jogged his memory to call her. He scrolled to her number and sat upright.

"Honey, what's doing?" he said as she picked up breathlessly.

"Oh, God, Mike. So freaking busy today, you have no idea. One thing after another but I'm good. How about you, baby?"

"Well, right now I'm trying to stay frosty. We're all over this Sandoval deal. Tomorrow's the big day. It's make-it-or-break-it time. Just gotta stay focused and keep the troops in line."

"You've been circling this deal forever, Mike. You'll get there. I believe in you."

"That's all I need, babe. Won't see you tonight, though. Gotta save my thunder for the early morning light. And if all goes well, tomorrow night we'll be taking the clients to the Yankee game, so I'll let you know."

"That's fine, Michael. We'll celebrate your success over the weekend. And, oh, don't forget, our anniversary is coming. Three years since we met."

"Oh really, it is?" he said, smiling to himself. "I almost forgot. Glad you reminded me."

"Nice. You forgot?" Courtney, sounding slightly hurt.

"No, never, baby, just kidding. Maybe we'll have a special surprise. Ya never know."

"I hate those jokes, Michael," she said. "Don't tease me."

"Relax, kitten. You'll see," he said with a smile. "Gotta go. Call you later, love you." He clicked off.

"Me too," she echoed to a dead line.

2

LORD'S PRAYER

Mike arrived at his office at seven-thirty sharp carrying his usual Starbucks in one hand and Italian leather briefcase in the other. The offices were still half-empty but as usual the trading floor was abuzz with activity. Caffeinated traders, most of whom had been there since 5 a.m., were staring at screens, typing on keyboards, or speaking on Bluetooth devices that hung from their ears like cigarette butts, gesticulating to no one in particular. The usual tension and ringing cacophony prevailed for the macho crowd that loved the game. Most were young, sleeves rolled up; many stood upright for most of the day. Despite the jacked-up air conditioning, dark underarm patches were already forming on their custom shirts. It was no country for old men.

Mike figured his game would pay better in the long run and hopefully not burn him out, as trading had for so many before him. It doesn't help to make money fast and be a basket case by the time you're forty, drinking in the daytime, expanding your waist, and losing your hair. The men he looked out on from the comfortable confines of the conference room were mostly new recruits; the old guard had been replaced or defeated, casualties of war. There wasn't a female trader on the floor. It was an exclusively male gladiator pit, and the testosterone was flowing this morning with its usual ferocity. The tension would continue to build all day until the closing bell. It was a marathon at sprint speed, with no letup, every single day.

Mike's phone vibrated. It was a group text from his secretary, Lara; the Sandoval group was in the waiting room.

"Showtime," Mike said to an empty room.

Joey opened the door and stuck his head in.

"You ready?"

"Ready for what?" Mike said.

"The big show! They're here," Joey said, hitting the high notes.

"Who's here?" Mike, grinning.

"Oh—fuck you. Get it together, man. Let's go," Joey laughed.

"This is going to be easy. Watch and learn, baby, watch and learn," Mike said as they headed down the hallway.

Mike strolled in and greeted everyone with a firm handshake. His eyes scanned the room for a friendly grin but was met with a sense of tension from the all-business group of underlings who had accompanied Sandoval.

"Buenos días," he said.

"Good morning, Mike. Please excuse me, my friend, but here we speak English," Miguel Sandoval said. "We don't want any misunderstandings."

"I was hoping you'd say that. That is, after all, the extent of my Spanish vocabulary." Mike sat down at the long walnut table and waited for a smiling response.

When none came, he continued. "May I ask? What did you think of our proposal?"

"Well, we liked what we saw—that is, if we can believe your numbers. But that, for us, is not the most important thing on our minds right now." Sandoval pushed his tortoiseshell glasses against his aquiline nose with a manicured forefinger and leaned forward. He interlaced his immaculate hands on the table in front of him as he spoke.

"What I mean is, of course we want this venture to make money and numbers are important. But there's plenty of time for that. There's more to this deal. What's most important for us—our family, our country—is to symbolize a new approach toward business and tourism for Mexico. It must represent the pinnacle of 'clean hands' and first-class business savvy. We want to show the world that we are open for new and modern business ideas. We are not just another third-world nation caught up in a messy and endless drug war." Sandoval's tanned, unlined face emphasized the whiteness of his perfect teeth.

"This is just the beginning of the new Mexico," he continued. "The one that welcomes families, wholesome values, and capital from around the world for investment. We want to build an entirely new image for our country. One that opens the door to gambling but brings it to a world-class level. And this deal is the first big step."

Mike saw his opening. "Señor, excuse me, but that is exactly what we believe we can deliver here."

He stood up as he expanded on the point.

"You may not be aware that we are the ones who put Steve Wynn at the pinnacle of the gaming industry. I like to think it was our input that made him uniquely successful in this business. And his attitude was exactly like yours—that is, finance it right, bring in only top-level operators, and take the whole enterprise to a world-class level."

Mike leaned forward, hands on the table. "You may not know this, but we convinced him not to put retail in front of the Bellagio—a very risky move at the time. I don't have to tell you, that is some prime retail frontage on that strip, and Wynn was very skeptical of foregoing that rental income opportunity. But we took the position that it would cheapen his hotel and reduce the uniqueness of his vision. We advised him to bring a new approach to Vegas, and he eventually agreed. He came to see the logic of keeping the entire experience upscale and completely different. He consulted with engineering experts, and then he put one of the most expensive and spectacular fountains in the world in front of the hotel. It drew people from all over and dramatically increased hotel traffic. To this day, he thanks us for that advice and for keeping his whole operation at the highest level. We believe we can do that for you, for your government, and for your country."

"That's very impressive, Mike. And no, I didn't know that. I've always been amazed at how entirely first class that hotel is. It's a world unto itself and it succeeds on every level. That is exactly what I have in mind, and I know that is what my father-in-law, the president, wants for the country."

"Miguel, I know we can do that for you." Mike sat down again and looked at Joey with a smile. The air in the room seemed to lighten.

"Mike, I want to make a call to the president today. He won't want numbers—he's a man that understands people. My sense is that he'll like you and your ideas. He will want to meet you in person if we go ahead with this, perhaps in a few weeks. Is that okay with you?" Sandoval asked.

"It's more than okay. It would be my honor," Mike said.

"Good. For now, I'd like my numbers people to sit down with your staff and take a closer look at your projections. Can they stay here and work together? Unfortunately, I must leave now," Sandoval said.

"Yes, of course." Mike was surprised that his part of the meeting was ending so quickly.

"What time is good for me to call you tomorrow?" asked Sandoval, standing up.

"We're here for you, sir. Anytime is good, but afternoons are usually quieter."

"Good then. It's set. I'll call tomorrow, in the afternoon."

"Before you go, sir. We have a little surprise," Mike said. "Do you like baseball?"

"Absolutely. My favorite," Sandoval replied with a broad smile.

"Great. The Yankees are playing Boston tonight at the stadium. They have a sensational new pitcher who, you may know, is Mexican, Alfonso Fernandez. We have a suite at the stadium and would like you to join us for the game."

"I'd love to," Sandoval said without looking at his associates, who had yet to utter a word. "I do know of him. He played in our minor leagues when he was young. I'll mention it to the president. He loves baseball too. I'm sure we could arrange to meet Alfonso in the locker room. Would you like that?"

"Yes, sir," said Mike. "We'd like—we'd like that very much." He glanced at Joey who smiled and nodded.

"Good. Then, gentleman, I'll see you tonight at the stadium," the handsome Mexican said.

"Please call me when you arrive. We'll have security escort you up to the suite," Mike said.

Mike and Joey walked Sandoval to the elevator. After the doors closed, they high-fived in the hallway.

"See? Simple," Mike said with a grin and upturned palms.

"How'd you come up with that Steve Wynn angle?" Joey asked.

"Creative license. I know Morgan provided some of the financing on his deals, so I just figured we'd add a little flare to that."

"Amazing. I always wondered why he put that huge lake in front of the hotel. Seemed like a waste to me. I think you explained it perfectly, even if it wasn't true."

"Maybe it is," Mike said with a wink. "Now get in there and convince them that the numbers work."

Mike's phone rang. "Hello."

"Michael, it's Murray. Your ring is ready. When you coming by?"

"Great, thanks, Murray. I'll be there in fifteen minutes."

"Good. I'll wait for you. You're gonna love it," said the merchant.

"Gotta go, baby," Mike said to Joey as he turned and slapped the elevator button. "Gonna see a man about a ring."

The four men kneeled in a circle on the gray-painted concrete floor of the visitors' locker room in Yankee Stadium, holding hands, heads bowed. Sandoval recited the Lord's Prayer in perfect English, then finished with the sign of the cross and an emphatic, "Amen." They all stood up, smiled, and shook hands.

"Amigo, we wish you luck tonight. Show them what our best Mexican talent can do," said Sandoval to the pitcher. "El Presidente will be watching this game on his television in the presidential palace. He told me to tell you that God will be guiding your pitches."

The barrel-chested Fernandez looked humbled and responded with a meek half-smile.

"Gracias, Señor Sandoval. I do my best for our country. Viva, Mexico," he said in broken English.

Joey and Mike wished the now teary-eyed Fernandez good luck and each shook his thick hand before leaving the locker room with Sandoval. They headed up to the suite to watch the game.

Within an hour-and-a-half, Fernandez had delivered on his promise. He struck out eight batters with a combination of whistling fast balls and slyly disguised sliders that would suddenly lose steam three quarters of the way to the plate and dive into the dirt. Red Sox hitters spent the evening glaring at him from the batter's box before walking off in disgust. By the time he was relieved at the end of the sixth, he'd held Boston to only two hits and no runs. When he stepped off the mound, he looked skyward and kissed the crucifix that hung on a gold chain around his neck. The Yankees went on to beat their nemesis 4-0. The stadium rocked with the sounds of Frank Sinatra singing "New York, New York."

As they rode down in the private elevator to the waiting cars, Sandoval smiled and turned to Joey and Mike. "That game was a symbol for me of what can come from our alliance," he said. "Today when I spoke to the president, he said he was eager to hear more from you.

He'd like you to come to Mexico City at the end of the month to sit down with him. We'll make all the arrangements. Will you be able to do that, gentlemen?"

Joey and Mike looked at each other. And then, to their embarrassment, they responded as one. "Yes, we'd love to," they chorused.

"Good. We'll set it all up." Sandoval's expression turned serious. "There are no guarantees here, but I think we can do business."

Once outside, Mike, who had been uncharacteristically quiet most of the night, said, "Señor Sandoval, we know this can work for you and for us. And we are the right people to get this done with you. We can absolutely deliver."

Sandoval smiled at Mike as he stood on the sidewalk next to his car. Three broad-shouldered men in black suits made a semicircle around them, forming a barrier from the rowdy throngs filing out of the stadium.

"I think so too, my friend. Remember, clean hands and world class. That's why I recommended you. We must have that. My people will call you tomorrow to make arrangements. Good night and God bless." Sandoval nodded and they all shook hands. Sandoval got into his black limo and was gone.

"Holy shit! I think this may actually happen," Joey said as the car disappeared into the traffic. "The fucking president of Mexico wants to meet us. Yes," he said, arms in the air.

"Told you, baby. And why not? We got the formula, we

got clean hands, and we can do this." Without hesitation, Mike said, "Let's celebrate. We deserve it."

"Mexican?"

"What else?"

3

CAN I TRUST YOU?

By the fourth tequila at Pablo's Cafe several blocks off River Avenue, Mike was more than buzzed. He'd also had several empanadas and a couple of Coronas to wash it all down, but now getting to the bathroom in the back of the adobe-colored dining room was somehow tougher than he had figured.

The place catered to a mostly local crowd. The jukebox blared with the brass horns of a mariachi band, and the wall decorations didn't go much further than a Mexican blanket or two and a few sombreros. Red-pepper string lights hung from the ceiling surrounding the bar, the wooden chairs were worn but brightly painted, and English was a decidedly second language. Hedge-fund types rarely found their way to this side of the tracks.

From his seat, Joey reached out a hand to steady his friend as Mike struggled to stand. "Don't worry, Joey. I'm fine. I don't need help to take a piss," Mike said, wobbling slightly.

As he headed toward the men's room, with a hand on some tables along the way, he came face to face with Larisia Diaz, a waitress skillfully carrying dishes to waiting customers.

He found himself staring at her and suddenly blurted, "You're the most beautiful woman I've ever seen. Will you marry me?" At that moment, abruptly and without any thought, Mike reached into his shirt pocket and pulled out his business card. He placed it in her hand, under one of the dishes she held.

"Please, call me . . . really, really . . . you're beautiful." He stumbled over the words. He leaned a shoulder against the wall for stability and stared at her with a crooked smile.

She looked at him like she was about to laugh at his awkward and oddly amusing pickup line. Then she rebalanced her dishes and headed toward her tables without saying a word.

Mike stood, dumbfounded and staring, for a long moment. He suddenly felt a strong slap on his back that jolted him back to the world.

"She's a hot one, eh, Mike?" Joey said. "Men's room is this way, Romeo. Better leave that one alone. You're almost married, remember."

"Ah, yeah . . . just looking." Mike felt in his breast pocket the bulge of the ring box that he'd picked up earlier. "Yes, you're right."

After a few more tequilas, Joey had to call it a night. "Come on, man. I'm done. We both gotta get up in the morning. There's work to do. Fucking great night, pal. My buy."

"You're buying? I gotta write this shit down. Never happened before, a fucking miracle," teased Mike.

"I'll remind you tomorrow, don't worry," Joey said.

"Yeah, if you can remember anything that is. Hang on a minute, I gotta take another piss. Be right back." Mike headed back to the bathroom, hoping to see the stunning waitress.

He got his wish. Larisia stood in the back, arms folded, head cocked to one side. Her raven hair, swept into a ponytail, gleamed with a deep chestnut sheen in the dim light. He walked up to her out of some instinct, trying to think of something to say. She didn't give him the chance.

"I don't call men, especially drunk ones, so take your card back." She shoved the business card into his shirt pocket and slapped her hand on his chest for good measure. Then, unexpectedly, she smiled. "But, if you want to call me when you're sober, my number's on the back."

Mike was rattled. "Ah, yeah, I'd like to see you ... er, I mean I will. Thank you."

He struggled for words. All the Irish charm, the blarney and the bullshit, fell away and he stood there silent and confused in the face of this enticing dark beauty. It had never happened to him before, and he couldn't understand why. It wasn't the tequila, which normally made him more gregarious and fearless. She had the opposite effect on him. It was a first. He was at a loss.

"My name is Mike, by the way," was about all he could get out. Awkwardly, he reached out to shake her hand.

"I'm Larisia. Nice to meet you, Mike." The touch of her hand sent an electric thrill down his spine that lit his crotch.

"That is a very beautiful name."

"Thank you. I'm named after my mother," she replied with a disarming innocence.

He stared and after an awkward moment of silence, blurted, "Ah, I gotta go. Get my friend home. He's not feeling too well right now. But it was really nice to meet you too, Larisia." He made a sign with his fist to his cheek, pinky and thumb extended, like calling on a phone, and mouthed the words, "I'll call you" as he walked away. He instantly regretted doing it and felt like a jerk by the time he got back to Joey, who now had his head down on the table.

"Man, let's get outta here. We gotta cut back on the booze. Startin' to lose it," Mike said, grabbing Joey by the arm, wrapping it around his shoulder, and walking him out the front door.

"Mike, what the fuck? You okay?" Joey said as he stumbled along with his friend's support.

"Me? It's you, man. You were out cold. I gotta get you outta here and into some fresh air. Let's walk."

With arms on each other's shoulders, they walked,

slightly off-kilter, for a few blocks toward River Avenue and the stadium. The night air felt soft and the streets were empty. As they rambled along, the putrid smell from a passing garbage truck wafted their way. Joey felt a nauseating wave hit him. He broke away and he leaned over a sewer grate, steadying himself on a parking sign pole, and upchucked his stomach's contents.

After a few wrenching minutes, he came up for air. "Ah, shit. That was fucking brutal. But I feel better. I'm calling an Uber . . . going home." Joey leaned unsteadily against a car and wiped his face with a cocktail napkin from Pablo's.

"Good idea," Mike said.

"What are you doing?" Joey asked.

"I'm okay. You're going to the West Side, I'll get my own car downtown soon as I get you going," Mike replied, trying to sort out his lingering feeling for the dark beauty he had just encountered.

Within ten minutes Joey was on his way home. Mike's last view of him through the side window of the Toyota was with his head back, smiling, eyes closed. Mike clicked open his phone to dial a car. He hit the Uber app and started to type in his destination. At that very moment the phone powered off with a faint musical sound.

"Ah, shit. Always the fucking way . . . now I got no choice," he said to himself as he walked up the block toward the elevated train. Though he hadn't done it consciously, his drunken route took him right past Pablo's and, at that moment, Larissa stepped outside, getting off from her shift. He saw her coming out the side door and held his breath as she walked onto the sidewalk. She stopped under the streetlight, looked up, and saw him standing there.

"You came back for me?" she said.

"Ah, well, sort of . . . that is, yes . . . I did. Couldn't help myself." Mike shifted from one foot to the other.

"That doesn't sound very convincing," she said. "I hear a lot of things. Don't believe them all."

He was thrown by her perceptiveness and her vulnerability. Her dark eyes looked wide and innocent. Her thick dark hair, now loose and down to her shoulders, shimmered in the dim light. She seemed to know him somehow. He was completely disarmed by her sensitivity and her sincerity.

"Ah, well, really? I was a little lost and didn't realize exactly where I was so . . . no . . . I actually didn't come back this way for you. I was trying to find my way to the train." He reflected for a minute. "I guess I shouldn't have said that. I'm sorry. But really, you were on my mind, and you have no idea how happy I am to see you now."

"Now that I can believe." She smiled at his unexpected vulnerability.

"Are you done for the night?"

"Yes. Long day for me. I'm done." She sighed. "Going home."

"Would you mind if I walked with you?" He felt like a kid in school.

"I don't live near the train."

"That's fine," he said.

"Ah, okay. Can I trust you to behave?"

"Yes, of course. Scout's honor," he said and held up three fingers.

"What is that—Scout's honor?"

"Oh that? It's an expression of honesty, like in the Boy Scouts."

"Were you a Boy Scout?"

He thought for a long moment and felt ashamed. "No, I actually never was a Boy Scout," he admitted. "Never wanted to be one ... too nerdy."

"Okay. Now you're getting it. I like that," she said. "I know your first instinct was to say you were—maybe you would have gone into one of your Boy Scout adventures. But no, you were honest." She smiled, grabbed his hand, and started to walk. "Let's go."

He walked along with her and felt like he already knew her. Like they were somehow meant to walk along these streets to get reacquainted with each other from some other time. Here, at this moment, on the empty streets of the Bronx, he forgot about everything else in his life. This was all there was.

"Do you like baseball?" he asked after a few moments of silence.

"Yes, but don't have much time to follow it, not with my schedule," she said.

"It's a great game, been a fan all my life. I was at the game tonight and, just before the restaurant, met the new star pitcher for the Yanks. What a wonderful guy. Alfonso

Fernandez—Mexican. We prayed with him, can you imagine that? We kneeled in the locker room holding hands together and recited the Our Father with him. Quite a night," he said. "So now I have three very special things that have happened to me on this fateful night."

"Am I one of those things?"

"Yes, absolutely. You may be the most special."

"Ah, there you go again. Always selling, but charming." She smiled.

He was floored by her perceptiveness and completely captured.

"Have you been to any games this year? You live around here," he asked, changing the subject.

"I may live close to the stadium, but I've never seen a game, never been inside. Too expensive. No different than most people in this neighborhood," she explained.

"Then I've got to take you to a game one of these nights," he said without hesitation.

"Really? I'd love that." Then after a moment of thought, "You're not making this up too?"

"No, I'd love to take you, really."

"So, you prayed with this famous pitcher. Are you Catholic?"

"Yes . . . well I was brought up Catholic. But as my Irish mother would say, 'You've fallen away from the church, my son,'" Mike said, imitating her light Celtic brogue.

She giggled. "I guess my Mexican mother would say the same. Only in Spanish."

After a few moments Mike asked, "Is waitressing your full-time job? Ah, not that there's anything wrong with that."

"No, I'm a full-time student at Fordham. Got a scholarship. This is my last year. I'm getting my nursing degree. I only work at the restaurant at night. It's been a grind."

"Wow, I love nurses," slurred Mike. "I mean, they are so great. My sister's a nurse. A healer, really. I admire her. Madeline. She's just a tremendous person."

"Glad you think so. My mother is a nurse too, in Mexico. She's also a healer . . . my rock." She seemed suddenly sad but said nothing as the moment passed.

They arrived at her building and sat on the front steps for a moment in the warm summer night air. They looked at each other—an unexplainable connection. It ran deep.

She was the one to break the silence. "Would you like to come up for a coffee?"

"I'd love to," he said. He took her hand and kissed it with a gentlemanly flourish. "You're very beautiful, Larisia."

She laughed. "Don't try to charm me. You're not staying. I gotta get up in the morning for early rounds."

"No, never entered my mind. Ehh, well, maybe a little," he said, smiling.

She looked him straight in the eye. "Can I trust you?"

"Totally," he said. "The real question is, can I trust you?"

"Maybe," she replied, smiling as she led him up the stairs.

4

SÍ, MUCHO DINERO

Mike awoke with a start. He sat bolt upright and looked around at the small apartment. Eyes out of focus, the room was mostly shadows. A distant streetlight cast a dim amber glow through the half-closed blinds, spreading a striped pattern across their discarded clothing scattered on the floor. He was completely disoriented. A digital clock on the night table read 3:12 a.m. in bright red numerals. He looked over and saw Larisia sleeping next to him. It all came back.

Shit. I gotta get home.

He quietly slid off the side of the bed trying not to rustle the sheets while she floated in dreamland. He padded to the bathroom, picking up his clothes on the way. Quietly he closed the door and snapped on the light. He turned and stared into the mirror over the sink. In the milky fluorescence his reflected image looked worn and gray. Mike turned on the faucet and tried to wash away the telltale signs of a long night along with an abiding sense of guilt. After drying his face on a thin towel, he picked up his Italian suit jacket. The ring box fell out of the breast pocket. He opened it and Murray's sparkling diamond dazzled, managing to upgrade his dingy tiled surroundings.

"What the fuck am I doing," he said to himself. He snapped the box closed and put it back in his pocket.

He turned off the light, quietly opened the bathroom door and, with a quick glance to a sleeping Larisia, slipped out of the apartment into the hallway and down the stairs. The night air was moist and pungent. The Bronx streets were deserted. With no charge on his phone and no cab in sight, he was in for a long, five-block slog to the train.

As he traveled along the gritty streets, he thought of the evening that now seemed like a dream. He was amazed at how Larisia's dark beauty captivated him. How he was able to block out everything else in his life and indulge his impulses. It seemed easy for him. He tried to justify it all as a singular moment in time, an isolated event that would have no effect on anything else in his life. No one would know. No one should know. Nothing would change.

I should just toss this number like it never happened, he thought as he looked at his business card with her name and number scribbled on the back. He was unsettled, trying to sort out his deep connection to this exotic woman he'd just slept with. His blood still ran hot for her.

Approaching the corner of River Avenue, he saw what looked like a gypsy cab parked half in the shadows by the curb. He tucked the card back into his shirt pocket, leaned over, and tapped on the driver's side window with a crooked knuckle.

"You free? You speak English? I need a ride to Astor Place, in Manhattan," he said. "Do you know where that is?'

The driver seemed slightly startled as he lowered the window. "Ah, sí, amigo. I know where that is. Near St. Mark's . . . the East Village, right? Sí, no hay problema."

"Yes, that's it. Right there, that's what I need," Mike said, opening the rear door and sliding into the worn Naugahyde backseat. Once in back he caught the driver staring at him wide-eyed through the rearview mirror, which was decoratively hung with a small Mexican flag, a soccer ball keychain, and a fragrant cardboard pine tree.

Settling in and inhaling the redolence of a fake evergreen forest, Mike watched the front passenger door open as another man got in. He turned to Mike and pointed a small silver pistol at his face. Mike's heart skipped a beat as fear suddenly jacked up his awareness. Blood surged in his head as his first instinct was to lurch at the man and fight for his life. But he held back and focused on the gun and the tattooed hand that held it. Survival instincts fought with logic as his mind went into overdrive.

"Hola, señor. Don't do anything stupid. If you do, I will have to blow your fucking brains out. Okay, amigo?" The man broke into a half-grin that showed a gold tooth.

Mike's mind froze. A surge of adrenaline flowed into his bloodstream and he had a strong urge to bolt, but he remained motionless. He stared at his adversary and nodded. The driver rolled up the windows and locked the doors with a click.

"Bueno, we understand each other then. You're not going anywhere for a while, comprende?" the gunman said. "Nice suit. I saw it from a block away. Beautiful cut."

"What do you want?" Mike asked.

"Fuck you. Shut the fuck up. I do the talking, señor. You don't ask the questions. You just shut the fuck up unless I tell you to talk, okay?" said the gunman, brandishing the undersized weapon and glancing at the driver.

Mike nodded to both of them. After a long moment of tense staring, the craggy-faced gunman, seemingly satisfied with Mike's response, pointed to Mike's wrist. "Gringo. Que hora es? I mean, what time is it?"

"About 3:30," Mike replied.

"No, estupido, the time on your watch?" The gunman smirked.

Mike pushed up his sleeve and peered at his Rolex. "3:34 a.m."

"Oh, nice watch. Take it off, I want to see it," he said, waving his gun in Mike's face. His thin body and deeply lined features spoke of a hard life. His breath smelled of liquor and he reeked of marijuana.

Mike unsnapped the clasp and slid the watch over his broad knuckles. He handed it to the gunman.

"Very nice, amigo, very nice. So generous of you,

gracias, señor." The gunman slipped the watch on his bony wrist.

"Ah, no, that's a gift from my—"

Mike hadn't gotten the words out when he saw a sudden flash of light and felt the gun butt smack against his face. He heard the bones in his nose crack and he fell backward into the seat. Blood poured from both nostrils. His eyes watered and his head throbbed. He leaned over and cupped his hand to his face, trying to stop the blood. Red streams snaked through his fingers and down his arm.

"Didn't I tell you to shut the fuck up? I'll tell you when to talk. Don't make trouble, or it will get a lot worse than that, you fucking stupid gringo."

The driver turned around briefly with a sympathetic stare but did nothing. He then turned back and adjusted the rearview mirror upward as if he didn't want to watch. He spoke to the gunman and they argued in Spanish. The gunman prevailed and there was a momentary silence. Mike pressed his head against the back seat to stem the blood flowing from his nose and tried to stay focused.

The gunman turned back around to Michael. With the pistol in his hand resting on the back of the seat, he smiled. His gold tooth reflected in the low light.

"This doesn't have to be nasty, really. But you can only listen when your mouth is shut, so keep it shut. We just want your money. I don't want to kill you. Paco here is right," he said, and nodded toward the driver. "He wants to help you avoid pain. Just give us your money, señor, that's all we want and this will all go away."

"What is that in your top pocket?" the gunman asked, as he reached for the business card in Mike's shirt pocket. He pulled it out and read it.

"Michael McGowan. Is this you?" he asked.

Mike nodded.

"Good. You know how to shut up. You're learning your lesson," he said as he read from the card, "Morgan Stanley. Vice President. Ah, an investment banker. Paco, we have a rich man here." They both smiled. The gunman put the card in his pocket and said something to Paco in Spanish.

"Sí, mucho dinero," Paco laughed, as if sensing the tension had slightly abated. The gunman laughed with him, but his intensity had not changed.

"Give me your wallet," the gunman said.

Mike reached into his inside pocket and felt the ring box. He withdrew his hand and reached into his other pocket trying not to betray his fear at the thought of giving up the ring. He pulled out his alligator wallet and handed it to Paco. The driver opened it and pulled out the cash and Mike's Citibank debit card. The gunman grabbed the card and left the cash in Paco's hand. Paco threw back the wallet to Mike and gleefully started counting the cash.

"Whaddaya got there, a few hundred? I got a better idea." The gunman looked over his shoulder at Mike, who was leaning against the back seat and putting his wallet away, the blood flow from his nose finally subsiding.

"Miguel, we can do a lot better than this, can't we," he

said grinning. His countenance reminded Mike of a skeletal skull, with bare, oversized teeth, thin lips, and dark holes for eyes.

"You got a lot more than a few hundred in this account, don't you, amigo." The gunman held up the debit card. "Don't fucking lie to me. You got money in there and you're going to give it to us. And not just this shit few hundred. Real money, my friend, real money."

"I'll give you whatever I can." He barely got the words out when the gunman reached over the back of the seat and punched Mike in the face. The punch landed high on his cheekbone and drove him back into the seat. It jolted him, but it wasn't the hardest punch he'd ever felt. For the first time Mike could gauge the man's strength. The thought entered his mind that given the chance he could take this guy. He sat back up from the blow and pushed his hair back. He took a deep breath and stared at his tormentor.

"You give us what you got, or we'll beat the shit out of you. It would mean nothing to me to put a bullet in your fucking head right now, you gringo piece of shit. In fact, I'd love to, but I want you to do something for us, and if it goes okay, maybe we let you go. No mas. No problemo."

"Tell me. What is it? I'll give you my money. I just want this over," Mike said.

"We're gonna go down to the Citibank at 165th Street and you're gonna to pull five thousand out of that cash machine and give it to us. You do that and you go home. You fuck around with us and I'll kill you on the spot and throw your body in the fucking river. They'll never find you. You got that?"

"I don't think I can take that much out of a cash machine. They put a limit on it," Mike said.

"Don't try that bullshit with me, señor. We go in together and we'll see how much we can get, okay?"

Mike nodded silently, but his mind was on how to get this guy alone. He'd have a better chance then, but decided, *if they'll just take money, fuck it. Take it. It's not worth my life.*

They drove along the deserted streets. A police cruiser drove past them going the other way. They stopped at the light a half-block away. Michael had the urge to leap out of the car and run for his life but Carlos, almost reading his mind, stared at him and shook his head just slightly. Michael stayed frozen. The cruiser pulled away when the light changed and Michael's heart dropped into his stomach as their taillights faded into the black night.

At 165th Paco pulled over. The gunman got out and opened the back door. Mike stepped onto the sidewalk and suddenly felt weaker than he had anticipated. His legs were unsteady and his gait was wobbly. *A long night and a couple of shots to the head can do that to you.* They walked up to the bank. He slid his card into the entrance reader and was buzzed in.

At the ATM he punched in his code and his balance came up. Mike tried to block him out but the gunman standing next to him leaned over and read the number. "$106,348.34 on account and available. Muy bueno, señor."

The cash machine allowed no more than two thousand to be drawn out in one day. Mike took four separate withdrawals of five hundred each and then the account was frozen.

"There's nothing else I can do. Here's your money. I can't get out anymore," Mike said.

"Okay, amigo, you're right. Let's get back to the car. You did your part," said the gunman. "That's enough."

Mike was surprised. "You can just leave me here. I'll get back on my own," Mike said.

"No, come with us and we'll drop you off. We don't want you running off to the cops," he replied.

"I won't. I'll just go right home," Mike tried to sound offhand. But he realized this was ominous. He was running out of time.

"Don't worry. It's finito, señor. No mas. We're done with you. Just come back to the car now." He pulled the gun out of his pocket and stuck it in Mike's ribs. "Walk." Mike went reluctantly. As they walked, he watched the man closely, taking stock, imagining how he'd hold up against this guy if he had to fight for his life. His mouth was dry and his stomach churned. Somehow it all felt much worse, but Mike tried to hold on to the fading hope that they still might let him go.

As they got back to the car, Paco was waiting with the engine running. Feeling a dark pit of dread in his stomach, Mike climbed into the back seat and watched the gunman get in front. They sped off into the night.

"Where are you taking me?" Mike demanded. "We had a deal."

"Paco, pull over. We need to talk to Miguel here," the gunman said. They pulled to the curb on a dark side street off River Avenue. Paco turned off the engine.

The gunman turned around, leaned his gun hand on the back of the front seat, and pointed the pistol squarely at Mike's chest. "Señor, we have a small problem now. I was just thinking, we need a little more money than what you gave us here. Now I see you got a lot more in your account," he said, smiling at Paco. "I think what we do is we wait till morning and you're going to go into that bank and get us fifty thousand in cash. We'll go in with you just to be sure. After we get that money then we can let you go, just like we said. Comprende?"

"But that just won't work. They'll be suspicious. They won't just hand me fifty-grand in cash to carry out. Banks don't do that. It's bullshit. It won't fucking work! Nobody does that," Mike shouted, sensing this was the moment to bait his captor.

The gunman instantly swung the gun butt at Mike's face but this time Mike was ready. He pulled back. The gunman missed with his swing, and Mike grabbed his hand and tried to rip the gun from his grip. The gunman jerked forward, almost pulling Mike over the seat into the front.

Now half-standing, gaining leverage in the struggle, Mike sunk his teeth into the gunman's wrist. The pistol went off with a deafening blast. Mike's ears rang as the bullet hit Paco in the right eye and exited out the back of his head. Bits of Paco's macerated skull splattered across the dashboard and side window. His body sunk backward into a motionless heap wedged between the door and the steering wheel. Acrid gun smoke fogged the tight space, burning eyes and intensifying the struggle.

The gunman, stronger than Mike had thought, reached over with his other hand, grabbed Mike's hair, pulled him forward, and jammed his thumb into Mike's eye. Half-blind, Mike managed to wrench the gun free. He dropped back, raised the pistol, and fired at the blurry shape before him. The figure fell backward into the floor well, leaving a crimson spray on the inside of the windshield.

Mike turned around, pulled up the door lock, and flung open the door. He fell out of the car sideways and slammed his head onto the concrete. Half-dazed, he got up and ran down the street without looking back. He ran in panic for several blocks under the elevated train. Though he could barely see, he realized the 149th Street train stop was close. Sprinting in the shadows, he looked down at his blood-spattered hand and realized he still held the silver pistol. Without a thought, he threw it down a sewer grate at the corner of 151st Street and kept running.

Hearing the rumbling of an oncoming train, Mike took the steps up to the platform two at a time and hopped the turnstile just as the train rolled to a stop. The doors opened to an empty car. He dropped down into a corner seat and wiped his face with the inside of his jacket, which he then pulled tightly across his body. He felt the bulk of the ring box in his inside pocket and took a deep breath of relief. He put his head down, pulled up his collar, and didn't look up till his stop at Astor Place.

He nodded at the doorman as he headed straight to the elevator of his modern building. He fell face down on his bed and welcomed his exhausted sleep, drifting off just as the warm sun rose, chasing the cold shadows away from downtown Manhattan.

5

TWO SKELLS OFF THE STREET

M ike's landline rang, jolting him awake. It never
rang except for unwelcome sales calls and he
tried to ignore it, pulling the pillow over his head. After
ten rings he picked it up.

"Hello?"

"Oh Christ, Mike, what the fuck are you doing? You okay?
I've been calling your cell all morning." An excited Joey was
once again hitting the high notes. "We need you here."

"Oh, shit, man, you have no idea." Mike touched his
throbbing cheekbone and winced. "But, yeah, I'm okay—
just forgot to charge my phone," Mike said, slurring his
words through swollen lips. "I'm sorry, I'm too fucked up
to get in today. I can't make it. You gotta cover for me."

"What? No! We got a meeting with the directors about
the Sandoval deal. I need you here. What the fuck
happened to you?"

"Joey, man, you know me. If I'm breathing, I show. Not today, I'm way too fucked up. You gotta put it off for me. Tell them I'm sick. Give me a day or two. You just have no idea."

"What? You're that sick? I'm calling an ambulance."

"No, no, don't do that. I'm not sick—I can't explain it on the phone. Why don't you come down here. I need to talk to you," Mike said.

"You mean now?"

"Yeah, like immediately. Believe me, I wouldn't ask if it wasn't really important. Do this for me, okay?"

"Yeah, yeah, okay. But what's the mystery?"

"I can't talk now. Just get here. You won't believe it."

"All right, okay. I'll cover for you here. See you in a half-hour." Joey clicked off.

Mike crawled out of his bed, plugged in his cell phone, and hopped into the shower.

The doorman buzzed and announced that Mike had a visitor coming up. Joey walked in wide-eyed. He stared, mouth agape, as Mike took an ice pack off his rearranged face. Both eyes were cherry red, no white sclera. A purple circle surrounded his right eye and swollen cheekbone, and his broken nose was red and off-kilter. A dark crust of dried blood lined his nostrils and the corners of his swollen mouth. He had a golf-ball-sized lump on the side of his head.

"What the fuck?" Joey let out a whistle. "You kidding me? Holy shit."

"Yeah, I know. Told ya." Mike tried to focus his eyes. Joey's face wobbled in his blurred vision.

"What shape is the other guy in?" Joey said, half-joking.

"Ah, the other guy? You mean the two other guys," said Mike.

Joey looked incredulous. "Two guys? Bet they're sorry they ran into you ... you kicked ass motherfucker. Tell me the whole thing."

"No, I didn't kick ass. I killed them. Shot 'em both ... with their own gun. Blew their brains out. Fucking dead!" Mike said grimly.

Joey stared in silent shock.

"Come on. Let's sit down." Mike put his hand on his friend's shoulder.

"Hold it, Mike. Shot? No joking around, what happened?" Joey said as they headed into the sleek living room and sat on the leather couch. The wide-screen TV was on, sound off.

"This is no joke," Mike said. "After I put you in the Uber, I got mugged in a gypsy cab by two Mexican guys. Nasty motherfuckers. They were going to kill me. Got my watch and two thousand I got from a cash machine. They wanted more. I think they were going to hold me until they drained my account. I knew I was fucked ... they weren't letting me go. I had no choice. I went for the guy's gun ... shot both of them in the struggle. A fucking bloody mess ... brains everywhere —a shit show. I really didn't think I was gonna make it."

Joey sat with his eyes wide, hand to his open mouth. After a minute he stood up and paced the room. "You shot two muggers? Oh my God, you're a fucking hero. Oh, Mother of God, you're amazing. Killed them both? Wow. The cops must have loved you! What'd they say? Two more low-life skells off the street? Right?"

Mike squirmed recalling the nightmare of it all. "No, no . . . I didn't tell the cops. I just ran. I was in a panic. Scared shitless. I just wanted to get the fuck out of there. I jumped on a train, came straight home. Nobody knows, except you, now."

"Hold it—you didn't tell the cops? Two guys are dead and you didn't report it?" Joey looked further amazed. "What the fuck, man. You gotta tell them. It's a crime not to. You can't hide it. You gotta call them—now." He sat back down and stared at his friend.

"No . . . no. I can't. Joey, hold on. Listen to me. I've been thinking about this. I can't tell anyone."

"Are you crazy? Why?" Joey was almost screeching.

"I'll tell you why," Mike said and leaned forward toward Joey. "Sandoval, that's why. Remember, we're meeting the president of Mexico, maybe this month. You think that'll go over at his house? Fuck no. We'll be out, and you know it. They'll cut us out immediately. Clean hands, world class? Remember? If they find out I was involved in a shooting in the Bronx at four in the morning, we're done. I killed two Mexican guys, no less. They'll think of drugs right away. Too dirty for them! Finito, señor, adios."

"Yeah, but they tried to kill you. It was all self-defense, right?" Joey said. Then, after a moment, he cocked his head. "Hold it. Four in the morning? I left you around midnight, didn't I? Yeah, I was home by twelve-thirty or so. What's with four in the morning? The fuck were you doing?"

"Exactly. What you just said is another reason I gotta keep my mouth shut."

"What? I don't get that—what?"

"Well, there's more to the story," Mike said.

"More? Like what?"

"You remember Larisia?"

"Who? Larisia who—you mean the waitress? At the restaurant?"

"Yeah, her. Well, skipping the details, I ended up in her bed last night. Didn't get out of there till after 3 a.m. That's when the shit hit the fan."

"What?" Joey stood up wide-eyed, his hands on his head. "Wow, you little devil. We had a very busy time last night, didn't we." Joey let out a half-giggle. "And why are we skipping the details? I want details."

"No, no details, we don't have the time for that bullshit right now. The point is I can't tell the cops 'cause they're gonna ask the same question you just did—'what were you doing in the Bronx at four in the morning?' It's the first thing they'll ask me. I can't lie, make up some bullshit story. 'I was just strolling along'—you know, with cops that doesn't work. I'll have to tell them where I was, what I was doing there, and with whom. And you may remember, I'm about to get engaged . . . to Courtney?" Mike looked down. "If she finds out about this little indiscretion I'm finished—we're finished." Mike shook his head and continued. "Look . . . I'm out, nobody knows I was there. I threw the gun away . . . no way to connect me to any of it. As far as I'm concerned, it never happened, nothing to do with me.'

Mike's phone rang. Courtney's name flashed on the screen. "I gotta take this." Mike tried to ignore the shooting pain in his side as he stood up and went into the kitchen.

Joey upped the TV volume with the remote, tried not to listen.

"Honey, no, I'm fine. Just a rough night. I know, I never miss work. But we had that big Sandoval meeting last night at the stadium and then we went out to celebrate, I guess a little too much." Mike took a long breath and rolled his eyes as he listened. "Yes, I promise, I'm cutting back on the drinking."

"Look, don't worry. Joey's here now and we're going over everything. Looks really good—we may be meeting with el presidente in a few weeks. That's how much they loved us." Mike paused. "No, I'm not kidding, the president of Mexico."

"Okay, honey, I'll rest today. Let's do our dinner and movie night tomorrow. We'll have take-out and binge watch 'The Walking Dead.' . . . I love Szechuan." Mike came out of the kitchen with the phone to his ear, gave a thumbs-up to Joey, and walked back in.

"Yes, baby, I love you too. Don't worry. I'm fine. See you tomorrow. Look, I gotta go." He hung up.

Mike smiled uncomfortably and gave a little shrug as he came back into the living room, grabbed the remote to silence the TV, and sat down. After a deep breath, he picked up where he had left off. "There's another reason for me to keep this quiet. More than anything, I don't want my picture on the front page of the *New York Post* as some hero who shot two muggers. Fuck that. My guess is, these two could be in some Mexican drug gang. Do you think I want those motherfuckers after me? Shit no! I got no choice here. The cops would probably call it a drug deal gone bad. Like you said, two more dead skells off the street. Let them worry about it. Fuck it, I just want out. Leave it there."

"Ah, man, I'm not sure that's the right thing. But I get it." Joey stared at Mike. "Look, this is your call. I'll keep my mouth shut, back you up if you need it. We're brothers, man; you've helped me. I'm there for you, the code."

"Yeah, thanks. The code," said Mike. They both stood, shook hands, and hugged. At that moment, as Mike looked over his friend's shoulder, the TV showed images of a green Chevy parked on a Bronx street near the elevated train. Cops were stringing up yellow tape. The blurry outline of a man slumped in the driver's seat could be made out through a blood-stained window, and the car's back door was open.

"Hold it. That's the car." Mike pointed to the TV as he grabbed the remote and raised the volume.

"Police report a shooting in the Bronx last night. The body of a man was found in a car off River Avenue. He was shot once. So far there are no witnesses to the incident and police have made no arrests. A police spokesman said they were investigating whether drugs were involved. Details at six," said the TV announcer.

They both stiffened in silence. After a long moment Joey turned to Mike.

"The body of a man?' What the fuck? I thought you shot two guys?"

"Oh, shit, that motherfucker, I don't know. I shot two guys, right in the head. Believe me, I shot them, there was blood all over the place," Mike said.

"I believe you, but it looks like you only killed one of them," Joey said. "One must've got out of there."

"How the fuck? Shot him right in the face, close range. What the fuck?" Mike paced the room.

"Wow. That's too much. Fucking cockroaches, ya can't kill 'em," Joey said.

"The son of a bitch who got away? He's the nasty one." Mike, mouth open, gently cupped the sides of his head and paced around his living room, then suddenly stopped and turned to Joey. "That bastard has my business card in his pocket—and my watch." He thought for a moment. "Shit, my card, it had Larisia's number on the back. And fuck me, I just remembered—he's got my bank card too."

"What?" Joey started pacing too. "You kiddin' me? Mike, man, this ain't good. I'm not sure you thought this through. Maybe you should call the cops now. Tell them the story—you panicked, ran home, passed out. Now you need to come clean. They'll get it. It's the truth. You can still straighten this out. Fuck Sandoval, we'll deal with him."

"No, no I can't. There's too much involved. It'll destroy my life, maybe get me killed. No, I can't do it. Let's hope he dies somewhere. I know he's hurt, badly. Probably dead in some alley. Maybe the cops will never connect him to this shooting."

"I don't know, man, right now you need more than hope," Joey said.

"I'm not going to the cops. That's it. I'll handle it. I'm not saying anything about this to anyone—you can't either. But I gotta talk to Larisia. She's gotta know. If that bastard is alive and has the card he might try to go after her, and me, somehow." Mike felt a thrill at the idea of talking to Larisia, even as he dreaded the warning he had to give her.

"Still think the cops could be your best bet. They could offer some protection," Joey said.

"Cops? Protection? Forget it. You think they're posting someone at my door? They're not a babysitting service. No chance," Mike said. "No, no cops. But I gotta warn her."

"What about the office address? It's on your card," Joey said.

"No, got lucky there. That was our old card with the Wall Street address on it. He won't be able to find me," Mike said. "I'll just make sure the office really screens my calls. Nobody gets a call through that I don't know. But that's when he'll go after her. I gotta call her, shit—just realized, I don't have her number—he's got it."

"Call the restaurant," Joey said after a minute.

"Great idea. See, that's why I love you . . . when I can't think straight, you do," Mike said. "You better get back to the office. Tell them I'll be fine. Make up some story. I'll be back in a day or so. I've got a woman I've got to talk to—right now."

After leaving his number at the restaurant and emphasizing "emergencia," Larisia called him back.

Mike's phone rang and he grabbed it. "Larisia?"

"Mike? I told you, I never call men. Why didn't you call my cell number? What's the emergency? Miss me already?" She sounded playful and teasing and he felt a surge of desire.

"Well, yeah, I can't take being apart from you for another minute." He laughed despite himself. "But listen, seriously, we've got to meet. I couldn't call you because I lost your number. It's a long story. I'll explain the whole thing to you later. But we need to talk, today. It's important."

"How important can it be?"

"Life or death . . . that important," he replied.

"Wow, okay, I've got to work tonight. Wanna meet me here?"

"Well, that's another part of the problem. I can't go

there. We've got to meet in Manhattan, away from your neighborhood. I can't explain it to you now, but you've got to take my word for it, it's really important, for you and for me. Seriously. Please," he said. "Something has happened and we've gotta talk, in person and not in the Bronx, right now."

"Now?"

"Yes, now, if you can. I'll meet you at the bar at the Campbell Apartment in Grand Central—it's in the back—in an hour. Can you be there?"

"Okay . . . I guess. Can you tell me anything about this?" she asked, and he could hear the concern seeping into her voice.

"Not on the phone. But please be there. It's really important." He clicked off.

As he approached the bar he saw her sitting at a table at the far end of the place, a textbook opened in front of her, wearing horn-rimmed glasses, with a marker in hand. She was just as beautiful as he'd remembered.

"What's this?" he asked.

"I've got a test. I normally do this in a library," she said as she looked up. "Oh my God, what the hell happened to you?"

"I know, I look like hell, right? That's why I'm here. This happened last night after I left you. I got mugged three blocks from your house. Almost got killed." He

54

stopped for a minute to let the words sink in. "Two guys put a gun in my face in a gypsy cab. Got my watch and some money."

"Oh, shit, Michael. I'm so sorry. The neighborhood is sketchy, I know. Jesus, what'd they do? Beat you up?"

"Yeah, that too, but it's much worse than that." Michael sat down and described how he fought for the gun and shot both men. "I thought I killed them both." He hesitated. "But I just saw on the news they only found the driver, Paco, dead in the car. It looks like the other guy got away."

Larisia sat silently for a minute trying to take it all in, then her eyes widened. "Wait—did you say Paco?"

"Yeah. Paco. Why?" he said.

"What'd the other guy look like?" she said. "The one you think got away."

"That bastard? Skinny, craggy face, gold tooth. Had a tattoo on his hand. Didn't happen to catch his name. We weren't formally introduced," Mike said with a half-grin.

"Oh, shit. Can it be?" she said with a distracted look on her face. "This could be bad. Skinny with a gold tooth. The tattoo? Was it an eagle with wings spread?"

"Not sure, but across the whole back of his hand . . . the right hand, with letters on it, like initials," he said.

"Oh, shit." Her face went pale. "It's Carlos. He's back!"

"What? Hold it. You know him?"

"Yes. Fuck . . . yes," she replied. Tears began to flow down her cheeks. She buried her face in her hands. "I can't believe he's back."

"What? No. You know this motherfucker?"

"I wish I didn't. I thought he was gone forever. This is bad." She began to cry again. "He haunts my life."

Mike leaned closer and held her hand for a long moment. She was shivering. Tears rolled down her face and stained the pages before her. She pulled her chair closer, trying to compose herself.

"Mike, there's a lot I have to tell you about me—my story—and Carlos. But first tell me more about what happened to you last night."

Mike stared at her for a minute, trying to take it all in. "Well, I think they wanted to kill me. Paco got shot when I grabbed for the gun and then I shot the other guy and ran. I thought they were both dead, but the news said that they found only one body, the driver. Looks like this Carlos must have gotten away."

Mike took a deep breath and a sip of water before continuing. "When I saw the news this morning, I remembered that he took my business card with your number on it. The one you put in my pocket in the restaurant. I had to tell you, to warn you. If he's still alive out there, somewhere, he may come looking for you, or me. He won't be able to get through to me—my office has security and I've got a doorman, but you? He may call you or try to track you down somehow to get to me. Who knows, he may want revenge. And now with what you just told me, well, shit, you know, this is not good." Mike fought to catch his breath. It was hard enough to relive the horror of the night before. But he'd taken comfort in thinking it was over.

"Ahh, shit." She looked away. "Have you reported this to the police?" Turning back, her brown eyes were wide in anticipation.

"Ah, no . . . no, and I can tell you why," said Mike.

She reached over and put her finger to his lips. "You don't have to tell me. I don't want to know." Her tears welled. "Listen to me. Don't call anyone. Keep it to yourself. And you can't mention me—to anyone. Please."

"You don't want me to report this?"

"No, I don't. And no matter what, I don't want to be questioned by the police. I can't be involved." She stared at him, stone-faced with fear. "A . . . lot has happened to me because of him. I have to stay out of this."

She sobbed quietly, his hand on her shoulder. After a few minutes she looked up. "You have no idea how dangerous he is. And not just him, it's the gang he's with— Los Sangristas. Drugs and shootings— that's all they do. They'll kill anyone. They terrorized my neighborhood," she said. "Most of them got arrested several years ago and got sent back. Last time I heard, Carlos was in prison in Mexico."

"What happened to you? What'd he do to you?"

She sat for a long moment and stared at Michael, eyes swimming in tears. She swallowed hard. "He raped me." He moved closer and she fell into his chest, sobbing. "When I was seventeen. That bastard raped me. I hate him. I hate him so much—"

"What? This Carlos? That fucking lowlife. Did you call the cops on him?" Mike was stunned.

"No. You don't understand. I couldn't. He'd have killed me if I turned him in. I was frightened to death of him. There was no chance for me." She hesitated.

"There's something else you should know. I'm not legal . . . I'm undocumented. I couldn't call the police. I have no rights—they'd send me back. My parents brought me across the border when I was six. They got sent back almost ten years later. They left me here. I'm what is called a 'Dreamer.' Aside from my aunt and uncle, who own the restaurant, I have nobody here. They saved me then. I was really alone, nobody to help me. I wanted to become a citizen but it's not easy, especially now. The government has made it impossible. If they identify me, I could get sent back."

He stared in amazement. "You were raped by this guy and no one could help you?"

"No . . . nobody. I was young and afraid of him and of the police. I didn't know what to do. I've only known America, since I was a kid. I feel American; I don't feel Mexican. I didn't want to get sent back—I hardly remember anything about Mexico—so I just shut up and hid it."

She stopped for a minute and took a drink of water. She was trembling. "Look, as a man you can't understand this but as a woman, as a person, I was completely humiliated. I had no power. No help. None! It was terrifying."

"Oh, baby, my heart breaks for you. Wow." Mike shook

his head. "No help, and now you have to worry about being deported to a country you don't even know!"

Trying to gather herself, she looked at Michael, inhaled a deep breath, and continued. "There's something else—I know this is a lot." She hesitated." I have a seven-year-old daughter in Mexico. Her name is Carmelita. She lives there with my parents." Larisia stopped and put her hands to her face. "She's his daughter … from that rape. I was a virgin. He doesn't know it. I never told him or anyone, including my parents, who her father is. She doesn't know. You're the only person I've ever told."

Michael, stunned, stood up. The gravity of what she had said washed over him. Her fear and suffering sunk deeply into him. He was astonished by her courage and strength.

"He doesn't know? Holy shit." He ran his hand through his hair and stared in amazement. Then he leaned down, grabbed her, and held her tight, over-whelmed by a swarm of emotion. She sobbed in his arms as he held her closely, feeling her body shiver.

After a few minutes, he quietly asked, "What happened after the rape? Did he contact you?"

"No. He knew I hated him for it. I avoided him in the neighborhood. He never knew anything about the preg-nancy. I heard that he wanted to be with me," she said, cocking her head and shrugging her shoulders. "Can you believe it? I was a kid. Latin men … they fuck you, they own you. The bastards."

She continued. "Then one day I heard he got arrested

along with the rest of that crew and was sent back to Mexico, ended up in a prison in Juarez. He's been gone for years. Never heard anything else. Thought he'd never be back . . . I thought it was all over . . . till now," she said with a sigh.

"Fuck, and now I walk into your life and it all comes back." Mike bit his lip as he sat down again. "But after hearing your story, I've got to tell you mine, and I'm ashamed. I feel like a shit."

She braced herself as he looked away for a moment. He took a deep breath and uncharacteristically made eye contact.

"I'm about to be engaged. That is . . . I mean . . . I'm getting engaged . . . in a month or so. For our anniversary."

Her face darkened. "Do you love her?" she asked calmly.

"Ah, well, yes, I do, I gotta be honest." He hesitated. "I never thought I'd be saying this, but till I met you it was never something I even thought about. Somehow just took it for granted that she was the one. Now I really have to think about that—"

She shook her head and put her hand up to stop him. "Please, Michael, don't say that to me. You don't have to. We just met. I don't expect anything from you. We're adults. I'm not in love with you, though I do really like you. I usually don't let anyone close; you're the first in a long time. But you have your life and I have mine." She smiled at him. "No, no regrets, please. We had our moment. It was wonderful but I don't want to—I can't—be a . . . a homewrecker."

Mike sat back in his chair and stared at her. Her olive skin was flawless and her dark hair shimmered in the low light. "You're unbelievable . . . really. I'm not just saying it. You are. You're a great girl."

"You mean woman."

"Ah, yeah, of course, I mean woman. You're right, a real woman," he said with a smile.

Larisia snapped back to reality. "Don't pull that charm offensive on me. Worked once, not again. You stay with your lady. We have a bigger problem right now. I can't live in fear. If he knows I'm involved, he'll come after me."

"Look." Mike reached out and put both hands on her shoulders. "I'll do everything I can for you. Don't worry. We'll stay close on this. It's not a bad idea to change your phone number, but make sure you give me the new one before you do. If you get any strange calls or you feel afraid, call me. I'll hire a bodyguard for you if necessary. For now, he doesn't know who the Larisia on the card is. He may never figure that out. Just screen your calls, don't answer any unknown numbers. And ask around the neighborhood if anyone has heard anything. Maybe we'll get lucky and someone will find him dead in an alley. I know he was badly hurt."

"Okay. Change my number—good idea. I'll call you if I have any problems or if I hear anything," she said.

She looked at him and smiled, and her brown eyes smiled too. She placed her hand on his. "We could have been great together—you and me. I haven't felt that way in a while, but it was not meant to be. Too bad." She gently squeezed his hand and blinked tears away.

"Yeah. Too bad is right." He looked down, shaking his head, thoroughly confused by a torrent of conflicting feelings.

6

WE'LL ASK THE QUESTIONS

The doorman rang up to Mike's apartment. "Food delivery."

"Okay, send him up please," said Mike. In two minutes, he was paying the Chinese delivery guy.

"Honey, food's here. Crank up *The Walking Dead*," he called out to Courtney as he opened the wire-handled food boxes and set up the plates.

She came out in her robe, barefoot and long-legged with her blonde hair in a towel. "Wow, you look like a shampoo commercial, a very sexy one," he said.

"You look like a boxer who just lost the title," she cracked.

"Ah, yeah, don't remind me. Rough night."

"You must have slammed into that cabinet door pretty hard to do that much damage. How drunk were you?" Courtney asked.

"I guess drunker than I thought. Hardly felt it. But

don't worry, I'm cutting back on the drinking, I promise," he said, handing her a plate. "Come on, dig in."

"You really should—cut back, that is. I worry about you, honey. Which cabinet did you hit exactly?" she asked. "I mean, were you running or what?"

"No, no, I just got up and didn't see the door open … right here." He pointed to a kitchen cabinet. "Just got up in the middle of the night and blam. Thought I kissed a moving freight train."

"Jesus. Good thing you didn't knock out any teeth," she said, piling the Szechuan chicken onto her plate.

"I'm fine, babe—now, with you here. By the time we go out for our anniversary I'll be as good as new. Got a special surprise for you," he said, changing the subject.

"Really, you didn't forget?" She smiled. With her wide smile and rosy cheeks, Courtney seemed to glow. She was a classic blue-eyed beauty and being with her now, after the trauma of the past eighteen hours, reminded him of how much he loved her.

"No, I didn't forget." He picked up his plate and headed for the couch.

They settled in, staring at the ragged zombies on the TV. He struggled to feel comfortable. With his thoughts in turmoil, he barely tasted the spicy food. A sense of dread clouded his mind.

"What time is it?" Courtney asked, once the show was over.

"I'm not sure," he replied, after reflexively looking at his bare wrist. "Check the clock."

"Where's your watch?"

He improvised. "Ah . . . oh . . . ah, I took it in for repair."

"What? That's brand new, honey. Still under warranty. Where'd you take it? I hope to Rolex," she said.

"Yeah, it was running a little slow, so I took it back to them for a little adjustment."

"They're impressive, aren't they, with the lab coats and all," she said.

"Yeah, classic German efficiency," he replied.

"Actually, Swiss, but close enough. Ya know, they have records on every watch they've sold for the last seventy-five years. When I was there a guy came in with a counterfeit one. They confiscated it from him right there and called the cops."

"Really? Busted him on the spot?"

"Yup. It was quite a thing. They don't tolerate those cheap Chinese knockoffs," she said. "When you getting it back?"

"Ah, next week. They're gonna check it out, and let me know if it's a cheap Chinese knockoff."

"Not at those prices, wise guy. Remember, it's under warranty." She smiled as she got up and headed into the bathroom.

After a few minutes, he heard her footsteps coming quickly down the hallway. "Jesus Christ," she called out as she came into the living room. "What the hell is this?"

He turned to see her standing in the doorway with her mouth agape, his bloody shirt and suit jacket balled up in her hand. "What the fuck? All this is your blood? I had no idea. Holy shit, you were a mess. It looks like you were in a goddamn war."

Mike's stomach dropped. "Ah . . . yeah. Guess I bled more than I realized. I know I hit the cabinet pretty hard," he said.

"Michael, how drunk were you? This looks like a lot more than banging your nose on a cabinet. You got blood splattered all over these clothes." She stared at him with one arm akimbo.

"Babe, really, I hardly remember the whole thing. I know I had a few too many . . . just didn't realize—"

"I thought you said you were asleep then got up and walked into the cabinet? How'd all this blood get on your suit jacket if you were in bed sleeping? And why were all these clothes balled up in the bottom of your closet?"

She stared at him, looking completely puzzled. His mind scrambled for something. He began to feel a numbing panic and felt his face begin to flush. He inhaled deeply.

"Ah, well . . . I was asleep, but not in the bed. I guess I came home and fell asleep in my clothes, on the couch. Got up in the middle of the night and ran into the door and fell on my face. Forgot to tell you that part. Yeah, I was really drunk. Didn't want to admit it. I was hiding the clothes. Didn't want you to see them and worry." His face now red, he looked down and shrugged.

"You guess you came home and fell asleep in your clothes? You're not sure? And this much blood? It's on your shoes too. You fell asleep with your shoes on?" She stared at him for a long time then turned around, shook her head, and walked back to the bedroom.

"You sure you weren't in a fight?" she said, sticking her head out from the bedroom doorway. "You're telling me the truth?"

"Yes, I'm sure, honey, please." He walked over to her, took her hand, and gently kissed her cheek. "I was embarrassed. Just got too drunk and slammed my nose on the cabinet door and fell. That's all, really. I know how much you hate my drinking. Felt like a jerk that I had to miss work and all. I promise to cut back—really."

She looked at him and exhaled. "You've got to. It's too much. You're worrying me to death."

Mike put his briefcase down on his desk and removed the plastic lid on his Starbucks cappuccino. He flopped into his chair holding the cardboard cup just as his cell rang. He sat up with a start. He recognized Larisia's number.

"Michael, hi," she said.

"You okay?" He felt jolt of adrenaline and put down the coffee. "Didn't change your number yet, huh."

"I may not have to. I've found out some good news."

"Really? I could use some good news right now."

"You were right. I asked around the neighborhood, you know, like you said, and a friend of mine who's an ER nurse at Lincoln Hospital told me they brought in a guy the other night to emergency. The cops found him unconscious in front of a bodega on River Ave. He was shot in the face."

Mike stood up. "Was it him?"

"Yes. The cops got his name. Carlos Estrada. They put it on the admissions report. It's him," she said, and he heard the euphoria in her voice.

"Holy shit. Son of a bitch managed to get away. Fuck, fuck! Will he survive?"

"Hang on. It seems the bullet went through his cheeks, took out some teeth but didn't hit any vital organs. Lost a lot of blood, but they listed him in stable condition. He'll probably make it," Larisia said.

"Shit. He would, that bastard."

"No, but listen, after they were working on him for a while, ya know, sewing him up and all, immigration cops showed up. ICE. They arrested him right then and there. Handcuffed him to the bed. Cops said he had an outstanding warrant in Mexico. My friend left that night at the end of her shift, but she heard that the next day they took him away. Sent him to the federal detention center in Newark. That's where he went last time. They usually send them right back to Mexico from there. I think he's gone . . . Can you believe it? I think we got lucky. Gone forever, I hope . . . again," she said, letting out a sigh of relief.

"Holy shit, mother. Thank you and all that's holy. Piece of shit got what was coming to him," he said. "Are you sure it's the same guy?"

"I'm sure. She saw him. Gold tooth. Skinny face. Tattoo on his hand. It's him," she said.

"Sounds like him. And he's gonna go?"

"Yep. Once they go to Newark, they don't come back. Fly 'em right back to Mexico City," she replied.

"Wow. That's great—unbelievable. What a relief. Maybe I should take you out to celebrate. What do ya think?"

"Ah, Michael. I'm happy, like you are, but I can't see you. Thanks, but no. I'm just glad he's gone and we can both go back to our lives. You're great, but we really can't see each other. You know why." She sounded resolute.

"Yeah, I guess I do. But I have to admit, I can't get you out of my mind," he said. "But okay you're right. It's better —maybe. But like you said, we could have been great together."

"Don't go there, please. I've got exams coming and a ton of work ahead of me. No time for distractions. And you, well, you have a lady you need to be right with. Don't screw it up," she said.

"Yeah, I'm a dog. You're right. I've got things set up for a few weeks. Our anniversary. Gonna pop the question."

"That's great. Hope she says yes. Does she know what she's getting into?"

"I think she knows. And I'm pretty sure she'll say yes. But you, really . . . you're a great woman. The guy who gets you is lucky. Somehow, I know you'll always be in my heart." Then, after an awkward moment of silence, "I guess this is goodbye. If you need anything let me know. I mean it—anything. I can be very helpful."

"Thanks, Mike, but enough with the heartstrings routine. Grow up and do right by that girl. You love her and she deserves it. Treat her the way you would want somebody to treat your daughter, that's always a good rule. Goodbye, Michael, and good luck," Larisia said as she hung up.

Michael sat there for a long moment and thought about her. "She's just a really great person, a terrific girl," he said to himself. His office phone rang, jarring him out of his reverie.

"Did ya see it?" Joey said.

"What? No, see what?"

"The email, from Sandoval. Don't you read your emails?"

"Yeah, of course I do, but I've been on the phone . . . with Larisia," Mike said.

"Oh, shit. Bad news?"

"No. Really good news, but I'll tell you later. What about Sandoval?"

"Read it yourself. We're going to Mexico probably at the end of the month, baby—to meet the big guy. We did it, somehow. You did it. They want us," Joey was yelling into the phone.

"We are?" Mike said. "Holy shit!"

"Yes, we are, numbnuts. Not that the president really

wants to meet you—you're too ugly. Mike, seriously, you made this happen. Fucking miracle. Let's celebrate tonight—ah, nothing too heavy."

"Yeah, man! Okay, just one drink. Oh, and more good luck. The cops caught that guy . . . you know, the nasty prick from the other night. They found him passed out and bleeding on the street a few blocks away. Cops took him to the hospital. Turns out he had a warrant back in Mexico and they're sending him back there. Outta my life forever, goodbye," Mike said.

"Wow, you lucky bastard. Looks like we're all going to Mexico now. Should we drop by while we're there and say hello to him in prison?" Joey laughed.

"Go fuck yourself," Mike replied.

"I love you too," Joey said, and hung up.

"It's a good news day," Mike said to himself as he opened his laptop and began to scroll through his emails. He had gotten halfway through the Sandoval email when his assistant Lara knocked on his office door.

"Mike, sorry," she said as she stuck her head in. "There are two men in the conference room who want to talk to you."

"Two men? Who are they?"

She looked and sounded distressed. "They're New York City police detectives," she replied.

A chill went down his neck. "Detectives? What the hell do they want?" Mike asked.

"They wouldn't give me any further information. Said they wanted to speak to you—now."

"What? Why?" Mike froze for a moment. Then, not wanting to look upset, he changed his demeanor. "Ah, okay, tell them I'll be right there. It's nothing, I'm sure," he said with the wave of a hand.

Now slightly panicked, he thought about calling his attorney, but decided against it. He wasn't sure he wanted to tell anyone, particularly a lawyer. He knew what any decent attorney would tell him to do: tell the whole story to the cops. He wasn't doing that. No way. In his mind, the whole thing was finished.

Fuck it, who knows what this is about? I can handle it. If it gets too tense, I'll just bail. Putting on his jacket and heading to the conference room he caught a quick reflection in the glass of the purple ring below his eye above his swollen nose.

Mike walked in and shook hands with two burly men who stood uncomfortably in the middle of the cavernous room. He invited them to sit down at the mahogany table surrounded by twenty leather chairs.

"Are you Michael McGowan?" The white, heavyset officer asked after getting settled. A dark ring of sweat stained the worn edges of his graying shirt collar.

"Yes, and you are?" Mike said.

"I'm Lieutenant Philip Krasnowsky and this is my partner, Detective Eddie Johnson. We're with Bronx Homicide." He slowly slid his business card across the table with two thick fingers. "We'd like to ask you a few questions."

"Yes. Okay. What's this about?" Mike asked. He felt a

warm flush of blood creep up his neck. His heartbeat pounded in his ears.

"We'll ask the questions, okay?" Krasnowsky said. "We won't be long."

Mike stiffened, nodding.

After a long moment seemingly assessing his prey, Johnson stood up and walked over to him aggressively. "Hey Mike, what'd you do? Huh?"

"What do you mean?" A startled Mike stared at the imposing Black cop.

"I mean, man, what the fuck did you do?" Johnson stood over him. "Come on, man. Ya did something, I know that and you know that. What kinda shit did you pull?" His face was stone serious as he stood glaring at Mike.

"I don't know what the hell you're talking about," Mike said. His mind raced as he recoiled against the back of the chair. He began to feel slightly nauseated as he locked eyes with the detective.

"Look, don't bullshit me. I've seen this before. Ya hadda do something—probably had it coming." Johnson leaned in close. His oversized teeth glistened white in stark contrast to his dark complexion and pink gums. He glared down at Mike with rheumy, bloodshot eyes and moved in closer. His breath smelled of beer and cigarettes.

Johnson took a step back with a half-grin and broke the mounting tension in the room. "The last time I got a shiner like that, she caught me with another broad—a white one. Hit me upside the head with a frying pan," the detective said with a laugh. "What'd you do?"

"Oh, this?" Mike put a suddenly shaky hand up to his eye. For an instant, he was at a total loss for words. "Ah, I had a few too many the other night and ran into a cabinet door . . . in my own apartment," he finally muttered. "She . . . she didn't catch me doing anything."

Johnson let out a laugh, slapped Mike on the shoulder, and sat down. "Gotcha, didn't I? I was just fucking with ya. Must've had more than a few to smack it that hard. That shit looks pretty bad—on a good hard run, were ya?"

"Yeah, it was . . . hard, that is," replied Mike.

"Sit down, Eddie," Krasnowsky said.

Mike felt his legs quivering under the table.

After Eddie took a seat, Krasnowsky turned to Mike who was struggling to focus. "You been in the Bronx lately?"

The question sent another chill down Mike's spine. He tried not to flinch.

"Yes, I was at the Yankee game the other night, when they played Boston," said a flustered Mike.

"Oh yeah, that was a great game," Johnson chimed in.

"Eddie, please," Krasnowsky said, looking him off.

"Do you have a credit card?" Krasnowsky asked, then wrote something down on a small note pad.

"Well, yes . . . I have several credit cards and a debit card," Mike said.

"A Citibank debit card?" the detective asked.

"Yes, Citibank. How did you know?"

The cops looked at each other and ignored him.

"I told you, we'll ask the questions, remember? Did

you make any transactions with the debit card the night you were in the Bronx? Just to be clear, that was three nights ago," Krasnowsky said.

In his mind, Mike scrambled to revise the events of the other night. "Ah, is that what this is all about? 'Cause, yeah, I lost my card that night."

The detective pressed on. "How'd you lose it?"

"I really don't know. Must've fallen out of my pocket. As I said, I had a little too much to drink that night." Mike rubbed his clammy palms against the light gabardine wool of his trousers.

The detective reached into his pocket and put a card in a plastic baggie on the table. "Is this your card?"

Mike leaned in and stared at it.

"Yes, that's it. You didn't have to come all the way here just to return it. Thanks, but I already reported it to the bank and they've sent me a replacement." Mike sat back in relief and exhaled.

Krasnowsky made another notation. "Well," the detective said, looking squarely at Mike. "Did you?"

"Did I what?" Mike said.

"Make any transactions that night? When you were in the Bronx—with the card, before you lost it," said the detective.

"Ah, I don't think so . . . as I said, I kinda don't remember much. We were celebrating—"

"Is that a yes or a no?" Krasnowsky cut him off.

"Not sure." Mike squirmed. "Probably not . . . usually use the corporate Amex."

"Probably?" The detective stared. "When did you notice it was missing, the card?"

"Oh, not till the next day," Mike said. "That's when I called the bank. New one's on the way. What, somebody found it?"

"What time did you leave the Bronx that night?" Krasnowsky skipped Mike's query and made another note.

"Oh, I guess about, oh, twelve-thirty."

"Cab, Uber?" asked Eddie, up now and pacing behind Mike.

"Subway. No cabs and my phone went dead so I couldn't set up a ride. Took the number four train home," Mike said.

"Live downtown, do ya?" Johnson asked.

"Yeah, how'd you know?" replied Mike.

Dead silence.

Krasnowsky was writing and staring at his pad. "You have a watch?"

Mike, rattled by the question, tried to improvise. "Yeah, but I didn't have it that night. It's in for repair. Beautiful Rolex, got it from my—"

Eddie, from behind, cut him off. "How'd you know what time it was when you left the Bronx? No phone. No watch."

"Ah, I don't know. A clock somewhere ..." Mike stood up. "Look, I've answered your questions. Tried to be cooperative, but I think that's enough. You brought me my card. Thank you for that."

He reached for the card and Krasnowsky grabbed his

arm. Mike felt the strength of the detective's meaty hands. "Sorry. You can't have it back. Evidence."

"Evidence? Of what?" Mike tried to sound collected as his heart skipped a beat.

"What kind of watch did you say you have?" Eddie's disembodied voice asked from behind.

"Rolex, Submariner, stainless steel," Mike replied, turning to the detective. "Black face," he added with a side glance. The pun was lost on Johnson, or ignored.

"Were you on the corner of River Avenue and 155th Street that night, when you were in the Bronx?" persisted Krasnowsky, playing detective double-team ping-pong.

"Ah, no, don't think so. I was pretty drunk," Mike said, turning back to look at Krasnowsky across the table.

"Well, your card was found by my detectives near the scene of a shooting off River Ave. Do you know anything about that?" Krasnowsky stopped writing and looked up. "There was a killing right there."

"Oh, I saw that on television. Maybe someone found my card and ended up losing it on the street somewhere. I don't know. I didn't have anything to do with it, if that's what you're implying." The room suddenly felt very warm and beads of moisture formed on Mike's upper lip.

"Implying? We're not implying anything—just asking, but it does seem strange that you lose your card and then somebody else finds it and, what, drops it near the scene of a crime?" Krasnowsky tilted his head and looked at Johnson with raised eyebrows.

"Look, I don't know. I lost it. That's all I know," Mike

got up and walked around to the far end of the table. He thought about walking out altogether but didn't want to look suspicious.

"Maybe the guys who were shot in the cab found it, or maybe they stole it from somewhere," Mike offered.

"Huh? That's interesting," Krasnowsky said. "What makes you say 'guys'? You think there was more than one?"

Mike felt dizzy as he realized his mistake. "Ah, well, that's what they said ... on the news—didn't they?"

"No, no they didn't," Eddie said. "We only found one guy. Nobody said anything about more than one. You know something about another guy?"

"Eddie," Krasnowsky interrupted him, sounding impatient. "Let me ask the questions, please."

Krasnowsky looked at Mike. "Well, do you?"

"Do I what?" Mike asked.

"Do you know something about another guy in the shooting?"

"No ...ah ... no. I just somehow thought they—on TV—said something about it. No, I don't." Mike hated this feeling, of stumbling, of stammering in front of these ordinary men.

"And why did you say 'cab,'" asked the detective, boring in. "What makes you think it was a cab?"

"I don't know," Mike said. He looked away and shifted from foot to foot. "It was on the news ... definitely. They said it on CNN or I heard it ... somewhere."

The cops looked at each other. Krasnowsky made another note.

"No, no they didn't," Krasnowsky said. "Nobody mentioned a cab."

"But it was a cab, wasn't it?" Mike asked.

"We've already told you, we ask the questions—not you." Both officers looked at him for a long moment, saying nothing.

Mike, staring back at them, felt the blood flush his face. "I'm sorry, but you'll have to excuse me now, gentlemen, I'm very busy. I've got to go. Thank you."

The cops didn't move. They continued to watch him.

He tried to gather himself and moved toward the door. "Look, I don't know anything about all this. I lost my card. That's it. How it ended up where it did, I don't know. That's your job to figure out."

He put his hand on the doorknob. "I have a lot to do today, and I must go right now. Thank you for your time. If I remember anything useful, I'll be sure to call you . . . okay? Please show yourselves out." Mike opened the heavy mahogany door and tried to collect himself as he walked toward his office on unsteady legs.

—————

Standing at his desk in his office and trembling slightly, Mike opened a bottle of Fiji Water and gulped it. He sat down and tried to think. His mind was a blur.

After a few minutes he gathered himself and picked up the phone to call his lawyer.

"Shelly," he said after being put on a brief hold. "You got a minute?"

"Yeah, Mike, of course, how ya doing?" Shelly sounded distracted, and Mike heard the shuffling of papers.

"Ah, I'm good, but I gotta ask you a sorta informal question," Mike said.

"Informal or confidential?" said the lawyer. "In other words, a client question or a friendly informal question?"

"Well, an informal friendly question," Mike took a breath. "You see I got this friend of mine with some possible police trouble. I'm trying to help. My friend asked if the police can get personal bank records, ya know, like deposits and withdrawals, and . . . er . . . bank ATM videos without permission?"

"Permission from who?" Shelly asked.

"From him," Mike replied.

"Oh, it's a he . . . not some dame," the lawyer said with a brief laugh.

"Yes, it's a he," Mike said, passing on the implication.

"Yeah, if the cops have probable cause of a crime, they can request a subpoena for all personal banking records and ATM videos from the bank. A judge has to sign off on it. Obviously, if they get the subpoena, the bank has to comply—this data is usually stored on the bank's servers. But, Mike, your friend would have to be in big trouble for the cops to go after that, only for a major felony. It happens, though. Which cops, the feds?"

"No, local New York City police," Mike answered.

"You mean street crime? Not like money laundering?"

"Not laundering. Regular street crime," Mike said.

"Well, for them it's not as likely, but they can do it too," Shelly said. "They're just a little less sophisticated. It takes a while with them."

"Well, okay, thanks. That's what I wanted to know," Mike said.

"Look, Mike . . . is there anything you want to tell me about this 'friend' of yours? I'm your friend, too, I'd be happy to help."

"No, not right now, Shell. I'll pass this along and I'll let you know. Okay?"

"Mike, remember, you—or your friend—can tell me anything. It's all confidential, lawyer-client privilege, remember," said the attorney.

"Shell, I love ya. Right now, it's nothing," Mike told him.

"And, Mike—ah, tell your friend, the number one rule: never say anything to a cop once he starts asking questions. Nothing. Clam up, especially if there's two of them and even with nothing to hide. Just tell them courteously, 'I've got to talk to my lawyer.'"

"I'll remember that, Shell, and I'll pass that on to my friend too," Mike said, hanging up with a shaking hand. A throbbing headache blurred his vision.

After the interview, Krasnowsky came back to his office disturbed and curious about the taxi shooting case. His mind churned. McGowan seemed nervous, maybe even lying, but he didn't seem like a killer. But, then again, *who can read minds*, he thought. He draped his light jacket on his worn office chair, sat down, and eyed the stack of folders on his desk. More cases piling up and always for the same reasons: drugs and gangs. In his opinion, the department was losing control of the streets.

For no conscious reason, he went to the bottom drawer of his desk, took out a dog-eared folder and opened it. A yellowed copy of the *New York Post* fell out onto his desk. He picked it up and stared at the front-page headline.

DETECTIVE'S DAUGHTER
KILLED IN GANG VIOLENCE

His mind flooded with the images of that excruciating experience. Identifying her body. Breaking the news to his wife, Gladys. News reporters hounding him day and night. The funeral at his Greenpoint church with tearful neighbors offering their condolences. The haunting bagpipes at her burial. His wife sobbing. The emptiness in the house.

He remembered being determined to find the killers. After weeks of grunt work investigating, he got a lucky break. He had made an arrest, in an unrelated case, of a low-level street drug dealer who, in an attempt to get his charges dropped, said he was at the scene when the fatal shots were fired. Krasnowsky pressured him to finger the killers, which he did. The detective found out that his daughter was simply collateral damage in a drug dispute, an innocent bystander. The *Post* declared:

HERO DETECTIVE
ARRESTS DAUGHTER'S
KILLERS

He had promised Gladys that he'd find the killers and bring them to justice. And he had done just that. Not that any justice would be good enough for what had been taken from his family, but at least he'd feel some sense of satisfaction.

But he was not prepared for the justice he encountered. He picked up another copy of the *Post* in the same folder.

CONFESSION QUASHED
DRUG GANG KILLER
FOUND NOT GUILTY

His eyes welled with tears for the horrid outcome. Part of him wanted to believe that slick lawyers had distorted the picture, claiming a coerced confession. An infamous judge at the time, Bruce Wright, also known as "Cut 'em Loose Bruce," saw the confession as a violation of defendant's rights because of "overzealous police interrogation." After heated arguments with the district attorney's office, the confession was never admitted as evidence in the trial.

Krasnowsky knew he had gone too far to get the confession. At one point in the interrogation he nearly punched the handcuffed defendant but was restrained by his partner at the time, Detective Gronkowsky. After the verdict, nothing made sense to him. His family was destroyed. Gladys never fully recovered and, he realized, neither did he.

Elbows on his desk, he put his hands to his face, wiped away any remnants of tears from the painful memories, and wondered why he even gave a shit about McGowan or these lowlifes in a taxi. But then, with odd clarity, he realized he had nothing else. Despite it all, the disappointments, the stark unfair courtroom decisions, to him the truth still mattered. *In fact,* he thought, *it was the only thing that did matter.* And probably the only thing that kept him going.

7

HIGH HEELS ARE FOR SEX

Several weeks later Michael was stewing over the details of his engagement plans. He wanted everything to be perfect. He called the restaurant to let them know it was his and Courtney's anniversary and, more important, he was going to ask her to marry him that night.

He made sure the maître d' had a quiet banquette in the corner ready for them and to be certain that at least two bottles of her favorite champagne, Veuve Clicquot, were chilled and ready, and that the menu had her personal favorites on it. And the lighting had to be just right, he'd told them, intimate but not too dark. She hated glaring lights. Mike didn't want intrusive music either, nothing schmaltzy, and certainly no rap.

He had planned to drop the ring into her champagne glass as she was about to drink but was told about another fiancée-to-be who had swallowed the ring, not noticing it in the glass, and spent her engagement evening in an emergency room getting her stomach pumped.

He'd also thought about giving her an anniversary present in a large box, hiding the ring in a box at the center of increasingly smaller boxes, but it all seemed too unwieldy. He had gone through several other possible plans but finally settled on simply putting the ring itself under the champagne bottle and having her discover it as he lifted the bottle to pour. He had spent more time on planning this night than any other event in his life. He enjoyed the creative concepts but hated the actual nagging details: not his makeup. That's what assistants were for.

He had also arranged for a group of their closest mutual friends to show up later at the King Cole Bar at the St. Regis for a celebration drink together. He didn't have much doubt about her answer but told them to wait for his call just in case. They were ecstatic for the couple, who were among the last of their crowd to be married.

Mike was determined to impress Courtney's parents, Robert and Martha McCallister. Their blue-blood heritage and tony Greenwich connections always intimidated Michael. He almost always felt uncomfortable in their presence. For them, he lacked real achievement and the family heritage they required. That fact had been not subtly implied to Michael on more than one occasion. It was clear they had wished for a better choice for their first daughter.

With her lithe carriage, beauty, and high-fashion good

looks, Courtney had her pick of the Ivy League boys that she'd grown up with. Her first boyfriend in high school, Bradley Weston, graduated summa cum laude from Harvard law and became a partner in a prestigious D.C. firm. Courtney's mother never let her forget what a success he'd become. Her dad, a partner at Sullivan and Cromwell, who had represented some of the country's biggest corporations, said that he would have been happy to have Bradley as a son-in-law.

"We could always use a good litigator in the family," he once said to his daughter.

Michael dreaded calling his father-in-law to be and asking for Courtney's hand in marriage. He finally broke down and did it, reluctantly, over drinks in the dark, wood-paneled lounge at the Metropolitan Club where Robert had been a member for many years.

"Sir, I love your daughter. I'm sure you know this. I would like your permission to ask her to marry me," Mike said, after two scotches, as he sat uncomfortably in an oversized leather wing chair in the imposing club room.

"I thought you'd never ask," McCallister told him.

"Well, I know we've been going out for a while, but with the way things are going for me in my firm I believe I'm now in a position to take care of her in the way she deserves," Mike said. "Much like you've been able to provide for your family, sir." He nearly gagged as he fawned over the autocratic figure who sat across from him.

The imperious Robert sat back, thumbed the bulbous

crystal glass he held, warming the rare cognac he so enjoyed. "Son, I'm glad you have finally decided to step up and act. I don't mind telling you that Martha and I have been concerned about your intentions toward our daughter. She's certainly had her pick of men before you came along, but it looks like you two are determined to be together and we do not want to stand in your way—it wouldn't do any good anyway. She's a wonderful girl, but headstrong, and I have no doubt you'll do your best," said Robert, struggling to come up with something positive to say about the match.

"Well, thank you, sir. I appreciate your support," said Michael.

Robert reached over and sternly shook Michael's hand, staring right at him. "Make no mistake, you'll have my complete support so as long as my daughter has a smile on her face."

Michael had the looks and the brains, but for the McCallisters that simply wasn't enough. He had done well in his New York City Catholic high school and had even managed to get a scholarship to Villanova. Though not at the top of his class, he did well enough to go on for an MBA in the school's highly rated business program. He was the first of his family to graduate from college, not to mention a postgraduate degree. His dad, Michael Sr., a handsome man blessed with a natural Irish charm but little formal education, had worked his way up to shop foreman at *The New York Times* printing plant in Queens. His mom, a deeply religious woman from a traditional

Irish family, was a dedicated homemaker. They both were very proud of their son.

Courtney and Michael had met in the city right after college, on a blind date set up by her best friend, Amanda. The girls shared a two-bedroom apartment on East 73rd Street and were full of excitement at being fresh New Yorkers, where all things seemed possible and love was around every corner. Courtney had just landed a job as a second-grade English teacher at the Dalton School and Michael, more established, was on the fast track with Citibank.

"He's really cute," said Amanda. "An investment banker. Works with my friend Bill. I really trust his judgment. Bill says he's a great guy."

They hit it off right away. Their romance soared with glitzy nights in downtown clubs, restaurant openings, and summer weekends in the Hamptons. It was nonstop and as the months went by, the love between them graduated into a deeper and more profound bond. Courtney announced as much to her skeptical mother after their first year together, but Martha remained unconvinced.

"Let's see a ring, darling," she would say with a dismissive wave of her jeweled hand as she drank her first—but not her last—martini of the day at five.

Two years into their relationship, Courtney had begun to feel sad that they did not seem to be heading toward marriage as so many of her friends had. She didn't want to think like her mother, but for her the pressure was building. Michael preferred things as they were.

He certainly loved her, but was somehow reluctant to take the next step. He even resisted moving in together. It went on like that, with Courtney trying to balance her love for Michael with her subtle feelings of rejection. By year three she had made her displeasure with their arrangement clear to Michael, so he viewed this evening as his chance to make it all up; to really show his love and good intentions to everyone, to really join the family.

When they showed up at the restaurant for what she thought was their anniversary celebration, it all seemed perfect. Courtney looked like a movie star in a low-cut silver dress and Jimmy Choo heels that showcased her long legs. Michael was dapper in a blue Brioni suit. Restaurant patrons stared as the handsome couple made their way to their corner table.

"You couldn't look more beautiful," Michael said as they settled into the red leather booth.

"And you couldn't look more handsome," she replied.

He sat back in the luxurious setting with his arm around Courtney and felt a surge of confidence. It was all turning out the way he had dreamed. Courtney was the right girl for him, and he loved her deeply. Even if other women had turned his head, he had remained faithful to Courtney. With the one exception of Larisia. *All men are the same. God made us this way*, he thought, conveniently. *We all slip once in a while.*

The Sandoval deal was going forward, and from all indications he and Joey would soon be in Mexico City signing the biggest deal of their careers. He was elated it was all coming together.

As the dinner went on through the second course, Michael signaled to the waiter for the second bottle of champagne. He slipped the ring under the bottle and decided now was the time. As Courtney held out her glass, he picked up the bottle. The ring glistened on the table, but she didn't see it at first. He poured her champagne, and placed the bottle back on the table next to the ring. She still didn't notice. Finally, he placed his glass right next to the ring, and she looked down and saw it. Her eyes lit up as Michael picked up the ring and got down on his knee.

"Court, honey, nothing in this life matters more to me than you. I'm sure you know I love you with all my heart." He took her hand and slipped the ring on it. "Will you marry me?"

She took in a deep breath and put her hand to her mouth in disbelief. After a brief moment they stood up together and she wrapped her arms around his neck and kissed him deeply. The moment was perfect.

"Michael, I love you and always will. And yes, I'd love to be your wife," she said with a big smile. The whole restaurant, which had gone silent when he proposed, broke out in applause. They hugged each other, slightly embarrassed, and toasted everyone in the room. They held hands as they sat back down and with broad smiles poured another glass.

At that moment Michael felt his phone vibrate with a

text. He resisted the urge to look at it and stayed with her until she excused herself and went to the ladies' room. Now was his perfect opportunity to call their friends who were waiting at the St. Regis, give them the good news, and check his messages. He dialed Joey.

"Dude, you're not going to believe this but against all odds, she said yes," Mike told Joey, who had him on speaker with the crowd listening in.

"What? Is she crazy? She could do so much better than you," Joey teased. Michael could hear the crowd behind Joey laughing.

"Come on over here when you two lovebirds get done. We're already half-drunk. We'll celebrate. And, Michael, man, I love ya, really, and congratulations to you both—from all of us." Michael heard the cheers in the background.

"Thanks, pal. Thanks everyone. It's all coming together," Michael said. He hung up and almost forgot to check his texts. He only had one. He recognized Larisia's number. He never put her name into his contacts; his way of keeping it all confidential. Courtney came back to the table before he had a chance to read it. He slipped his phone back into his pocket.

"Any news?" she asked with a smile.

"Well, yes, my lovely fiancée, our presence is requested by a rowdy bunch of friends over at the St. Regis who have been waiting for our big announcement. They want to celebrate with us," he said smiling, holding up a glass of champagne.

"Wow, you set all this up in advance? I'm impressed. What if I said no?" she asked.

"Then they would have stayed there all night getting drunk while I went and jumped into the East River," he said.

"Ah, now, Michael. I would never have let you do that." She smiled and hugged him. He held her close and felt his phone vibrate again.

Ignoring it, he jumped up excitedly. "Honey, let's pay the check and beat this pop stand. Our friends are waiting."

"Okay, my handsome fiancé," she giggled. "Sounds good, don't ya think?"

They dashed out into the warm Manhattan night and hailed a cab for the quick ride to the King Cole Bar. "No chance you're walking in those heels," he said.

"They're made for sex, not for walking," she replied with a sly smile as the cab pulled up. He got an instant hard-on as she grabbed him by the crotch in the back of the cab. He in turn discovered she had no panties on. Both found the intense cab ride way too short.

"There they are," said Joey, as the couple walked into the crowded bar. Everyone swarmed. The girls surrounded Courtney, giggling and ogling her bling. The guys grabbed Michael with hugs and back slaps. The drinks flowed. It wasn't till an hour had passed that Michael had time to head to the bathroom and check the text from Larisia.

Michael, please call me. I have to talk to you.

She had sent it three times.

He had no chance to call that night. The party went on and by three-thirty, back in his apartment, the newly engaged couple were too tired and a little too drunk to have the sex that had been on their minds since the cab ride.

"We have a lifetime to catch up," he said as they fell asleep in an embrace.

His cell phone rang at 7 a.m. He picked it up out of a dead sleep and saw Larisia's number. He clicked the hang up button and went back to sleep.

"Who was that?" a groggy Courtney asked.

"Oh, nothing . . . unknown caller . . . probably selling something," he replied as he turned over his pillow and drifted off. In a minute the phone dinged a voice message. Courtney reached over him and picked up the phone. The screen showed a voicemail and just a number. She gingerly put the phone back down and tried to go back to sleep. She was slightly disturbed by the early call but said nothing and after twenty minutes she drifted off, too exhausted for further conversation.

"Michael, I have to talk to you as soon as possible. Please, call me," Larisia's voicemail said. He was walking toward the subway on his way to work when he finally dialed her back.

"Hello, Michael," she said.

"Larisia, what's going on? Is he back?"

"No. Not that I know of—but no, this is not about him. I'm sure he's gone, but I've got to talk to you in person. It's important. When can we get together?"

Mike wondered what the fuss was about. "Can't you tell me on the phone? I gotta go to work. We got that big deal going and I'm leaving for Mexico in a few days. No time, I'm swamped—oh, and I thought you should know, I got engaged last night. Took your advice and she said yes. That's why I couldn't call you."

Larisia took a deep breath. "Well, that's good. I'm happy for you Michael, but you gotta make time for me. We have to talk in person."

"Okay, okay, if you insist. Can we meet in Grand Central again? It's close and with the subways—"

"All right," she said, sounding annoyed. "I'll meet you there. Same place as before?"

"Same place. In the corner of Grand Central—the Campbell Apartment. It's cozy," he said.

"Yes, fine. See you at one? That okay?"

"Yes, that's good," he said, and hung up.

When they met at the bar Michael looked harried and unusually disheveled for a guy who took a lot of pride in his appearance. Larisia was composed but dour. Umber shadows circled her dark eyes. The stained-glass windows and wood-paneled room seemed a perfect setting for her mood.

"Larisia," he said, "what's the matter, baby? What's so important?"

"Funny you should call me that—baby," she said after a pause. "How are you? Or should I say, what's wrong? You don't look well."

"Oh, I'm okay. Just running hard ... busy," he replied.

"Well, you look like hell. But at least your face is healed," she said as she touched his eye.

"Yeah, that's like ancient history at this point. Did all that really happen?" he said with a wry smile. "Right now, I'm just swamped. Leaving in a few days for Mexico. Getting ready for this deal and I'm badly hungover, barely functioning. We had the big engagement party last night —wasted. But never mind me. What's going on? You sounded so stressed."

"Well, I'm not feeling too great either," she said with an almost theatrical pause. "I'm sick every morning."

"What? A cold coming on?" he replied, missing the hint.

"No ... morning sickness. I throw up every morning," she said, staring at him, waiting for it to sink in.

"A flu? What?" Michael was blank-faced.

"No Michael," she kept staring in disbelief. "I'm pregnant."

"What?" His face turned pale.

"Yes ... pregnant." She gave him an incredulous look, as though he was beyond dense.

"What? When did this happen?" he said, in denial.

"When did it happen? Shit, you know when it happened—about eight weeks ago now. Remember? It's your baby—I mean it's our baby. I just did the test yesterday. It was positive."

He seemed unable to comprehend the words. He stared at her for a long moment.

"What? Are you sure?" he muttered. "You're pregnant?"

"I did the test twice. It came up positive both times. I'm going to the doctor this afternoon to double—triple—check, but I know my body. I've been through this before," she said.

"Are you kidding?"

"I wish I was, but no, I'm not." Larisia shook her head in disbelief.

"Are you sure . . . ah . . ." He hesitated and looked down.

"What? That it's yours?" Her face turned hurt then angry. "Yes. It's yours. I don't sleep around and believe me, I'm not happy about . . . ." She hesitated, already very conscious of the new life she carried. "I mean, this is not something I wanted either."

"Ah, I'm sorry, I didn't mean that. But are you sure, you know, that you're pregnant?" Mike said, taking her hand.

"Yes, I am. But I'll know for certain this afternoon." She pulled her hand away from him and a lone tear slid down her face. "Michael, look, I don't want anything from you if that's what you're worried about. I'm not gonna cause you any trouble. You can go on with your own life. I can do this on my own. I've done it before," she said as her voice quivered. "But I thought you should know."

Michael was stunned at her implications. His mind raced ahead as he tried to collect himself. He was simultaneously struck with fear and, suddenly, felt a deep desire for her. He put his arms around her and held on tightly.

"Larisia, honey, I'm sorry. I don't doubt you. I'm just floored. Sorry." The words came out haltingly and as he held her, he felt her body heave with a deep, quiet sob.

After a long embrace, Michael said, "Look I'm here for you completely. You know I have feelings for you but this . . . ." He stumbled. "This is something—"

"I don't want you taking pity on me. I don't need that. I can handle this. I've been there, remember? And don't ask me to get rid of it. I can't do that. I'm having this baby. It's God's gift to me, to us, and I can't go against that."

"No, Larisia, I know that, and I respect that. Look, don't worry. I'll help. If it's my baby—"

"If? If? It's yours," she shouted as she pushed him away and put her hands to her face to hide her tears. She held onto the bar and a few patrons stared at them.

After a minute or two, he tried to embrace her again but she would have none of it and pushed him off.

"I'll take care of you. Don't worry. I'll give you money, I'll help with the baby, I'll do whatever you need. I want to. Please don't push me away," he said quietly.

She began to cry again and relented, allowing herself to lean into him. He held her close as her fragrant dark hair flowed across his arm. His emotions swirled. He could hardly admit to himself that all he wanted that very moment was to make love to her.

"I mean it, honey. I'll be there for you. We'll do this together. We'll get a babysitter—daycare, whatever. I'll pay all your doctors' bills. Don't worry. I'll take care of you. I wouldn't let you do this on your own. I'm there. I promise."

"Thank you for that," she said, softening.

"I'll always help you. Whatever you need. Believe me," he said.

They embraced for a long time and then, after calming down a bit, ordered drinks. The bartender, who had kept a respectful distance, came over with two whiskeys. They clicked glasses and locked eyes.

"I'm not sure I should drink this—probably not good for the baby, but right now I really need it," she said.

Eventually the tension passed and they settled into a quiet moment.

"How do you think your new fiancée is going to handle this?" she asked.

"Oh, God . . . I have no idea. I'm not sure I want to break it to her right away." Even the thought of telling Courtney was too much for him to take on right now.

"I understand, Michael, but don't put it off. She has a right to know. You are going to tell her, aren't you?"

"Yes, yes, of course. But I'll handle it. I gotta let all this sink in, give it some time. It's a lot to digest." His heart pounded as he thought about the future.

"Yeah, for me too." She looked down and inhaled deeply.

He put his hand under her chin and gently brought her face up to his. "No matter what, I will take care of you and your—I mean, our—baby. Believe me, I will." He kissed her on the cheek. As he leaned in and inhaled her scent, it gave him an instant hard-on. He fought the urge to kiss her full lips. He felt her respond to the sexual energy before she gently pushed him away with a half-smile.

"Sorry, but we're better as friends. Just stay true."

"You have my word," he said, staring into her tearing eyes.

After a long pause and a brief hug, he finished his drink and said he had to get back to work. She nodded and kissed him gently on the cheek. She looked up at him as he gently brushed away a tear and smiled.

"I want to be part of this—I have to be," he said.

"I'll let you know what the doctor says. We can talk about other things later." She paused and held his hand tightly. "Michael, remember, I'm not asking anything from you. And I definitely don't want your pity. I'm too proud for that. I'll have this baby with or without your help. I've done it before. I can do it again."

She smiled as she slung her bag over her shoulder and headed off. He watched her as she walked out, never having anticipated the depth of his feelings as she disappeared into the crowd.

The next day she called him to confirm what she already knew.

Less than a week later, settling into their first-class seats to Mexico City, Michael ordered a drink from the flight attendant before takeoff. He asked Joey if he'd like one too.

Joey looked at him. "Dude, I'm not drinking on this trip till we have a signed deal. I don't know how you can, but please, do me a favor, let's minimize it. Okay?"

"Have I ever screwed up anything 'cause of drinking?" Mike narrowed his eyes at Joey.

"No, never. But you know what I mean. Anyway, you seem down … something's off. What's on your mind? You didn't hear anything about, ya know, that night—did ya?" Joey asked.

"Well, shit, now that you asked … fuck yes. I got a problem." Mike turned to Joey. "You're not going to believe this one. You remember Larisia?"

"Yeah, of course, the waitress," Joey said. "The hot one?"

"Yeah, her … well, guess what?" Mike asked.

"What? I'm afraid to guess," Joey said.

"She's pregnant!"

Joey nearly jumped out of his seat. "What? No—you gotta be kidding me!"

"No, not really …" Mike said.

"It's yours? I mean from that night?" Joey asked.

"Yup, that's what she says," Mike replied.

"And you believe her?" Joey said.

"Yeah ... actually, I do."

"Jesus and holy shit. What the fuck are you gonna do now?"

"I don't know ... I'll help her. Got to. She's not asking me for anything. But I want to help. I don't really know. Haven't really had time to figure all this out ... been a little busy with all this stuff ... the wedding, Sandoval," Mike said as he finished his scotch. "But I'll tell you, she's a really great girl."

"What? You drinking the Kool-Aid too? Great girl or not, this is a shit show," Joey said. "What the fuck? How are you going to tell Courtney?"

"Don't know that either. I'll handle it, somehow. For now, I'm just pressing ahead with our wedding plans. There's no stopping that now," Mike said calmly. "Can't tell her now. I'll just have to figure something out."

"Can't tell her ... no shit." Joey looked at him and grabbed him by the neck. "Of course you can't tell her—she'll rip you a new one. Jesus, man, you're unbelievable, nothing slows you down. I'd be a fucking wreck."

"Shit, what else can I do? I just gotta keep pushing," Mike said.

"You sure it's yours?" Joey asked.

"Well, not really. How can I be? For now, I've just gotta go with it. But, you know ... I believe her. I actually do. She doesn't want anything from me. What I do know is

I've got to help her, any way I can." Mike shrugged his shoulders.

Joey looked askance at his friend and changed the subject. "Did you ever hear anything else from those cops —ya know, the ones that came to the office?"

"No, I think I handled it okay. Well, mighta fucked it up a little, but they just went away . . . doubt they had anything," Mike said.

"Hope so," Joey replied, then after a long pause. "Whaddaya say we just concentrate on this deal for now. We'll worry about the rest later." Joey smiled at Mike. "Look, pal, I'll help you any way I can . . . really want you to know that. We're brothers. I don't know what I can do for you with this one, but just want you to know I'm here for you, whatever you need, man, I'll do it, okay? Anything. But please, try to remember—you gotta keep that thing in your pants, you putz."

"Thanks, dude. I know you will . . . and you may be correct about the pants thing but you're a putz too," Mike said.

"Okay, I'll give you that. For now, put it out of your mind and think about the good stuff coming."

"Yeah, right, I can't think about her right now. I need a drink and a nap. Let's talk about the deal later." Mike smiled as he settled back in his seat and ordered another drink. His mind was racing but he closed his eyes and tried to think only of the business at hand. Joey sat next to him, staring into space with sweat beads forming on his brow.

On the ground in Mexico, Sandoval greeted them with a smile and brought them to the presidential palace in black limos flying presidential flags. Their meeting with the elderly president himself was brief but positive. They sat in an imposing marbled conference room with high ceilings and crystal chandeliers, oversized flags of Mexico and USA at one end, behind where the president sat. Once the president entered the room everyone stood in silence as the old man was helped to his gilded chair at the head of the long, marble-topped table. He seemed a little confused as Sandoval explained to him in Spanish the reason for the meeting. At first Mike got the feeling it was all a formality, window dressing. Sandoval was really in charge, and the decision had already been made. But the wily old man asked several questions about employment opportunities and overall financial benefits to the country.

"Señor McGowan," the president asked in Spanish. "Do you feel there is room for growth in this industry we are now bringing to our country on a larger scale than ever before?"

"I think you have an opportunity to grow this business enormously in the coming years, as they have in China, where the size and number of casinos dwarf anything in Las Vegas. Our research has shown it has become a major source of revenue for that country, not to mention a major international tourist magnet. The benefits for the country have a multiplying effect, providing jobs for all the businesses that supply these casinos, from construction and maintenance to finance, banking and the creation of ancillary businesses, like restaurants, supplies, and transportation."

After Sandoval translated, the president asked, "Do you see this business as a positive support for our vital real estate and tourist businesses?"

"Sir, from my point of view, nothing could be a better fit for increasing growth in both those economic areas. It will also raise the international profile of your country if the casinos are done on a world-class level as we have advised," Michael said.

His proposal was relatively simple. Morgan would act as a fiduciary in financing the deal and underwriting it, help raise money from investors by issuing bonds, and provide extensive consulting services to guide the Mexican government with managing the entire project. The fees would be hefty and there would be a series of percentage incentives for Morgan if the casinos hit their numbers.

The president paused and seemed to be thinking about the deal. After a long moment he unexpectedly rose from his chair and thanked both men with a warm handshake. Speaking in perfect English for the first time, the president announced, "We'll only have this project on an entirely world class level or we won't do it." With that everyone got to their feet as he smiled and left the meeting with a gracious nod and an informal "adios."

· · ·

Sandoval later said the president was impressed with them. He also said the president felt their character and had a good feeling about them as honorable men.

Later that evening there was a small dinner party at the palace with Sandoval and his wife, who was the president's oldest daughter, the president himself with his wife, Michael and Joey, and an aide. Most of the conversation was in Spanish, with Sandoval periodically giving them a brief English translation as a courtesy. The president and his wife left early. Sandoval explained that the old man needed his sleep.

"Our deal goes forward as planned. As you can see, the president is leaving a lot of this to me, and as far as I'm concerned we're on the right track, gentleman. The president will sign all the documents in the morning. There will be no ceremony. The president is not certain this will be highly popular with the electorate, so he has decided to keep it low-key. No reporters or pictures." Sandoval he got up and shook their hands. "We've made arrangements to drive you to the airport tomorrow. You'll be on the 3 p.m. flight to JFK, first class."

By three twenty-five the next day, Michael, was relaxed and ordering a whiskey on the Aeroméxico flight back to New York, signed documents in his briefcase.

"The old man was sharper than I thought. He asked the right questions," Michael said after takeoff.

"Really, I don't know how you do it. You spun out those answers like you knew what was coming. Just incredible, but with the shit that's happening in your life, man, I don't know how you can even think straight," Joey said.

"Yeah, sometimes I don't know either," Michael said with a half-grin.

They both settled into their seats with their drinks. Joey tried to sleep but he couldn't quiet his mind and enjoy the moment, despite what seemed like a stunning success. He appreciated that he would not be here without his friend and mentor, Mike. But his partner's tendency to press the limits and sail through hair-raising situations sent Joey's blood pressure soaring. He tried to let it all go as the plane climbed into the clouds and Mike snored next to him.

8

CANCÚN HONEYMOON

Diego Hernandez, eleven years old, was riding his bike along River Avenue in the shadow of the elevated train. He stopped for a minute, put his leg on the curb at the corner of 151st Street for stability as he waited for the light, and looked down into the sewer grate under his wheels. He saw a shiny object. He got off his bike, leaned it against a parking sign, and got down on his knees on the curb to get a better view. Pressing his face against the cast-iron street grate and inhaling the rancid sewer fumes, he still couldn't get a clear view. But he saw something reflecting light that intrigued him.

He got back on his bike, went home, rigged a broom handle with a hook made from a wire coat hanger, fastened it with duct tape, and came back to the grate. On his knees, he struggled to hook the object without knocking it farther down the drain. It teetered at the edge of the dark hole, half-covered with garbage, rank street debris, and saturated newspaper. He could hardly make out what the object was. With an unsteady grip on the last three inches of the broom handle, he hooked it and felt its heft as he gingerly pulled it up, hand over hand, out of the sewer. A silver pistol emerged from the darkness, dangling from the improvised hanger hook. He examined it closely, knew it was real and, popping out the small magazine clip, saw it was loaded with copper hollow-point rounds. He slid the cartridges back into the pistol, wiped it off with his shirt, and slipped it into his pocket. He had a good idea who would want to see it.

"Juan, I've got something you're gonna wanna see," Diego said to the local drug dealer standing on the corner.

Diego reached into his pocket and pulled out the silver .25 caliber "Saturday Night Special." It glistened in the afternoon sun.

"Whoa, little man. Where'd you get that?" said the skinny, tattooed Juan, smoking a cigarette and holding the crotch of his 501s.

"Found it," said Diego. "It's real. You wanna buy it?"

"Buy it? I'll just fucking take it from you, you little prick. You shouldn't be walking around with no fucking gun ... get yourself in a motherfucking bunch of trouble. Gimme that thing." Juan reached for the gun.

Diego jumped back and pointed the pistol at Juan. "Fuck no. You ain't taking nothing from me."

Juan stood back. "Hold it, kid. Don't point that thing at

me." Then after a minute, "Okay, come here. I ain't gonna steal it from you. How much ya want for it?"

"A hundred dollars."

"A hundred? I'll give you fifty," Juan said. "Let me see it."

"No good. You think I'm stupid. I want a hundred, man. You know you got it, selling shit on this corner every day. Give me the money, then you can see it," Diego said.

Juan, shaking his head, reached into his pocket, took out a roll of cash, and peeled off five twenties. "You're a tough little bastard, aren't you? Here kid, take it and gimme the piece. If it's good, I'll let you keep the money."

Diego reached out, took the money, and handed the gun over.

"Hey, not bad. It's got bullets in it too. Nice and small." Juan stuffed the gun into his hang-down waistband and covered it with his long T-shirt. "Keep the money, kid. And keep your mouth shut too. Okay?"

Diego pushed the bills into the pocket of his jeans. Juan watched him as he got on his bike and pedaled off, smiling.

The drug trade had grown in the neighborhood as the Mexicans had taken over. In his three years as a street dealer, Juan never made more money than now. The demand never stopped for the newest rage: black tar heroin. The drug had been brought in by Mexican nationals who had direct ties to the poppy farmers in Xalisco. It was a less purified but more potent form of heroin that was responsible for the huge spike in overdoses that had plagued the Bronx in recent years.

Though Juan considered himself Mexican, he was born in the US. He was bilingual so he was allowed to sell the product that was normally restricted only to a tight knit group of men who were rotated back to Mexico every six months. The cartel-aligned group had mastered the American corporate model of vertical integration: They controlled the entire supply chain from growing the poppy, to harvesting the tar, refining it, importing it, and finally delivering the finished product to towns and cities all over the United States. They set up safe houses or local businesses that acted as central distribution points. Street picked up the product in bulk and repackaged it into small quantities for retail sale.

Juan would take the black tar, roll it into BB-sized balls, put five to ten of them into a balloon, and tie it off. He'd then hit his normal street spots, carrying the balloons in his mouth. He spit them out one at a time for his customers. If ever approached by police he'd swallow the balloons, which would stay intact in his stomach. Later he'd take some castor oil and shit them out.

The demand grew every day, but for Juan it wasn't enough. He was a hustler and a moneymaker for the Xalisco group, but he knew the real money was further up the chain. He wanted his own franchise of dealers, each bringing in two grand a day. But not being a true Mexican, he was never allowed to move up or expand.

He had an idea to change all that.

Juan stood in the alley across the street from the bodega. In the shadows, he watched the hand delivery of a box marked "milk" by a guy he recognized from the neighborhood. He knew it wasn't milk, and he knew now was the time to move on his plan before the drugs got into the hands of local dealers and put out onto the street. As soon as the courier got back into the waiting SUV, Juan checked the pistol and cocked a bullet into the chamber. He cupped the small gun in his palm, pulled down a black stocking cap over his face, and made his move.

He walked in and immediately went up to the startled clerk at the counter. Pointing the gun in his face he yelled, "Give me the box. I know what you got. Do it now, motherfucker."

"What box?" the clerk said in a quivering voice.

"The fucking drugs, you piece of shit. I'll kill you right now!"

The clerk reached below the counter with a sudden jerky movement. A jittery Juan panicked, stepped back, and squeezed the trigger. He froze as he heard a dull click. The misfire emboldened the clerk, who jumped over the counter swinging a bat. Juan half-turned to avoid the blow but it caught him on the shoulder with a deadening thud. He felt his bones crack as a stunning pain exploded across his neck and back. Juan spun around, re-cocked the pistol, and managed to fire a shot. It hit the muscular clerk high in the chest, but the small-bore round seemed to have little effect. The clerk kept charging. With a wild swing his bat crushed the side of Juan's face. The force of the blow knocked Juan through a shelf of canned goods and slammed him up against the refrigerators, rattling the bottles of beer and Gatorade. Half-dazed, Juan fired again, hitting the clerk in the forehead right above his right eye. It dropped him in his tracks. Juan slid down the glass doors and passed out on the tile floor, bleeding from his ears and mouth.

Krasnowsky sat behind a low stack of papers at his battle-scarred desk in the four-two precinct. He held a black phone to his ear as an oscillating fan on a cluttered windowsill swept back and forth, occasionally blowing loose papers onto the floor. His forehead and upper lip were beaded with perspiration and lines of sweat tracked down the side of his face following the edge of his long sideburns. Occasionally he'd dab at the droplets with a folded, graying handkerchief. The delicate gesture seemed oddly effeminate in contrast to his meaty hands.

"Eddie, anything from Forensics on that cab shooting?" he asked his partner on the other end of the phone.

"Yeah, just got the report. Got a prints match on a guy named Carlos Estrada. A rap sheet two miles long, a real fucking gangsta," Eddie replied.

"Okay, so what's the delay?" Krasnowsky asked. "Let's pick him up."

"We can't. He's in prison."

"So? That's good," Krasnowsky replied. "Where?"

"No, not good. Prison in Mexico."

"Mexico? Aw shit, that ain't good," Krasnowsky said. "Fucking extradition, takes forever."

"We may also have his blood in the car and—you're gonna love this—that night, the night of the shooting, he was found unconscious on the street not far from the scene with a bullet hole through his face. Precinct guys brought him to Lincoln Hospital."

"Perfect. A prime suspect. How'd he end up in Mexico?"

"Our guys ran a warrant check on him. As soon as they red-flagged him they called the feds. ICE took over, had him patched up, and sent him back," Eddie said.

"Did he have anything on him?" asked the lieutenant.

"Yeah, well, no gun, but according to their report that they found him with two grand in cash in his pocket and sporting a new Rolex, probably hot. The bad news is it all went back to Mexico with him," Eddie said.

"This could be our guy. I think we need to reach out to our friends south of the border and start the process to get him up here. Let's talk to the chief."

"Yeah, good idea. Another thing, we got other blood in the car too—in the backseat, along with prints, different from Estrada's or the driver. No matches so far," Eddie said. "And we got hair too."

Krasnowsky laughed. "Hair? Of course you got hair. It's a fucking gypsy cab, Eddie. Probably got half the hair in the Bronx in there."

"Not this kind of hair—like a clump, a handful, like in a fight," Eddie said.

"Oh, okay, a fight. Hmm, so now it looks like we had a trio of skells in that car, who really didn't like each other," Krasnowsky said.

"Yeah, the fucking Wild West. What'd ya think? Drugs?"

"Maybe. Did they find any in the car?" Krasnowsky said.

"No. Just a joint."

"How 'bout the trunk?"

"No. Clean."

"Then it's just about money . . . it's always about the money," Krasnowsky said.

"What now?"

"Let's see if we can get Estrada up here. That may take some time, but we gotta talk to him. My question is: who's scumbag number three, the shooter?" Krasnowsky teetered back on his chair, cradling the phone with his shoulder and staring at the ceiling.

"Oh, and Eddie, in the meantime, call Lincoln Hospital to see what you can get from them. We need the full medical details on Estrada—blood type, description of medical procedure, all that."

"You got it."

"Hey, did you ever dust that bank card for prints? You know, from that bullshit hedge-fund guy," Krasnowsky asked.

"Bank card?" Eddie said. "Did you give that back to me?"

"Ah, shit—you know I did. Don't tell me you fucking lost it?" screamed Krasnowsky.

"No. If you gave it to me, I got it . . . don't worry," Eddie said.

"I am worried. Find the fucking card, would ya," Krasnowsky demanded. He slammed down the phone shaking his head. "How the fuck did that guy ever get a gold shield?"

Within a minute the phone rang again and Krasnowsky, expecting to hear Eddie's voice, picked it up with a barking, "What?"

"Ah, lieutenant?" A timid voice came over the line.

"Oh, ah, yeah, who's this?" said Krasnowsky, backing off a little.

"It's Sargent Cooper at the front desk. We just got a report of a shooting at a bodega on Jerome Avenue. We got the perp. Looks like he killed the clerk. Robbery guys are there already. You wanna go over or do you want me to call Johnson?"

"Yeah, send Eddie. Let's see what he comes up with."

"How about those fucking Yankees? Looks like they're in the playoffs," Joey said as he sat in his office sharing a sandwich with Mike.

"Yeah, thanks to our friend Fernandez. He seems to be

getting stronger as the season has gone on. We've got what, maybe six games left? I think they're in. Could take the whole thing this year," Mike said.

"Yeah. With strong pitching, I think they got it," Joey replied.

"Hey, Sandoval is really moving fast on this," Mike said, changing subjects.

"They're hoping to break ground by spring. They don't play in Mexico. They go. I'll bet we have another deal with them in less than a year," Joey said. "It may even be bigger."

"Yeah, let's hope," Mike said. His cell rang. It was Larisia's number. "I gotta take this," he said, turning away.

"Hey, babe, how are you feeling?" he asked.

"Hi, Michael. I'm okay, I guess. I'm over the morning sickness but starting to show just a little—almost four months now," she said, "But, I had to call you, 'cause I'm getting frightened about my nursing license."

"Why, what's the problem?"

"I'm afraid. They want to fingerprint me for my license application. They may find out that I'm not legal. What the hell do I do then?"

"Do you have to do it?" he asked.

"Yes. I'm sure I do. The state requires fingerprints to issue the license. I've still got a little time, but sooner or later I'll have to do it. The school has asked me already. Do you think they'll find out and send me back?" She started to cry. "Mike, I've been working so hard for this . . . and I'm so close to graduating."

"Hold on, baby. Just cool down. I think I can fix this. I got an idea. Let me try to get some information for you first, maybe call an immigration lawyer. Give me some time, okay? I'll come up with something. You're not going back," he said.

"Oh God, Mike, this has been so hard. Thank you . . . thank you for anything you can do."

"I'll get back to you. Just take care of yourself and that baby, okay?'

"Okay, Mike. And thank you for that check. It helped a lot," she said.

"You're covered. I told you I'd take care of you. I'll let you know. Talk to you later." He hung up.

Mike sat back and thought for a long silent moment. He looked at Joey with a focused stare while Joey stared back with a quizzical look on his face.

"What now?" Joey asked, trying to go back his tuna.

"Oh, she's panicked that the school will find out she's not legal. She's actually very exposed. The school may be obligated to turn her in to the feds if they find out. I don't know. I gotta help her." Mike was still looking at Joey, sizing him up.

Joey rolled his eyes. "What the fuck? Every time you pick up that phone with her it's another problem. Man, you gotta do something."

"Yeah, I know." Mike stood up and walked around the desk. He stared at Joey and put his hand on his shoulder. "Look, I've got an idea, and I really need your help. You're the only one that can do this."

"Oh, boy. Here we go," Joey said, abandoning his sandwich. "What is it this time?" He leaned back and folded his arms across his chest.

"You know, like you said, we're buddies . . . you're there for me? Remember that?" Mike smiled.

"Yeah . . . I guess." Joey sounded wary.

"Look, you said it, you know it—you did."

"Okay, yeah, so . . . what scheme have you got cooking up in that fucking distorted brain of yours?" Joey asked, forefinger at Mike's head.

"You gotta do me the biggest favor in your life. Not just for me, for her—for my baby," Mike said.

"Ah oh, here it comes." Joey shook his head. "I'm already getting scared. Spit it out, will ya?"

"Okay. You ready?" Mike paused dramatically. "You gotta marry Larisia for me. Keep her and my baby here. Otherwise, shit, who knows. They'll send her back and my kid becomes a Mexican. I'm out. What the fuck do I do then?"

Joey leaned back and widened his eyes. "What? You're fucking nuts? I got a girlfriend. Remember Melissa, numbnuts? How the fuck do you think she'll feel with me marrying some Mexican broad? Plus, I don't want to marry her. I don't even want to know her. No way. You're crazy."

Mike was up now, pacing and undeterred. "Melissa doesn't have to know. We'll keep it a secret. No one will know, just us three. Anyway, you know you're not going anywhere with Melissa. You said it yourself. She's just not the right girl."

"Hey, fuck you, man. I told you that in confidence. I was half-drunk."

"Look, it doesn't matter ... you'll get divorced in a few months. As soon as she gets her green card you're out. I'll pay for everything—won't cost you a dime. You don't have to do anything with her, just show up, say 'I do,' go back to work. In a few months it's over, nobody knows anything. Stay with Melissa, it's fine," said Mike.

"You know you're out of your mind, don't you?" Joey asked, shaking his head and looking skyward.

"Please, man, please. I'm begging you. I just don't want my baby to go back to Mexico and be born there. My only child so far. Shit, I can't let that happen. You gotta help me here." Mike held his palms together in mock prayer.

"Aw, fuck, how do you even know it's your kid?" Joey asked.

"Well, okay, I don't—not for sure, but if it is I'll never forgive myself for letting my baby leave here and be born in another country. I may never see him or her again. I'll have no rights as a father at all. Shit, I can't take that chance. I'll find out if it's mine after it's born, but for now look how many people you're helping. If it's not mine, no harm done. She shouldn't go back anyway—too good a person to have her dreams crushed. It's a nightmare for her. And the kid ... you're saving his life too, whether it's mine or not—and I'm pretty sure it is—the kid will be able to live here as a citizen and have a real chance in life. I'll make sure of it."

"Mike . . . shit. Really? How the fuck am I gonna do this?" Joey slumped his shoulders in exaggerated surrender.

"Joey, baby, leave it to me, okay, I'll set the whole thing up. I'm getting to be an expert at this shit. I'm in the middle of my own wedding, ya know," Mike said with a laugh.

"Yeah, yeah, I know."

"So come on, dude . . . you in? Please, man, you promised you'd do anything for me. You'll be saving my life and theirs too. You're really helping someone. She's a really good person, too, you'll see. Joey, I need you to come through on this, man. I'll pay you if you want," Mike said.

"Aw, fuck you, another shit show thanks to my buddy, Mike," Joey said, shaking his head and heading toward the door. "And I don't want your fucking money."

Mike grabbed him by the shoulder. "Is that a yes?"

"I gotta think about this . . . you're rushing me," Joey said, half pushing him off.

"I know I am, but I gotta. She's scared to death and needs a break. It's been on my mind for weeks. Let me call her and take this thing off her back. She'll be forever grateful—we both will."

"Oh, man," Joey said with a dejected look. He mockingly banged his head against the wall. After a minute, "Okay, fuckface . . . only for you. Her, I don't know at all, and right now couldn't care less, but as long as I get out quick and no one knows. And it's not gonna cost me anything, right?"

"Baby, my pal, I love ya, man. Thanks, really. And no, it's not gonna cost you a dime. And when you get to know her, you'll see, she's a great girl. I mean it," Mike said. "You're really doing good for her and me and the baby—and the country. We're better as a country with people like her here."

"Okay, okay, enough already. You handle it. Tell me where to go and we'll get it done." They high-fived and Mike bear-hugged him in elation, hoping to squeeze any doubt away, as Joey stood limp. "I guess you really need this."

"Yeah, I really do. You're a lifesaver," replied Mike.

Mike's phone rang. He released Joey, saw it was Courtney calling, and clicked into the call. "Court, honey, I was just talking about you. What's the latest?"

Mike smiled as he turned away from a Joey. "Wow, that's great. So the St. Regis confirmed the date, then? Great, they got the cancellation? We're solid for November 15? Unbelievable. Luck o' the Irish. It was meant to be then. Great news." Mike gave a thumbs up to Joey as he continued talking excitedly with Courtney.

Joey started to head for the door. Mike grabbed him by the collar and dragged him back in.

"Honey, baby, I'm in the middle of something right now," he said. "Yes, great news . . . let me call you back a little later. Love you, baby." He hung up.

He turned to Joey. "Come on, man. You're the best.

Can't thank you enough." Mike put his hand on his friend's shoulder.

"Looks like we're both getting married very soon, huh?" Joey said with a crooked smile. "Maybe we should all go on our honeymoon together too. How about Cancún, all four of us, almost five?"

"Yeah, great idea, ass-wipe," Mike said with a half-grin. "I love Mexico."

"Me too—or should I say—I used to." Joey, head down, walked out.

9

A BROKEN TOOTHBRUSH

"So the perp shoots the clerk here?" Eddie Johnson asked, pointing to a crimson puddle in the middle of the bloody and chaotic scene inside the bodega. The clerk's lifeless body had just been removed by the forensics team and the place looked like a bomb had hit it. Red stains were splattered across the glass of the refrigerator doors and the wall.

"Yeah, the clerk took two shots. One in the chest and one in the head—-looks like that was the kill shot, but he did manage to make our job a lot easier by crushing the shooter's skull before he died. We found the perp out cold in the back by the refrigerators—still had the gun in his hand," said the uniformed officer, reading scribbled notes from a leather-covered duty pad. "We sent him to Lincoln."

"What kind of gun?" asked Eddie.

"Here it is," another officer said, holding the silver pistol in a large plastic baggie.

"Oh, of course, another 'Saturday Night Special' piece of shit. Did you get to talk to him at all?"

"Talk? I don't think so . . . lucky he's alive," said the cop.

"Okay, good. I'll go over later to see if he makes it, maybe have a little chat with him if he wakes up. Give me the gun. I'll have ballistics check it out," Eddie said. "Anything else?"

"Well, yeah, we found six bricks of black tar heroin under the counter if you find that of any interest," said the other cop.

Eddie looked at him with a sly grin. "Oh, yeah, I get it now. So, we got a simple hold-up for drugs and money, a dumb perp with a shitty gun, and a dead clerk who should've been the lead-off batter for the Yankees. Nice." They all laughed as cops sometimes do in the face of incredible carnage.

At that moment a radio call got the robbery unit's attention. "Hey, Eddie, we got another call over by the Stadium. Can you finish up here? And could you do me a favor—check the drugs and gun into the property clerk's office? We gotta go—oh, and don't forget the Louisville slugger."

"Yeah, sure. Gimme the whole thing. I'll check it in. No problem. Not much more to do here anyway. You guys go ahead."

"Thanks, Eddie," said the cop as he jumped into the

unmarked car and stuck a red light onto the roof as they
sped off.

A few days later Eddie stopped by Krasnowsky's stuffy
office. The overweight detective was dabbing his sweaty
brow again as Eddie came in.

"So, what's with that bodega shooting?" Krasnowsky
asked.

"A drug holdup. The victim fought back and got the
chance to hit the killer with a bat before he died. Knocked
him cold. I just left the perp in the hospital; looks like he'll
be okay. We got him dead to rights. He knows he's
screwed, but the interesting part of the story is the gun."

"Yeah, what's so interesting?"

"Well—you're gonna love this—ballistics just told me
the gun used in that holdup was the same gun that killed
the cab driver over on 155th Street and, my guess, put a
hole in Estrada's face too," Eddie said.

"Same gun—what? You mean we got a two-for-one?"
Krasnowsky said. "Wrap up both crimes with one jerk-off
lowlife?"

"Well, no, I wish," Eddie said, sitting down and putting
his feet up on Krasnowsky's desk.

"Meaning?"

"Well, it's the same gun, but this guy—the one in the
hospital—is not the guy that killed the cab driver. He was
in Rikers at the time of that shooting," Eddie said.

"Rikers, huh. So, same gun, different shooter. This shit never stops." Krasnowsky shook his head. "So, where'd he get the gun?" He pushed Eddie's oversized feet off his desk.

"Just finished tracking that now. The perp, whose name is Juan, said a kid, a Diego Hernandez, sold it to him. I talked to the kid, and he said that he found it in a sewer on 151st Street and sold it to the shooter. I believe him. He's eleven." Eddie said, now sitting upright with his feet on the floor.

"What? Found it in a sewer … an eleven-year-old … fucking unbelievable," Krasnowsky said, scratching a crusty scalp of thinning red hair and lost in thought. Flakes of dandruff dusted his shoulders.

Krasnowsky was up now and pacing. "But, okay, makes sense with the cab homicide. So, somebody's trying to get rid of evidence after shooting the cab guy on 155th. But they're either stupid or in a panic. They dump the gun in a sewer but it's a place where it's easily found—not thinking. Gotta be an amateur."

"Yeah, probably," Eddie said with a shrug.

"Any prints?"

"Not really, nothing clear. Too many hands involved," Eddie said. "But the lab guys found some blood under the butt handle of the gun. O-positive, same blood type as in the back of the cab."

"Good. So it looks like we may be able to connect the gun to the perp and the cab. Wonder how the fuck blood got under the gun handle." Krasnowsky knitted his brow.

"Maybe in the fight somehow—somebody got cracked." Eddie shrugged again.

"Yeah, probably. Mighta been in a fight for the gun," Krasnowsky replied, after more scratching and dandruff. "So the gun ends up in a sewer on 151st Street?" The overweight detective muttered to himself as he walked over to the yellowed precinct street map tacked on the wall. "Where's the closest train stop to 155th Street?"

"I think 149th Street." Eddie pointed to a spot on the map.

"Hmm, 149th. So the gun was found on 151st and River Ave, in between the shooting and the train stop." Krasnowsky traced his finger along on the map. "You think that's a coincidence, or was our shooter heading for the train when he dumped the gun?"

"Beats me. Who the fuck makes a getaway on the train?"

"A guy with no car obviously—and not a local," answered Krasnowsky. "Probably the same guy who hailed the cab in the first place."

"Makes sense," Eddie nodded.

"Okay, so we got a weapon and a victim. We got blood and hair—clumps. We got a suspect coming up from Mexico—I hope. Now we just need the shooter." Krasnowsky continued to pace. "Any ideas?"

"I got nothing," said Eddie.

Krasnowsky stared at him and just slightly shook his head in disgust. "Well, start thinking. We need a break in this fucking case. This gun may be it?"

Two weeks later, on a rainy Tuesday afternoon, Joey and Larisia stood awkwardly in the lobby of City Hall waiting for Mike. His presence was needed; he was going to be their witness. Larisia wore a simple navy dress with low heels. She held a small bouquet Joey had bought at the last minute at a local Korean grocer. Her dark hair was pulled up and back in a long ponytail. It made her long neck look even more graceful. She had slightly widened at the waist. Her olive skin radiated but her dark eyes were sad. Joey, wearing his work suit with a white carnation on the lapel, was struck by her beauty.

"You don't have to do this," she said. "I'll manage."

"No, don't feel that way. I want to help, and you need this right now," he said smiling. "And I promise to make a great short-term husband. Very few demands."

She laughed and, almost unconsciously, straightened his tie and brushed some lint from his dark suit. "Good. I'll make a great short-term wife. You can watch all the football and drink all the beer you want. No problem."

"Hey, that's terrific. This could work out." They both laughed.

Mike showed up, late as usual, shaking off his umbrella with a big smile. He put his arm around Larisia and kissed her gently on the cheek, then turned to Joey and shook his hand.

"Ya know, you two really make a beautiful couple," he said. Then, looking at Joey, "The bouquet ... nice touch."

"Gallantry is not dead despite rumors to the contrary," Joey said, handing Mike a carnation. "Here, I even got one for you."

"Great, let's look the part," Mike said as Larisia pinned the flower on his lapel.

Mike took out his iPhone and snapped a few shots as Joey and Larisia stood uncomfortably in front of a massive green marble column in the bustling municipal building. Then they tried a few selfies, pasting on awkward smiles amid the damp dreariness of the institutional setting.

"Do me a favor, don't send them to *Page Six*," Joey said, trying for a laugh. It bombed.

"Okay, I doubt we'll make the gossip columns," Mike said. "Let's head upstairs . . . the ceremony awaits."

"Okay, honey," Joey said to Larisia, reaching out his hand. "Let's get a little married." She giggled as she took it.

As Joey and Larisia stood before a balding and disinterested city official, holding hands and declaring their intentions to love, honor, and obey, Mike felt a strange mix of jealousy and relief. He wanted her, yet he wanted her out of his life. Joey was his friend but now, oddly, his rival. His mind spun at the unlikely turn of events that had landed them all here on this rainy day in this strange and unwelcoming setting.

As the clerk declared them husband and wife, Mike threw a handful of rice and cheered. The clerk asked that he not do that and expressed hope that he would clean it up. Mike laughed.

"Hey, dude we're happy for them," Mike said as he kicked some rice under a bench.

"We have another couple coming in immediately and they won't appreciate this mess all over the place," replied the clerk.

"Let's go have a quick lunch and celebrate," Mike said, ignoring the fussy bureaucrat.

Larisia smiled but declined. "I gotta get back to work," she said, slightly sullen. "No time."

"Okay, honey. I understand. We can talk about the honeymoon later," Joey said playfully.

She giggled and gave him a peck on the cheek. "How about Tahiti?"

"I was thinking about Cancún but considering recent events, forget that. I've always wanted to go to the South Seas," Joey said, with a laugh.

"We'll have to talk about it later," said Larisia with a half-grin. "I gotta go. But I just gotta tell both of you guys how much I appreciate your help. Really." She squeezed both their hands, then kissed them each on the cheek, and headed out the door without looking back. Joey watched her shapely legs as she rotated through the revolving brass door.

"Ya know, Mike. She is quite a girl."

"Ah, see? Told you. Don't get any ideas, okay?" Mike said, pointing his finger.

"Relax, pal. Just playing the part."

Santiago had received his orders. Rolls of sweaty flesh hung over his belt as the obese Mexican sat on the metal toilet in his cell and held a flame to the end of a plastic toothbrush handle. The green plastic softened, then bubbled in the heat. He reached his tattooed hand under his mattress for a hidden, single-edge razor and gently seated the razor into the softened plastic, blade side out. He doused the weapon with cold water, inspected it, and tugged on it, testing its strength. He sharpened the blade quietly against the bare cinderblock wall; after a few minutes of scraping he felt the edge. He held the blade tightly and shaved off a tiny, curled layer from his fingernail. Satisfied, he got up, placed the weapon into a folded towel, and headed to the bathroom.

The metal detector at the end of the hall stayed silent as he walked through and stepped heavily down the stairs. COs watched him on video screens as he entered the tiled bathroom. Fully aware of state law, he knew there were no cameras inside.

Once in, he surveyed the scene. One guy in a stall, another washing his hands at the sink, and a skinny kid taking a hot shower in the corner. Santiago waited in the entryway. The hand washer picked up the vibe, as inmates do, and stared at the corpulent Mexican for a moment. Without saying a word, he finished up quickly and left.

Santiago knocked on the stall door. "Que pasa?"

"What the fuck? I'm taking a shit. Leave me alone," said the voice from inside.

"You're finished now. Get the fuck out," was the reply. Santiago pounded on the door again.

The inmate opened the door impatiently. Seeing the assassin's eyes, he changed his demeanor and left immediately, holding up his pants with one hand.

The steam rose in the corner shower as Santiago approached. *Good*, he thought, *hot water gets the blood pumping. He'll bleed out in a minute.*

Juan was rinsing the soap out of his eyes, when suddenly a heavy knee pushed into his back and slammed him up against the wall. A powerful hand grabbed his chin from behind, pulling his head up and angling him backward and off balance. The other hand came around with the flash of a blade and sliced through his carotid artery and deep into his extended neck. Juan reached back, struggling as the thick hand came around again for another even deeper cut. A crimson cascade spread down his chest.

Juan was losing consciousness as he struggled for air. He reeled off balance and fell backward onto the floor. Santiago stepped on his chest with one foot, his massive weight pinning down the young man as he gasped for breath, arms flailing. Juan gurgled out a muted sound, but his severed windpipe prevented him from calling out. His own thick, warm blood flooded into his lungs. It gagged out of the gaping hole in his throat as he writhed on the floor. Steaming sanguine water flowed in florid swirls down the shower drain as Santiago stood silently over the body of his victim until the slim figure was motionless.

After a minute or two he stepped back, assessed his work, then broke the toothbrush in half and flushed each half down different toilets. He washed his hands and calmly walked out. COs monitoring video screens noticed nothing.

Two weeks later Bronx police responded to a frantic call from a sobbing mother. Felicia Hernandez had found her eleven-year-old son, Diego, dead in an alley behind their building. The boy had been strangled. There were no witnesses or suspects.

10

A GIFT BASKET OF TACOS

C iudad Juárez prison was hot and dusty, situated among scrub brush and cactus on an open plain of high desert outside the city. There were few trees or hills. The guard towers had sight lines for ten miles in every direction and the guards had high-power rifles with scopes and bulletproof vests. The perimeter was patrolled by guards with trained dogs. Escape was next to impossible. The few who got over the razor wire were usually shot by sharpshooters or died of thirst in the desert.

The prison was overcrowded, treacherous, and controlled by Mexican drug gangs. The leader of the country's top drug cartel, Pedro Lieja, was housed in a suite of air-conditioned cells on the second floor of E-block along with his wife, some of his children, and his own cook. He made all the important decisions about what went on behind the prison walls and everyone, including prison officials, knew it.

Carlos Estrada walked through the sun-drenched courtyard into the crowded cafeteria. It was bustling, hot, and smelled of fried tortillas and sweat. He got his plate of rice and beans and went to his usual table. He knocked on the table then stood silently, all the while looking down, waiting for the customary reply knock before he sat down. He kept his eyes only on his plate while he ate, knowing full well how dangerous it was to make eye contact with the general prison population. More than one hardened criminal overestimated his status and never saw the shiv coming. Hearing a return knock of acknowledgement, he sat down.

As he ate, he felt a hand on his shoulder. He stiffened with anticipation. Any touch is a threat. An assault is always a surprise.

"Amigo, Pedro wants to see you now. Leave your food. Come with me," said the voice in perfect English. Carlos didn't look up. He knocked again to leave, waited for the return knock, then got up and followed the man to E block.

Pedro was sitting on his bed in the back of one of the cells he and his family occupied. The barred door was swung wide open and a rattling air conditioner blew cool air into the small space, to little effect.

"Carlos, I have a job for you. The laundry truck leaves tomorrow at 7 a.m. sharp. We'll make sure you're on it and get you across. You'll be dropped off by The Cantena outside El Paso to pick up a backpack; bring it to our safe house in New York. Ricardo will set everything up for you from here."

"Sí, gracias, patrón," said a humbled Carlos. "You can trust me completely. What else do you want me to do?"

"Once you drop off your package your job is done for now. We'll contact you in New York." Pedro handed him a burner phone.

"Sí, bueno. I have some unfinished business there." Carlos pointed to the bullet hole scar on his face.

"I heard the whole story," Pedro said. "We have people in there that can take care of that for us."

"No please, patrón, I need to do this myself. I have a score to settle and I know how to find him. If I have a problem, I'll ask for help. Gracias." Carlos reached into his shirt pocket and pulled out a dog-eared business card. He handed it to Pedro.

"This is the guy?" Pedro said, as he read Michael's name.

Carlos nodded and smiled as he drew his index finger across his throat. He took the card back and put it in his pocket. "Sí. If I don't come back, you can finish him for me."

"Okay, amigo. We'll call you once you're in New York. Keep the phone close and make sure you answer it when we call," Pedro warned.

"It will be with me every minute. If I don't answer, you'll know I'm dead," Carlos said as he backed out of Pedro's cell. "Muchas gracias and God bless you."

The crowd gathered in the sumptuous ballroom on the second floor of the St. Regis. Chairs were set up in rigid order and an aisle was laid out, with a white runner leading up to a silk-draped altar in the front of the gilded, high-ceilinged room. Dramatic floral displays had been arranged on each side of the altar and the tall, flowered sprays were lit from below, casting imposing shadows on the hand-painted walls, adding to the sense of fairytale grandeur.

The families filed in and, after much excited chatter, found their seats. The McGowans and the McAllisters, in gowns and tuxedos, laughed and waved to each other from across the aisle. A priest in red-and-gold vestments stood in front. He held a leather-bound book of prayers and wore a beatific smile as the room fell silent and music began to play. Michael stood at the altar, facing the crowd in a black tux. He smiled at the gathering as he looked up the aisle.

The double doors in the back of the room opened after a few moments and the bridal party emerged, walking in cadence down the aisle. Six bridesmaids in royal blue gowns were followed by two diminutive flower girls in cream-colored dresses with blue sashes. The young girls smiled at their adoring families as they gently dropped pink flower petals on the white runner. A six-year-old blond boy in a navy suit and red bowtie carried a blue velvet pillow down the aisle. The pillow bore two gold wedding rings tied together with a white satin ribbon. The crowd approved with smiles and gentle words of encouragement to the slightly embarrassed youngsters.

Finally, the bride entered the room on her father's arm to sighs and tears of joy. Courtney, with her blonde hair up, skin glowing, and long, veiled train, stunned Michael with her beauty. She smiled at him from the back of the room and didn't take her eyes off him as she seemed to float down the aisle in her radiant white satin-and-lace gown. His eyes welled up as did hers. Neither had anticipated the depth of the emotion that the lavish ceremony had created. They were swept up in the all-consuming and loving energy of the moment.

At the altar, Courtney's dad blinked through watery eyes as he lifted her veil, kissed her gently on the cheek, and symbolically handed her over to Michael. He smiled at the couple and stepped back. The touching gesture was for Michael the most emotion he'd ever seen from either parent in the rock-ribbed McAllister family. It gave him a moment of hope that he might be accepted into the clan after all.

They reached for each other's hand as the priest smiled down from the elevated step of the improvised altar. He spread his arms and invited everyone in the room to join into the palpable energy that permeated the room. Michael, embarrassed, wiped away the tears that traced down his cheeks. His heart was pounding as he stared at Courtney.

"Please be seated," the priest said as the crowd rustled

into their seats. He reached out his hands slightly, turning his palms upward.

He smiled and waited for the room to settle down. "We've come here, all of us, friends and family alike, to witness the joining of Courtney and Michael in the Holy Sacrament of Matrimony. There can be no more joyous an occasion than the lifelong pledge to love another person more than oneself. In a sometimes difficult world of disappointment and often downright cruelty, this declaration is the foundation of our lives. Without it we are doomed to a world of selfishness and narrow interests. Instead, through this sacrament, our Lord has given us a way to understand his message of universal love and caring that expands our hearts to another and, by extension, to the whole of humanity. It is, in the simplest terms, a way to save the world—to love another more than you love yourself. To give more than you receive. And yet mysteriously, ironically, through God's grace, the bounty of gifts we inevitably receive in return are immeasurable."

The priest paused and looked directly at his audience whom he held in a breathless silence. He smiled broadly as he continued. "And of course it invites into the world new life through the children who, with God's grace, will be brought forth from this union into this love and into our world. No gift is greater than this renewal, this extension of life and love, and the commitment to sacrifice all for the sake of another. To give all for those we love and have that love ripple through the world. It is the surest and truest path to the Kingdom of Heaven. It is God's way. It's God's gift to us. All we need to do is follow his path."

The crowd stirred at the priest's stunning words and Michael, at that very moment, pledged to himself to heed the words and committed himself to a more honest and less selfish life than he had lived before this day. No more lies. No more deception. The impact of all he'd been through weighed on him. He felt his perspective had changed. After these current issues were settled, he promised himself, he would live in a way that hewed closer to the high standards of his traditional Catholic upbringing.

He looked over at his mother, whose eyes were filled with love and the joy of the occasion and at his dad, whose ruddy Irish face glowed with pride. He then smiled at Courtney and found himself overwhelmed with the deep love he felt for her. The room crackled with the loving energy between them.

Then the priest led Michael and Courtney to read their own handwritten vows to each other. They held their sheets with trembling hands. Halfway through his vows Michael had to stop and wipe away the tears that made it impossible for him to see his words he had written. Joey stepped forward and gave him a handkerchief. By the time they declared their "I dos" there wasn't a dry eye in the house.

The priest stepped back and raised his open hands to the sky. "I now pronounce you husband and wife." They kissed and the entire crowd stood and clapped. The beaming couple turned around and headed up the aisle to thunderous applause.

Photographers snapped the happy couple hugging and kissing family and friends. The little ones, happy it was all over, played hide-and-seek under the tables in the crowded cocktail hour. After an hour of hors d'oeuvres everyone headed upstairs to the fifteenth-floor ballroom and a fantasy world of splendor. Tables had been set with towering flower arrangements, simmering crystal, and the finest silverware. The gilded and hand-painted room was bathed in soft pink lighting.

Courtney's dad, as the host, stood at the entrance, holding a glass of champagne and greeting everyone. When the room filled, the crowd quieted down just before the couple entered the ballroom.

Mr. McAllister stepped into the center of the room. "Hello, everyone, and welcome to all you dear friends and wonderful family. I wanted to tell you how happy we are that you're here to celebrate with us this fabulous occasion—the marriage of our lovely daughter, Courtney, to our wonderful new son, Michael, who we welcome into our family as one of our own."

Michael held hands with Courtney, standing just outside the ballroom, listening to his new father-in-law's warm welcome. Maybe he was finally going to get the acceptance he had always wanted from the McAllisters. At that moment, he looked around the room and saw a standing Sandoval smiling as he held his champagne glass. An ebullient Joey stood next to him.

Mr. McAllister continued. "We couldn't be more excited about this wedding, and I'd like you to join with us in raising a glass and toasting them and their beautiful love. Let's wish them a long, happy, and loving life together. So please, help us welcome the best-looking couple in New York. May I present to you the new Mr. and Mrs. Michael McGowan."

With that, the double gilded doors swung open, and the new couple came marching in like royalty. The crowd broke into spontaneous applause as the band struck up the chords of "I Feel So Close to You Right Now" by Calvin Harris. Immediately, everyone got up to dance. Michael hugged his new bride and swung her around in the center of the dance floor surrounded by family and friends. The hugs and kisses kept coming all night.

The next day Michael and Courtney sat in the first-class lounge of Emirates Airlines at JFK airport waiting for their early evening flight. Courtney leaned over, kissed Michael on the cheek, and excused herself to go to the bathroom. At that same moment Michael's phone rang.

"Joey, how ya doing," Michael said.

"Oh, man. The real question is how are you doing?" he replied. "What a fucking shindig that was. Man, it was the best, absolutely. You good?"

"Come on, I'm on the moon. I'm just great. We're getting on the flight soon. Flying off to a new life with my new wife. Couldn't be better. Man, we had a great time." Michael said.

"Well, shit, yeah. Me too. Looks like your new father-in-law went all out for you guys, and what a great speech he made. You finally got what you wanted. You're in—he loves you. The mother-in-law too," Joey said.

"I know, I was really touched by all that. They're great now, but I get it. They were tough on me but just wanted to make sure I was the right one for their daughter. I'd probably be the same way with my own daughter, if I had one."

"Well, speaking of that, you may have one soon enough. Have you heard anything from Larisia?" Joey asked.

"Well, no. I guess she's okay, I hope so. I think she didn't want to bother me during the wedding and all. Joey, do me a favor and check up on her while I'm gone. I won't be back till early December. She might need some help," Michael said.

"You mean check up on my own wife?"

"Yeah, that's it," Mike whispered, cupping his hand around the phone. "Be a good husband and check in on your wife who's pregnant with my baby, will ya?"

"Well since you put it that way, sure. No problem—er, well, small problem. But it will get fixed, right?" Joey said.

"Yes, it will. I'm gonna turn a corner and fix all this shit. Cutting out my drinking ... it's too much. I'm gonna come clean with Courtney too—very soon. Just deal with the truth. I'm gonna make sure Larisia is good, and the baby is too, and I'm gonna get you straightened out too. Don't worry. That priest got to me," Michael said. "He was right. I think I lost my way a little."

"Wow, I'm glad to hear it man, really. You got religion . . . a little. That's good. I hope you do it. But before I forget I gotta tell you the best news of the night," he said and paused for dramatic effect. "You know our friend Sandoval?"

"Yeah of course, he was at your table—I put him there. How'd it go?" Michael asked.

"Well, I guess it went okay. He told me to tell you before you go off on your honeymoon, that he wants us to meet him for lunch when you get back."

"Yeah, and?" Michael said.

"Well, he's taking an option on twenty acres of prime waterfront in Cabo. He's convinced the president to go ahead with another casino project, only this one he says is gonna be even bigger than Cancún. He wants us to put together a proposal for the financing. He said the timing is right with the old man, who's got only two more years left in his term, and he wanted to move now before political winds change and the rates jump. He also mentioned— are you ready for this one—he might consider running for president of Mexico. Wants to keep that confidential— really confidential—but said this project is important for his future plans."

"No! You got to be kidding me. President," exclaimed Michael. "Wow, I'm guessing he needs this project just as much as we do. He needs it for his run. This will put him on the map. And that explains his emphasis on 'clean hands.'"

"Yeah, you're right. He needs to make this happen—clean and world-class. He also said we're on the top of his list. He's very happy with what we've done so far. He loves us, man, he really loves us." Joey said, almost squealing with excitement. "I knew it, man, I knew it would happen. Just not this soon."

"Holy shit and thank you, Jesus! He's been watching us. He's got a big future planned and he wanted to see if we were legit. Maybe last night put him over the top . . . fucking unbelievable. I was hoping that would work. Only one more reason for me to do the right thing here with Courtney and everyone. Man, this is it, we're there, baby. This is incredible," Michael said. "And, oh man, you're not going to believe what he gave us for a wedding present."

"A gift basket of tacos?"

"Yes, how'd you know," Mike laughed. "No fuck-face, a check."

"A check? For how much? A hundred pesos," Joey said, cracking up.

"Yeah, make that dollars and add two zeros."

"What! Ten grand, for your wedding? Shit, you asshole —I'll marry you for that," Joey said.

"Sorry man, I'm already taken—oh, and now that I think of it, so are you." Michael grinned into the phone.

"Yeah, thanks, and no one gave me any checks for it either. Now you really owe me, man."

"Hey, baby, you'll get yours, don't worry. We're rolling,

baby. President, can you believe it? No stopping us now," Michael said, as their flight announcement came over the PA. "Ah, oh, our flight. Gotta go."

"Where you going again?"

"We're flying to Dubai for a few days—gotta see it—then to Kenya for a six-day safari. Then we fly to the Seychelles for some real downtime. See you in a few weeks."

"Unless it's an absolute emergency, I won't be emailing you, okay. Just enjoy," Joey said.

"Great. Just keep the bad news to yourself till I get back."

"Don't worry, man, it's all good news from here on out," Joey said, as they ended the call.

———

Krasnowsky was sitting at his precinct desk when his cell phone rang. The screen showed the name Jimmy Gronkowsky, I.A.

"Whoa, a call from Internal Affairs. What, am I in trouble?"

"You? Always. You've been in trouble since the day you were born," answered a familiar voice.

"Me? What about you? You're no better, ya dumb Polack," Krasnowsky cracked back.

"Yeah, the last two dumb Polacks in the New York City police department," Jimmy said.

"Probably a good thing for the city," Krasnowsky cracked. "So, uh, what's up, Jimmy? It's been a while."

"Mostly good stuff. I wanted you to let you know I'm getting ready to hang up my spurs," Jimmy said.

"No shit. When?"

"Few months, end of February," Jimmy told him. "I just figured it was time to kick back and let the mayor send me a monthly check for doing nothing—just like him."

"How is that any different from what you're doing now?" Krasnowsky laughed. "Whaddaya gonna do?"

"Well, we're thinking North Carolina, like everybody else," said Jimmy. "Maybe a place by the beach. Do some fishing."

"What? No golf?"

"Golf? You know I hate golf. Can't stand the whole thing."

"Yeah, I know. It's for old guys—just not us old guys. Ya know, I heard there are more NYPD now in the Carolinas than in New York," Krasnowsky said. "Everything's changed."

"Yeah, you're not kidding. Not like it was. How's Gladys doing?"

"Ah, shit. She had an X-ray and they found something on her lungs. I'm worried. I told her to cut out the cigarettes. She says she has, but I'm not so sure. Tried the patch. The gum. Hypnosis. It's useless. She's going back in for some more tests. We'll know better in a few weeks," Krasnowsky replied.

"Oh, man, I'm sorry to hear that, Phil. Give her my best, will ya?" Jimmy said.

"Yeah, I will. She always liked you, Jimmy," Krasnowsky said. "Is Mary good?"

"Yeah, she's fine. She'll be getting social security this year," Jimmy said.

"Wow, seems like only yesterday we were both newlyweds. Man, those years went fast, didn't they?" Krasnowsky said. "Remember what we were like when we first got on the force?"

"Do I? Two fucking Polish cowboys from Greenpoint. They didn't know what to do with us. We figured we'd arrest every scumbag in the city. Clean it up for our neighbors, no mercy. Miracle we didn't get killed . . . came close a couple of times. It was fun then but now, well . . . ." Jimmy trailed off, sounding sorry they were talking about the past.

"Jimmy, I know this isn't the time, but I know you did everything you could do to help me back then. It was my fault. I pushed that shitbird too hard. I know I did, but the court should never have thrown out the confession. They did it. You know it," said Krasnowsky, starting a rant.

"Phil, don't do this to yourself. Ya gotta forget it. It's over. They cried coercion and the judge bought it. It was bullshit. We know that," Jimmy said. "They got theirs anyway, still serving time for that other shooting in Fordham, fucking lowlifes."

"Yeah, but I had 'em. They shot my daughter. They did it. A father has a right—"

"Philly, please. It wasn't your fault. You gotta let it go."

Phil took a deep breath, trying to let go of the searing memory. "Okay, okay, you're right. I can't let myself go back into that. I'll go nuts. It's already taken too much of a toll on my family."

"I know, I know. It wasn't right, but it's done. Gotta move on," Jimmy said quietly. "But I called you because I wanted you to know we just listed the house and we're getting some nice offers."

"Good for you, next steps," replied Phil, trying to calm down. "How's your end of the old neighborhood holding up?"

"Great. It's changing—filled with yuppies. Brooklyn is the new Manhattan. Construction everywhere. New money coming in. You won't believe this, up by me, they closed Visali's Kielbasa store, after all these years. The old man died and, ya know the story, the kids sold the building. Guess what's in there now?"

"What?"

"A taqueria," Jimmy said.

"What the fuck is a taqueria?" Krasnowsky asked.

"It's a fancy name for a Mexican restaurant," Jimmy said. "High priced tacos—and shitty at that."

"Really? Well, you won't see me there, but I'll miss the kielbasa store," Krasnowsky said. "Fucking Mexicans, killing everyone up here. Can't stand them. The Bronx is a bloodbath, and the drugs are out of control."

"Yeah, well now that you mention that, Phil, I did want to ask you something else," said Jimmy, turning serious.

"Did you investigate that shooting in the bodega on Jerome Avenue?"

"Ah, yeah, well we covered it, but I didn't go over there myself if that's what you're asking. I let my partner Eddie Johnson handle it. He needs the experience. Why?"

"Yeah, I thought so. Look, keep this to yourself, but the six bricks of black tar heroin they found at that scene turned out to be six bricks of baking soda and molasses," Jimmy said.

"Oh shit—what? The old gypsy switch?" Krasnowsky said. "Or maybe it was bad shit anyway."

"No, it wasn't bad shit, that makes no sense. That was one of their main distribution spots. The Mexicans would never put garbage on the street, it'd kill their business. No, someone grabbed the real stuff, mixed up a fake batch, and did the switch," Jimmy said. "And I'm sure the real stuff ended up back in the hands of the Mexicans by the time it was all over."

"Yeah, probably. No one would be stupid enough to try to sell it on the street themselves—not on Mexican turf. That's suicide," Krasnowsky said. "Got any thoughts?"

"Yeah, but I can't say right now. We're checking with the PD's property office on chain of possession, but my advice for now is to watch your back. We think the cartel's got someone inside the department—they just seem to know too much. It's not like the old days. You can't trust anyone now. We're looking at everybody involved," Jimmy said.

Then came a long moment of silence where it seemed

Jimmy wanted to say more but couldn't. "Look, Philly, you're the last of the old guard—I can trust you—but keep your eyes open. All I can say is don't trust anyone. Call me if you have anything. I'm around for a few more months and I'd love to nail this fucking rat before I go. Okay? Take care of yourself, pal. Good talking."

"Yeah, Jimmy, take care—and thanks," Krasnowsky said as he hung up.

The thought of someone in the department who would betray his brothers, who was willing to sell out the trust and honor of the job, devalue their sacrifice, and barter with the truth offended Krasnowsky on the deepest level. But it wouldn't have been the first time, and he knew it wouldn't be the last. His only thought now was to find that rat and bring him to justice.

11

ALL IN THE GAME

When Larisia saw Joey's number light up her phone she answered on the first ring.

"Hello, Joey, or should I say, my new husband?" she said.

"Yeah, that's it. You can call me hubby."

"Oh, please, let's not," she replied with a laugh.

"Yeah, you're right . . . stupid—but still cute," Joey said.

"To what do I owe this nice call?"

"Oh, that's cute too. Well, I was wondering what you were doing for Thanksgiving? I was hoping you'd be free and thought maybe you might like some company," he said.

"Well, that's nice of you, but I've got exams coming and I thought I'd do some studying," she replied. "And what about your girlfriend?"

"Well, we're kinda on the outs, so she went back to celebrate with her family in Ohio."

"Oh, sorry to hear that. Hope you're okay with that, but I'm just a little busy," she replied.

"I'm fine with it, but c'mon, wifey, you need a break. It'll only be for a few hours. I'll have you back by eight, eight-thirty the latest and you can study for the rest of the night. I know a great restaurant in the Bronx called Joe and Joe. It's right off the Bruckner. We'll have turkey with some cranberries and maybe a little lasagna and some penne arrabbiata. They're like family there. It's the best," he said.

"Wifey? Really?" Larisia laughed. "But, you know, that actually sounds good. Maybe . . . ." she trailed off.

"You'll love it. You can't stay home on this most American of holidays. And now that you're becoming one, you gotta celebrate like an American, only Italian-American style," he said.

"Okay, why not? But home by eight. I have a lot of work to do."

"You got it. Pick you up by four. We'll need at least a few hours—the food just keeps coming."

"K. I'll be ready," she said. "And Joey, thanks. I know Michael put you up to this."

"Larisia, please don't think that. No. This was my idea. He did ask me to check in on you, yes, but really this is on me—really," he said. "I'm looking forward to it. We'll have fun."

"Well, okay. Free food, I'm in," she laughed. At that

moment she heard a beep on her phone. "I gotta grab this. See you Thursday, four sharp."

She clicked over. "Hello?"

Long silence.

"Hello," she said. "Who's this?"

"Larisia?" said a vaguely familiar voice with a Spanish accent.

"Yes . . . who's this?"

The line clicked off.

"Hello? Hello?" A chill went up her spine.

Joey was there promptly at four. He called her cell as he waited in his Cherokee double-parked outside her building.

"Okay, I'm here. You hungry?" he asked.

"Yeah, famished, and you're right on time. Be down in a minute," she said.

Thirty seconds later, she seemed to bounce out of the front door of the tattered walk-up, full of energy: jacket open, showing a slightly enlarged stomach, dark hair flowing, and holding her scarf. She hopped into the passenger seat, leaned over, and gave Joey a peck on the cheek.

"How you doing, wifey?" he asked with a big smile.

"Great. Thanks, hubby. I feel good, and I'm starving," she said, rubbing her belly.

"Well, yeah, eating for two."

"Yup, constantly hungry lately. I think that's a good sign," she said.

"Well, you look great, that's for sure—and healthy." Joey put the car in gear and headed to the restaurant.

Joe and Joe was packed with holiday activity but Joey, an old customer, managed to get a table.

"Okay I was hungry before but now I really need food to stave off malnutrition," Joey said as they settled in and he rubbed his hands together in anticipation.

"Me too. Since you seem to know this place, I'll let you do the ordering," she said. "Give me the works."

A waitress named Josie came over and recognized Joey. She knew all the regulars, having worked there for fifteen years.

"Hey, doll," she said to Joey. "What'll ya have today?"

"Okay, Josie, we're talking about the whole holiday menu, turkey, all the fixings and the lasagna special. And bring us a bottle of your best Chianti."

Larisia held up her hand. "That's only for you."

"Oh, sweetheart, I see you're expecting. Congratulations," said Josie. "You make a beautiful couple."

They looked at each other, giggled, and let it pass.

"Thanks, Josie," Joey said, as she wrote down the order and left.

"There must be a reason why people keep saying that to us," Larisia said.

"I think 'cause it's true. We are. They'll just never guess the reality of the whole thing," Joey said. "But, ya know, this is going to work out. You'll get your papers, we'll make sure of that, you and your baby are going to be American citizens."

"I can't thank you enough for that." She reached across the table and patted his hand.

Joey tingled and felt his body light up at her touch. "No need. I'm actually enjoying being married—for now," he said with a smile. "So, tell me more about your life. Do you remember anything about your time in Mexico?"

She hesitated for a minute, not eager to bring it all back. The pain of the memories had never relented. The agony seared in her heart showed in her face as her eyes reddened and filled with tears, but it was important that he know.

"Well, yes, some of it. I had just turned seven when we left. We had a terrible time. My parents were heartbroken to leave, but we had to. I remember my mother crying almost every night," she said. "Before we left, we lived in a house close to the water just outside of Acapulco. It was beautiful. I remember being happy and playing on the beach. My father was a waiter in a restaurant at a resort that catered mostly to Americans. He spoke English very well and made good money. My mother was a nurse at the local hospital. I had an older sister, Carmelita," she stopped and looked down, holding back tears.

Joey leaned forward and put his hand on her arm as comfort. "Look I didn't realize … please don't cry. Sorry I asked."

"No, I want to tell you." She gathered herself with a deep breath. "At that time, the drug gangs were becoming more and more powerful in that town. The tourists stopped coming as the shootings became more common. One day coming home from school my sister, who was nine, was caught in a crossfire between two gangs. She was shot three times. She died in the middle of the street. My dad said he couldn't even go out there to get her body. It was too dangerous. She was just lying there dead in the hot sun for hours. The police were no help, he said. No one was ever arrested for the shooting. At that point they knew we had to go. After the burial, my parents closed up the house. We left everything behind—even my dog, little Poco. They gave him away. I remember crying about that for weeks. My dad paid a man to get us across the border to the US. We had nothing, just what we could carry. We came to the Bronx because his brother was here."

"Holy shit … I had no idea," Joey said.

"Thank God for my uncle. He saved us. My parents worked here in America but were always off the books. They could never really make much. By the time I was fifteen, ICE caught up with them and sent them back to Mexico. We had no papers. They wanted me to stay and somehow managed to keep me out of it. I lived with my aunt and uncle, but they were so busy with the restaurant I was pretty much on my own. I did some waitressing at the restaurant during high school. That was when Carlos began to chase me. He's the guy that Michael … well, you know," she said.

"Yeah, that part of the story I know. The good news I hear is he got sent back," he said. "But can you believe the crazy chance of it all? You meet Michael—and me—at the restaurant that fateful night, and then Mike manages to stumble his way into a cab with this guy Carlos a few hours later? Then the whole shooting—"

"Yeah, it's just unbelievable. Carlos had been arrested and sent back to Mexico years before. I had lost track of him. I didn't even know he was back in the neighborhood until Michael told me the story," she explained. "When Carlos was a young kid, he got involved with drugs and that gang. He was very violent and everyone was scared of him. Michael was right to save himself that night. They probably would have killed him. They have no qualms about murder."

"Yeah, he said that. They weren't letting him go . . . he knew it," he said. "Mike's a pretty tough guy actually."

"How do you know him?" she asked.

"Well, we grew up in the same neighborhood in Queens and we went to the same high school—Bishop Loughlin. He's two years older than me. When I graduated from college, was looking for a job, he was building a financial team at Citibank. He reached out and brought me into his group. We did well for them at Citi and when Morgan Stanley saw what we were doing they hired us away. That was over two years ago now. I owe Michael a lot for what he's done for me and my career. He's kinda been a big brother to me," he said.

At that moment the food showed up and they dug in with oohs and ahhs.

"You're right about this Italian-American Thanksgiving thing," she said with a laugh. "I'm starting to feel more American with every bite—and Italian too."

The food kept coming and by the time the coffee and pumpkin pie showed up neither could eat another forkful.

He reached over and put his hand on hers. "You're a good eatin' girl. My Italian mother would love that. She had no time for those picky types."

"Yeah, my mother too. If she made it, she wanted you to eat it and enjoy it. Nothing made her happier than people enjoying her food."

With full stomachs they both sat back for a long moment and smiled at each other. Joey had the irresistible urge to kiss her. She stayed right there as he leaned in, but once their lips met, she pulled away slightly.

"I don't know if this is a smart thing right now," she said.

He stared at her. "I don't know if I'm thinking too clearly at the moment. Between your beautiful face, the food and the wine, I'm a little foggy," he replied.

"Okay then," she said. "Let's just take this slowly."

"Yeah, this is complicated enough . . . even though I am your husband," he said smiling.

"Exactly my point. Do we need to make it more complicated?" she said. They each took a deep breath and silently tried to gauge the depth of these sudden feelings.

"Yeah, let's let the food settle."

On the ride home he reached over and held her hand

for a few moments. An oldies station played Tommy Edwards' "It's All in the Game." Joey sang along.

"'Many a tear has to fall'—that's love, and such a great line," Joey said. "They just don't make them like they used to."

She smiled. "Maybe that's a good thing, but I do love that song. And you have a pretty good voice."

He pulled up to the curb in front of her building. "Here you are, señorita. Right on time. As promised, eight-fifteen. May I escort you to your apartment?"

"Ah, no thanks. We'll take it slow, right?" she said. "I'm fine."

"Okay, you're right. I'll just stay here till you're inside, safe and sound."

"Well, thank you, Joey. You're a gentleman. I'm glad we did this . . . hubby," she giggled.

"That's my girl. Call me if you need anything, okay?"

He leaned over and kissed her full lips. She didn't pull back this time. She smiled and squeezed his hand.

"Night," he said.

With a quick, "Night, honey," she was gone and up the front stoop, two steps at a time.

He pulled away, still humming the tune and inhaling her subtle fragrance.

Amused and distracted by her date with Joey, Larisia fumbled in her bag for her keys in the dim light of the second-floor landing. As she turned the key in the lock, a tattooed hand came from the darkness and wrapped around her mouth. Another hand encircled her neck. She felt herself pushed into her apartment. The door slammed behind her and a familiar, terrifying voice whispered into her ear.

"You, puta, you make a sound, and I'll kill you right now . . . you understand, you fucking slut bitch?" Carlos raised a glinting straight razor to her eye.

Paralyzed with terror, she barely nodded. Her mind spun; she couldn't comprehend. A few moments passed in silence. He turned her around and held her back against the wall with his hand pressed against her nose and mouth. She took a shallow breath. He jammed his knee into her crotch and felt the bulge in her belly against his. Her eyes widened. He stared at her impassively as tears tracked down her cheeks and over his hand. Her body trembled. She was too terrified to move as he pressed the cold steel against her cheek.

"I will take my hand away now. If you scream, I swear I'll cut you up. I would love to see you bleed." He smiled. "You deserve it, you whore. You've been fucking more guys. How many men do you fuck? It means nothing to you, does it, bitch? I should know."

Suddenly enraged by the renewed memory, he grabbed her by the throat and slammed her against the concrete wall. Her head flew back with a dull thud, her knees buckled, and she crumpled to the floor like a ragdoll. After lying at his feet for a minute or two, she groaned as she slowly came to.

He kicked her in the ribs. "I told you not to make a sound," he shouted.

"I'm sorry, Carlos—I'm sorry," she cried as she rolled over and began to vomit.

He kicked her again. "Quiet. Shut your mouth, you understand."

Trembling while lying in her own vomit, she whispered, "Sí."

After listening for any sound outside, he grabbed her by the hair and dragged her into the bathroom, stumbling over her bag and sending its contents skittering across the floor. Holding her by the hair, he pushed her face to the mirror. The dim light of the streetlamp filtered through the frosted transom glass, leaving half the room in shadows.

"You see that face . . . that face. You think it's beautiful," he said, speaking in Spanish and holding the glinting razor close to her eye. "I will rip it apart. I will make holes in your face like your boyfriend did to my face." He turned his head slightly revealing a dark crater in his right cheek. "Your scars will be much worse than mine."

She shook her head slightly. "Please no. He's not my boyfriend," she whispered.

"Oh, so you know who I'm talking about." He stared at her as she trembled. "He's not your boyfriend? Yeah, you got lots of them, don't you . . . fucking whore. He's your baby daddy? Isn't he?"

She closed her eyes in surrender, expecting to feel the blade.

"Is he?" he hissed.

"Yes, yes, he is," she said, tears flowing. "But I don't love him … I'm not with him."

"No of course not. You're just a whore." He glowered at her. "Ya know, I knew it was you right from the beginning … when I saw the name … then I heard your voice on the phone."

He tightened his grip on her hair. "You'll fuck anybody."

He slammed her forehead into the mirror, shattering the glass which rained down onto the sink and floor. Her mind went numb. Blood from tiny cuts tracked down her face and into her eyes. Her legs quivered and she could barely stand. He held her face to the shattered mirror, shards still dropping.

"You devil bitch, you make men love you and you ignore them. You think you can control us, make us your fool. No, not this time. This time I control you. I cut you up—no one will want you. You'll beg me to stay with you and your little bastard." He backhanded her across the mouth with bony knuckles, knocking her against the wall. Blood began to seep from the corner of her mouth.

"Tell me where he lives."

"Carlos, I don't know … please, please don't hurt me. I swear I don't know. I was never at his house," she begged.

"Tell me." He leaned into her.

"I don't know . . . please, believe me. I don't," she sobbed.

"You liar. You are useless to me." He stood in stony silence for a long moment and then, squinting his eyes slightly, he pushed her against the wall with a forearm across her throat.

"Tell me or I'll cut you open," he said with a menacing grin. "Tell me, right fucking now, or I'll slice you open and kill that baby in front of you." He placed the cutting edge against her bulging belly. Her eyes widened.

"No, I don't know. Carlos, please . . . please, you must know something, now before you do this." She coughed out blood and tried to take a full breath. "I—we—have a daughter together. We have a child."

"You lying pig. You'll say anything to save yourself," he said.

"No, no, I swear. I can prove it to you," she said. "Look at my phone . . . on the floor. Turn it on. You'll see her face. She looks like you . . . your Carmelita. Look at her. You'll know her."

Stunned and visibly moved by her revelation, he pressed his hand to her chest to keep her against the wall. "If you move, I'll kill you."

He turned, picked up the phone, pressed the on button and saw the face of his seven-year-old child. He knew immediately she was his—the facial structure, the hair. He stared at her picture for a long time, the glowing screen highlighting the crags of his gaunt face. His eyes began to fill with tears. At first he seemed enraged, but after a while his shoulders slumped and he bowed his head. He looked at Larisia, eyes red.

"Why, why? You never told me? You never told me about her. How could you do that?"

"No, no Carlos ... I ... I was afraid of you. I was just a child myself when we were together, just seventeen. I didn't know what to do. I hid it from everyone, and then you were sent back to Mexico. I couldn't reach you. I was too afraid," she said. "There was nobody to help me."

"Where is she now?" he asked.

"She's back in Mexico, with my parents. She's a happy, and wonderful girl. She's in school. She always asks me about you, and when we can come to get her—you and me. Bring her to America. She wants to see you—her daddy. I told her you're very busy ... and that you love her. That you are a good man and will come to see her soon."

He dropped his hands to his side. "You made a fool of me. I wanted to love you, but you were cold to me ... a bitch."

"No, Carlos. You scared me. I was too young," she replied. "You raped me."

"No, you liar. You wanted me to fuck you. You teased me with your body. Your eyes begged me. I helped you to grow up. Made you a woman ... you were my woman and you shamed me. I loved you and you turned your back on me. My friends laughed." He approached her again.

"No, Carlos ... I was too scared," she implored, reaching out for him. "I was too young and frightened then . . . but I'm not anymore." Sensing a break in the threat she took a towel from the rack and wiped her face. She looked at him with her dark eyes. "I'm a woman now, not a child. I'm not afraid, not now."

He stared at her in the half-shadow. He watched her breasts, nipples protruding, rise and fall with each halting breath. He stepped forward and inhaled her. The faint light outlined her profile in black and white, her slender form a silhouette through her translucent blouse. She smiled and opened her arms as he got closer. She leaned back on the edge of the sink and spread her legs. Without thinking he dropped the razor, grabbed her, and kissed her deeply. She opened her lips and felt his tongue explore her mouth. His breath smelled of beer and cigarettes and she could taste the sour acidity of his saliva. She reached down and felt him getting hard.

"We can try again, Carlos," she whispered as she gently squeezed him. "We have a family already. We can be together again, now."

She unbuttoned her blouse and he buried his face in her full breasts. He traced his hand along the inside of her thigh. She jolted slightly, holding her breath as he pushed her legs farther apart and jammed his fingers inside her. She arched back. With his other hand he fumbled with his belt then dropped his pants to his ankles.

At that moment, legs spread, blouse open, she reached behind her into the sink. Her hand found a shard of mirror. As he suckled on her enlarged nipple, she jammed the jagged glass into his neck, once, twice, three times, ignoring the pain as the glass cut into her palm. It broke off in his neck and she felt the warm blood spraying out from the now gaping wound.

He pulled back wide-eyed, both hands to his neck, blood shooting between his fingers. He teetered unsteadily, legs tangled in his pants. She leaned back, crooked her leg, and kicked him in the chest with everything she had. He careened off balance across the room, arms flailing, and falling backward, slammed his head on the edge of the toilet with a dull thud. He slumped onto the floor. The blood pumping out of his neck wound formed a growing crimson puddle around his crumpled body. Larisia stood frozen in the shadow, listening to the gurgling sounds of his last breaths as he lay motionless on the cold tile. She didn't move, standing there in the dead silence, staring into the darkness in disbelief, out of the realm of time.

Finally, realizing it was over, she fell to her knees and sobbed. She cried till she was dizzy and shivering and exhausted. Her only thought was of Carmelita and how deeply sorry she was for killing her father. There was no malice. No revenge in her heart, only sorrow for sins never to be forgiven.

Almost half an hour passed before she had the strength to gather her thoughts and get to her feet. She winced as she put her bloody hand under the cold water and picked pieces of glass out of her cuts. She wrapped her hand in a towel then stared at the body that lay in a dark halo of blood on the black-and-white patterned floor.

She threw a towel across it; partly to cover the carnage, partly to cover her guilt. She dialed Joey.

"Hi, baby. Don't tell me, you miss me already, right?" he laughed.

She couldn't laugh. "Joey, something terrible has happened. I need you here, now," she said, voice quavering. "I can't explain it to you on the phone. Please, please just come here now."

"Honey, are you all right?"

"No ... yes ... barely. Just get here, please."

"On my way." He clicked off.

Larisia opened the apartment door when Joey knocked and fell into his arms as he walked in. Tears streamed down her face. He stayed silent, holding her and looking around.

"It's okay, baby. I'm here ... I'm here. Don't worry, I got ya," he said, as she shook in his arms. "It's okay, try to relax. What the hell happened?"

"Joey, you have no idea ... it was horrible."

"What? What was horrible?" he said. "What's with your hand, your face ... what happened?"

She took a deep breath. "Carlos. He was waiting for me when I came up to the apartment after you dropped me off. He grabbed me ... tried to kill me ..." She broke down crying.

"Carlos? What? Where is he?"

She walked him over to the bathroom, opened the door, and flicked on the light. He looked in, then slowly went over to the body and picked up the blood-soaked towel.

"Holy shit. You did this? You're amazing," he said as he stood back from the carnage. "So this is the motherfucker . . . good. Fuck you, man."

She stepped out and he followed. "How the hell did you do this? You're unbelievable, really," he said.

"I was fighting for my life. It was horrible." She buried her head in his chest. Then after a minute, "We've got to get rid of him."

"Wait, what? Call the cops. He tried—"

"No, you don't understand. It'll destroy my chance to become a citizen. No. I'm afraid—his friends in the neighborhood will come after me. Please, no . . . I can't." She turned away from him.

"Aw, shit. I've heard this before. This is not good. Forget the neighborhood. Come live with me. Get the fuck outta here," he said.

"No, no they'll find me. They do that. I don't want it on me. We've just got to get rid of him, dump the body somewhere. Probably no one even knows he's here," she said, turning cold.

"Oh, shit, this is fucked." He walked around the room. "It's a crime. We don't want to do this." He shook his head, hands on his hips.

"Okay, okay. I'll do it myself then," she said. "You don't have to be involved. It's okay. I understand. I'll rent a car and I'll dump him. I'm not going to the cops. No way."

"Do you even have a license?"

"I don't care. I'll do it somehow."

He grabbed her by the shoulders. "Oh, honey, no, please don't do this. It's not good." He felt her shudder as fear crossed her face. He realized he'd been too rough with her.

"No, no cops. If you can't help me just leave—now. I'll handle it." She pulled away from him and sat down on the battered couch. She crossed her arms and he saw her determined resolve.

He couldn't believe her strength. Her will. He went over and embraced her. She was still shaking. He realized he'd never felt this way about a woman before. She had more courage than anyone he'd ever met and at that moment, beat up and shivering, she looked more beautiful to him than ever. He realized, just then, that he was totally, fully in love with her, and that there was no turning back. No matter what. Suddenly it all became simple and easier.

"Okay, okay. I can't let you try to do this on your own. Too much. I'll help you, even though it's against everything I believe. I gotta help you." He shrugged his shoulders, then after a moment. "Have you got any duct tape?"

She nodded with a half-smile.

"Good. Let's pull down the shower curtain ... I'll wrap him," he said. "How about Clorox?"

She nodded again and gave him a hug.

"Rubber gloves?" he asked.

"I'm a nurse, remember? Plenty of rubber gloves—disposable too," she said with a smile. "I won't forget this ... thank you."

"He looked at her. "But wait," he said. "Your hand, it's bleeding. Let me—"

"It's nothing," she interrupted. "I'll disinfect it."

"Okay, good. Gloves on, start mopping up the blood with towels. Run the cold water and squeeze the towels out into the tub. Cold water washes out blood. Use the bleach to wipe down the walls and floor. Don't forget under the tub and behind the door and the bowl. Blood splashes, so wipe down the whole wall—top to bottom—even check the ceiling. We can use a broom handle and a damp towel to get anything out of reach. At the end we'll soak everything, especially your clothes, in cold water and bleach. We'll bleach out everything and then dispose of it all. Don't worry, honey, I'll buy you new stuff." Then he stopped for a minute and glanced around. "What happened to the mirror?"

"My head." She touched her forehead. "I can't talk about it ... not now, please."

"Okay, okay, don't worry about it—but we gotta clean up the glass. I'll replace that mirror," he said, his tone matter of fact.

She looked at him, then looked around. "How the fuck do you know all this?"

"I watch *NCIS*. They're always doing this kind of shit," he laughed.

After a few minutes of scrubbing, she asked, "Where we going with him?"

"The City Island Bridge. I've fished there. It's got a heavy current and it's deep. We'll toss him into the middle of the channel," he said. "They'll never find him."

"City Island? Shouldn't we just dump him on the street ... just another murder in the Bronx?"

"No, if you don't want to be involved, then it's better that he just disappears. Nobody will know what happened to him, especially his local friends," he said as they were doing the final tape wraps around the body. "Oh, and don't tape it off too tightly at the top or the bottom. Also, we'll need to make some holes in the shower curtain. Gotta let the air escape—don't need him floating to the surface."

She looked at him and shook her head. "You're unbelievable."

"Only for you, babe."

He sent her down the stairs first, holding a blanket. She popped open the rear hatch, looked around, then gave him the all-clear sign. He grunted as he hoisted the wrapped body onto his shoulder and struggled to hold the banister as he carried it down the steep hallway stairs and out the front door. He laid it down with a thud in the back of the car. "This skinny fucker is heavier than you think." She quickly covered the body with the blanket and closed the hatch.

"Get in and wait. Keep the lights off. I'll be right back," he said.

He went to the back of the building and cut off a long piece of laundry cord from an empty wash rack, rolled it up, and put it in his pocket. Then, in the darkness, he managed to find a half-broken cinder block. He came back to the car, threw the block on the floor behind the driver's seat, jumped in, and drove off.

They traveled along the empty Bronx streets in silence, then took the on-ramp for the Bruckner. "How the hell did he even know it was you?" he asked.

"Tracked me from Michael's business card. He said he thought it was me from the very beginning. Then knew for sure when he heard my voice," she replied.

"Yeah, and how many Larisias can there be in this neighborhood?"

They continued south and took the City Island turnoff. The road was empty at the end of the Thanksgiving holiday. He pulled off the road at the foot of the bridge, turned off the car and the lights, and looked around.

"Well, this is it. Looks right and we're lucky; the tide is high and no moon." He scanned the quiet road. "I'll tie the block around him. Once I get him out, you grab the block. Then we'll get him up onto the railing and toss the whole thing over. Okay?"

"Yeah," she nodded. "You sure you've never done this before?"

"Maybe . . . ." He smiled.

She got quiet for a moment and looked at him. "Do

you think God will ever forgive me for using the name of my daughter to save my own life?"

"I think he will. He gave you the strength to save yourself for your family. He wanted you to live. You did what was necessary. Gotta try to forget it for now." Joey stared at her. "Ah, can we talk about this at another time?"

She nodded. "Yeah, okay, no problem."

Just then a cell phone went off with a strident ring.

Joey turned to her. "Shhh! Is that yours?"

"No, is it yours?"

The phone kept ringing.

"No, not mine. Ah, no—it's his. Shit, we never even emptied his pockets. Fuck."

At that moment, a lone car slowly drove by. The headlights blinded them for a moment. The driver glanced over briefly and kept going.

"Shit, what the fuck was that?" he said in a slight panic.

"I don't know ... but what do we do now? Should we empty his pockets? We'll have to unwrap him to find it," she said, looking over her shoulder, out into the darkness.

"No ... no good. Let's just get this done, now. They'll never find him—and the salt water will destroy the phone anyway," he said, opening the door.

Then the phone went off again, for another cycle of ten rings. The ringing seemed particularly loud, echoing off the water on this quiet, moonless night. They stood frozen in silence for a long time after it stopped.

"Fuck," Joey said as he wrestled the dead weight onto his shoulder. "Grab the block," he said, puffing, as she closed the hatch. They struggled to the center of the bridge. He managed to lift the body onto the wide railing, placed the cinder block on top of it, and tied it on tightly with the laundry cord.

"Ready?" he said, looking at her wide-eyed and catching his breath. She nodded and together they pushed it over. It splashed and sank into the dark current.

"Go straight to hell, ya bastard. You've caused enough problems," he said. "And fuck you!"

Larisia quietly made the sign of the cross and lingered for a moment, whispering to Jesus for forgiveness while she stared into the black water.

"Let's get out of here," he said.

They jumped back into the car and drove off. Joey, uncomfortable and wary, maintained a moderate speed to blend into the light traffic on the Bruckner. They headed north and stopped briefly to throw the blanket and some towels into a dumpster behind a local supermarket.

"Hey, babe, I just realized, you can't sleep in that apartment. That's no good for you. You gotta come back to Manhattan with me, just for tonight. Okay?"

"I thought we were going to go slow," she replied.

"Honey, no obligation. We can go as slow as you like. I'll sleep on the couch if you insist. No problem. But remember, we're partners in crime now. Everything has changed," he said, and gave her a tense, oversized grin.

"That's not funny . . . but you're right. I can't go back

there, not tonight," she said. "Can I trust you to be a gentleman?"

"Me? Sure. Can I trust you?" he replied as he looked over at her.

She shook her head with a sly grin. It all sounded too familiar.

12

A NECKLACE OF TWINKLING LIGHTS

J oey was Michael's first call from the car as he and
Courtney drove home from JFK. He couldn't wait to
share the good news.

"Dude," said Michael, squeezing Courtney's hand.
"We're back."

"Yes, dude, glad to hear it," said Joey. "We missed you.
How was the trip?"

"Well, let's just say we had a ball. Dubai is unbelievable. It's our next place to do business. The money there is
off the charts. Africa, insanely beautiful. And the
Seychelles are paradise. We loved the whole trip," said
Michael. "How's things here?"

"Ah, let's just say it's been interesting in your absence,"
Joey said.

"In a good way?" asked Michael.

"Yes, mostly . . . but I think we got to sit down and talk,
just you and me—there's a lot to discuss."

"Don't tell me the deal is falling apart," Michael said.

"No, no, nothing like that, all good news there. In fact, Sandoval wants us to meet with him tomorrow. The Cabo deal is all ahead full. He's moving on it and we're definitely his guys," Joey said.

"Okay, great. I'll be jet-lagged, but anything for our guy Sandoval. Set it up for like one o'clock. I'll come in a little late and we can talk afterward," Michael said. "But before any of that . . . I called because I wanted you to be the first to know—"

Joey cut him off. "What? You're joining a monastery and you want to repent for all your sins?"

"Well, yes, that too," replied Michael, not missing a beat. "But more importantly, numbnuts, Courtney and I are having a baby."

"What? wow . . . I . . . I wasn't expecting that," Joey said. "What the hell? When did you find this out?"

"We just got the news. We have the results of a test Courtney took just before we left. We were purposely out of radio contact for a while there, so we got the news at the end of our honeymoon. A great way to finish it all off," Michael said.

"Well, congratulations are in order here. I'm really happy for you—both of you. Really. That's fabulous. Well done," said Joey, briefly feigning an English accent. Then after a moment, "I'm guessing you didn't mention anything about—"

"Ah, no . . . not yet." Michael was holding the phone to his ear as he looked over at Courtney and smiled. "So, ah

. . . thanks, man. We're over the moon. A whole new life ahead of us."

Michael continued after a moment. "Listen, we got a lot of people to call, so I'm jumping off, but you got it first. I'll see you in the office tomorrow. We'll talk then. Okay? Gotta go."

"Yeah, yeah. Don't worry about it. Great news. Talk tomorrow." Joey clicked off.

There was a light dusting of snow on this crystal cold December night. A necklace of twinkling lights strung across the Verrazano Bridge reflected off the roiling black waters of New York Harbor as the couple's limo sped along the Belt Parkway toward Manhattan. The windshield wipers swung in hypnotic cadence as the exhausted newlyweds snuggled in the back seat, each holding so much within themselves.

"Beautiful isn't it," Michael said. "It's good to be home."

"Yes, back to reality," replied a contemplative Courtney. "What did Joey say about 'not mentioning something'?"

"Oh, no," replied a surprised Michael, scrambling. "No, he was just talking about the office. We may change some of the office procedures . . . it's nothing really."

"It seemed like something important from what I could hear," she said.

"No . . . no, you know Joey. He's always worried. Takes everything so seriously. Believe me, it's nothing."

"Michael, are you happy? I mean happy with me, with

us—and now with the new baby? Are we gonna be okay?" she asked quietly.

He took her hand and stared into her pale blue eyes, which at that moment seemed slightly teary. "Honey, I couldn't be happier. I love you with all my heart. You know that. And now, with a little one coming, babe, really, there's nothing better than us, right here, right now. I'm the luckiest guy in the world—we're the luckiest people." He leaned over and kissed her.

"You wouldn't lie to me or do anything that may hurt us . . . especially now . . . would you?" she asked, her tender smile turning fearful.

"Never, ever. I promise. Haven't I been cutting back on drinking, for you, for us?" He smiled and hugged her as their limo crossed the Brooklyn Bridge into Manhattan.

The meeting with Sandoval dug into specific details of the deal. Joey explained the outline of the financing, which he expanded on with extensive and highly detailed spread-sheets. Michael went over scheduling, talked at length about projected numbers, and did some hypothetical comparisons to other casino operations. The meeting went on for more than two hours. By the time it was over, Sandoval was fully on board.

"Gentleman, we want to move ahead as soon as possible with all this. And I want your team to take the lead on putting this all together," the gentlemanly

Sandoval said. "We were going to bring in the Wynn Group to manage the facility, but with these recent accusations about sexual harassment by him we've decided against them. Can't be associated with that on any level. We're calling in MGM and we'd like you to participate in those meetings. So, let's go to the next level."

"We're here to help with anything you need," said Michael, cutting short his usual oratory. Sandoval seemed quietly confident, and everyone shook hands at the elevator.

"That was great," Joey said after the elevator door closed. "A minimum of bullshit. And it's clear they don't want anything to do with any scandals."

"Yeah, squeaky clean," Michael said. "We got 'em where we want 'em and too much talk can only hurt us. We said enough."

Michael walked into his office and closed the door. He turned to Joey.

"All right, so what's so important that we gotta talk?" Mike said abruptly. "And, oh yeah, before you start, you gotta be careful about what you say to me on the phone. Courtney heard some of what you said, and I had to do some dancing. I don't need more problems."

"Ah, yeah, I'm sorry. Shouldn't have mentioned it, but it's on my mind," Joey said.

"You talking about Larisia's baby?" Michael said. "Why is it on your mind?"

"Well, it's the whole thing. Larisia, the baby, the marriage—"

"Hold it," Michael said. "What exactly are you saying?"

"Well . . ." Joey hesitated. "In the last few weeks, I think I've begun to fall in love with Larisia."

"What? Really? In love?" Michael sounded incredulous. He all but dove onto the couch, staring at Joey, who stood like a statue in the middle of the office.

"Yeah." Joey nodded. "Yeah, really."

"Wow, that's one I didn't see coming. But I told you she's a great girl, didn't I?" Michael said, shaking his head.

"I didn't see it coming either. And yeah, she is, and sexy too," Joey said. "But don't get me wrong, this is more than just some pussy for me. I'm hooked. I feel more for her than any girl I've ever met. I love her, wanna take care of her. Tremendous person."

"Dude . . . she's pregnant with my baby," Michael said. "Get real."

"I know, I know. I have an idea about that too. That's why I wanted to talk to you." Joey halted and stared at the floor. "Look, it's a good thing that you didn't mention anything to Courtney. Don't. Don't say anything to her, or anybody else."

"Well, I gotta come clean about the baby sooner or later. I plan to talk to her, it just wasn't right during the honeymoon," Michael said. "I'm not looking forward to it but—"

"No, I understand that but, ah . . . ." Joey swallowed hard. "Look, I want to stay married to Larisia and I'll be the baby's father—if you agree to an adoption. Let the new baby be part of our new family. No one has to know.

It's not the first time a husband brought up another guy's baby."

"What? You want to do what? My baby. Now you're the father?" Michael got up and paced the room. He loosened his tie and gulped down some water. "You want to take this kid from me? Take my kid? What the fuck?"

"No, no, you can't look at it like that. The baby needs a home—a family. You've already got one and I'm afraid that if you tell Courtney at this point . . . well, shit, I don't know, but she may dump you right now. With this new one coming you've got what you want. Everyone's happy. And I'll be a great dad. No one would be a better dad to your kid than me. Right? It'll be our secret. You can see the kid whenever you like. We'll have other kids and probably so will you. We can all be one happy family. No one ever has to know. And you don't have to worry about losing Court, especially now with the new baby coming. She'd never forgive you. You know it. It won't work. It'd be all over. Do you want to risk losing everything?"

"You know, you can really talk some shit," Michael said, putting on a smile as he struggled with his own confused feelings.

"No, it's not shit. It's the truth and I think this is the only way that we all get what we want. I'd hate to see you and Court come apart over this. But it's your call, man. I only want to help. I'll love you either way, but I'm not so sure about Court," Joey said. "But no matter what, I don't want to lose Larisia."

Michael stopped pacing, took a long look at his friend

and shook his head. "Wow, you're that far gone, huh? All this in a few weeks?"

"Yeah, but ah . . . there's another thing that I haven't even told you yet," Joey said. "A big thing."

"A big thing? Bigger than this? What the fuck?"

"Okay, get ready. You're not going to believe this one."

"Hold on," said Michael, sitting down again. "Okay, go . . . this better be good."

"You remember your little friend Carlos?"

Michael nodded, slightly wide-eyed. "Yeah."

"Well, he returned . . . to the Bronx. Looking for you."

"That fucking animal. What the fuck happened?"

Joey stared at Michael. "Well, he found Larisia—from her number on your card—he found her, waited in her hallway, and attacked her with a straight razor. He was going to kill her to get to you. He wanted to know where you were—where you lived."

"Are you kidding me?" Michael said. The thought of Larisia in danger horrified him.

"No, I'm not. She refused to give you up and fought him—fought for her own life and yours. She battled this fucking piece of shit with a razor in his hand and, believe it or not, managed to kill him—dead."

Michael jumped up. "What the fuck? Killed him?" He pounded the desk with his fist. "Oh my God!"

"She called me in a panic right after it happened. Asked me to help her," Joey said. "We dumped the body in the river. Doubt anyone will ever find him."

"Holy shit . . . fuck," Michael exclaimed, pacing again.

"That motherfucker, she got him—wow . . . unbelievable. He got what he deserved, that bastard!"

"That's what I said. Unbelievably brave dame. She's unreal, but I'm telling you, she saved your ass. You owe her. He was coming after you," Joey said.

"So, shit, how the hell did it all happen?"

"Well, like I said, he waited for her in her hallway and attacked her. She said she tricked him as he was about to rape her and stabbed him with a shard of glass from the busted mirror. Right after that she called me, totally distraught, obviously. Blew my fucking mind, but had to help her get rid of the body. Crazy but I fell for her at that moment. We completely bonded. Anyway, he's gone now. Forever. It's over," Joey said, frazzled from the recall.

"She didn't want to call the cops?"

"Are you actually asking me that question? You, Mr. Coverup? No, she wasn't going to the cops. And if I didn't help her she would have done it alone, somehow, I'm sure." Joey said. "Told her we'll just make him disappear. No one will know anything."

"Goddamn it. How the fuck did she—?"

"Doesn't matter now. She's too traumatized to go into details but, trust me, it was a mess. Can you imagine, she stayed there as he bled out. She's got more balls than you and me put together," Joey said.

"Unbelievable. She's something. And I guess you're right, I owe her, actually. Brave girl. Is she okay?"

"Yeah, she's good mostly . . . some cuts and lumps . . . but good."

"And she's okay with you being the baby's father and you guys being together?"

"Yes, she is. We're good—really good. It's like everything changed between us that night. We've been together ever since, partners in crime," Joey said with a laugh. "I'm in love with her, Michael. Probably more in love with her than I've ever been with any woman in my whole life. I'm all in."

"What about your girlfriend?" Michael asked.

"Oh, that's over. You were right. It wasn't going anywhere."

"You know this is a lot to ask from me. Come on, man . . . giving up my baby?" Michael said. "I just don't know. Tough call for me."

"I know, Mike. But isn't it better that I be the father of your child rather than anyone else? This way we all keep it in the family, all together." Joey said. "Look, no rush right now. Let's not have it ruin our friendship. I only want what's best for all of us—and what can work. And I think this can work." Joey reached over and gave Michael a hug. Michael remained limp, eyes unfocused.

"I'm not so sure," Michael said, his mind reeling.

"Give it some time, man. We'll figure this out."

Eddie Johnson called his lieutenant on a snowy day in mid-December. "Hey, Phil, Merry Christmas. Santa just left us an early present."

"Oh, really, what? You've decided to leave the department and take that job in the post office?" Krasnowsky said.

"No, I found the bank card."

"Bank card?" Krasnowsky said, scratching his scaly pate. "You mean the one from that hedge-fund guy? What's his name ... McGowan?"

"That's it. You were right, I did have it. Found it under my desk. Must've fallen out of my pocket," Eddie said.

"Still in the bag?" asked the lieutenant.

"Yep, untouched."

"Good. Get it to Forensics. Run some prints. And while you're at it, see if you can get a read on activity on that account on and around the night of the shooting. Find out if there were any cash withdrawals. I'd like to know how that fucking lowlife Estrada got that two grand in cash that went off to Mexico with him," Krasnowsky said.

"You got it, chief," Eddie said. "I'll get to it tomorrow. Got a headache today."

"Just fucking do it, all right. And, ah, did you get any word from the Mexican authorities on Estrada's whereabouts?" Krasnowsky asked.

"Are you kidding? No one in legal answers my calls. I left three messages," Eddie said.

"Okay. Keep trying. Something will turn up."

13

LOVE FINDS A WAY

L arisia made a traditional Mexican Christmas feast for Joey at her apartment on Christmas Eve which included a red posole, an aromatic stew of shredded pork in a red chili broth with cheese tamales, and a roasted pork loin rubbed with mild peppers on white rice with a fresh salad of tomatoes, lettuce, and onions. They had a toast to Christmas with the Chianti Classico that he brought, but she only had a sip.

For dessert she pulled out all the stops with her specialty: traditional marranitos, a sweet molasses gingerbread cookie, and as an added treat, a delicate caramel flan with whipped cream. She topped it all off with her version of Mexican hot chocolate infused with a touch of cinnamon and chili powder.

"My mother taught me how to bake these cookies as a little girl. They are some of the few memories I have left of our life before . . . ." She hesitated and looked down. A tear formed in the corner of her eye. Joey walked over and held her for a moment. She looked up, gave him a quick kiss with a smile, and headed back to her cooking.

The apartment smelled of her exotic food mixed with her light floral perfume. As she toiled in the kitchen, he watched her slim form fill out her ruffled skirt and simple cotton blouse. Joey was moved to a new level of love and lust for her.

"I had no idea you're such a good cook. And so beautiful too."

"Muchas gracias, señor. Cooking is in our soul—and don't forget, I work in a Mexican restaurant," she replied with a coquettish smile.

They had decorated the tree together and after dinner, got ready to exchange presents while sitting on the floor in the glow of the lights. But first he poured two shots of caramel-colored reposado tequila. He took her hand and raised his glass.

She smiled. "Joey, you know I can't drink," she said, placing her hand on her bulging stomach.

"Yes, but just a taste. And, with a new baby coming, let's upgrade our marriage with a little bling." He handed her a small blue box.

Eyes opening wider, she opened the ring box to reveal a sparkling diamond wedding band.

Her eyes filled with tears as she took the glistening ring and gave it to him. "Please put it on me."

He slipped it on her ring finger and tears tracked their way down his cheeks too. Sitting there at that moment, both of them crying, feeling so much love for her, Joey felt transformed. The world was a different place, and he was a different man, because of her.

"Sweet girl . . . I love you so much. There's nothing I wouldn't do for you. You've changed my life completely. You saved me and I'll never be the same. It's us, for now and for forever. Merry Christmas." He leaned over and kissed her deeply. She melted into him.

"Joey, you have it wrong," she said, staring into his eyes. "You saved me and now, for us, everything is possible. I have not felt this way in my life. You are the first and only man ever to enter my heart." As they drank and kissed on the floor, he pulled up her skirt and they made love in the warm glow of the tree, shaking the delicate glass ornaments that tinkled with their passion.

They went to bed together that night, sleeping in each other's arms. In the morning, she made a light breakfast for him in her modest kitchen. The smell of strong coffee and huevos rancheros wafted through the apartment. He walked out of the bedroom in his boxers and socks, groggy, scratching his head and smiling as he surveyed the scene.

"Ya know, I haven't felt this at home since I was a kid, living with my parents in Queens. All the kids would get up on Christmas morning—I got two brothers and two sisters—and we'd make breakfast for my parents as they got up. Just like this, only not with the Mexican eggs."

She laughed. "Even before opening your presents?"

"Yes, my parents were strict," he said. "They wouldn't

allow us to open anything till we all ate together and cleaned up. Yeah, I hated it ... but it's funny, ya know, the anticipation made us enjoy the moments even more. We always said we were lucky they didn't make us get dressed and go off to Christmas mass like the Donahues next door. They were really strict."

"Who could sit still and pray when all you can think about is presents?" she laughed.

"I know, for us that breakfast was fun but after we cleaned up we tore into those gifts. Everyone was ripping wrapping paper, giggling. The girls tried on new clothes. The boys laughed at them. One year I got a new bike and my brother got a baseball glove. We'd hang around all day like that. My mother usually cooked a turkey. My aunt and uncle would come over. They were pissers. My uncle Jimmy usually got drunk, but he was a fun Irish drunk, not a fighter. My father and he would watch football on TV. I didn't realize how much I enjoyed all that till now. I'd like to do that with our family." Joey leaned over to kiss her.

"I thought you were Italian."

"Half ... the lower half," he said with a grin. "My father's Italian and my mother is Irish. That was Queens in those days. Most of the families we knew were different nationalities. The Italians, the Irish, and the Germans all mixed together. It depended on your exact neighborhood, but it was mostly Irish. Didn't matter. We all had a great time."

She smiled but a hint of sadness crossed her face. "I

guess I never realized how much I missed those kinds of days with my parents. Me and my sister and our dog . . . he was really my dog. We had to give him away—that I remember—but the rest is so faded in my memory now." She smiled. "I want to remake it and have that kind of life for our family too."

She hesitated for a moment and stared at Joey. "I'd like to bring my daughter Carmelita to America to live with us. She's such a sweet child. Are you okay with that?"

The question startled him a bit, but he nodded. "She's your daughter . . . she'll become our daughter. I want her here too. You wouldn't be happy without her, would you?"

"No. I miss her every day," she said.

"That's it then. Once we get settled, we'll get her here." Joey smiled, hiding any doubts he had about living with the child of the man who had almost murdered his friend Mike and assaulted his love and whose body he had just recently thrown into the river. He wondered about how he'd feel about the innocent child who carried her father's genes. The daughter of a possible murderer. The thoughts lingered with him and made him uncomfortable, but his feelings for Larisia seemed to wash them all away.

He stayed with her the next few days and they made plans to celebrate New Year's Eve together. They looked forward to the new year and a new life for both of them. Larisia, for the first time in her adult life, began to feel the possibility of a bright future in America. For her, Joey represented stability, and his love provided her with a growing sense of optimism. She no longer worried about living in the shadow of American life, being afraid and alone, but rather participating in it and realizing the dream of reuniting her family. For the first time in a long time, she found herself deeply happy.

Eddie Johnson's phone rang just before he left his disheveled studio apartment heading to work.

"Hi, Ma, how you doing?"

"Well, Eddie, I never received that check you said you were sending me." Her displeased tone emphasized her usual disapproval of him.

"Oh, sorry, Mom. I've been a little stretched this month."

"Well, I need my medicine. My blood pressure is too high and I'm getting these horrible headaches. It's just got me at the end of my—"

He cut her off. "Yeah, yeah, I know, Ma, but I got my problems too."

"Ya know your brother, bless his soul, would never talk to me like that," she replied. "He was making the same money in the fire department as you are but he'd never—"

"Mom, Mom, I really don't have the time right now. I know, I'm not like my brother, but I gotta go to work. I'll send you the check." He clicked off, grabbed his wrinkled jacket draped on the couch, and slammed the door behind him as he walked out.

Head pounding as he stomped down the stairs, he

stopped to check his mail. He opened a letter from his wife's lawyers, Weinberger and Katz, who unceremoniously informed him that he was again behind in his temporary alimony payments and they were about to commence a legal proceeding to cut off his visitation rights with his twelve-year-old daughter. In addition, his wife was unhappy with the amount she was getting and she was demanding a substantial increase in his payments, since she was saddled with most of the household bills. And finally, she had instructed them to ask the court for an extension of the restraining order she had gotten against him.

As he read the letter, Eddie's neck began to tighten and a ring of acrid underarm sweat seeped through his shirt. He inhaled deeply, crumpled the letter, and threw it on the floor. Instead of going to his car for the sixty-minute drive from Hempstead to the Bronx, he walked around the corner to the quiet refuge of Duke's Lounge, had a breakfast of vodka and Heineken, and made some phone calls. An hour-and-a-half later, he strolled into the precinct house feeling much better.

On his desk sat the forensic report on Mike's credit card. After reading it, he picked up the phone and called Krasnowsky.

"Phil, I got the report on that guy McGowan's card."

"Yeah, and?"

"Well, we got both his prints and Carlos's prints on the card. And there's blood on the card that matches Carlos's. There's also other blood on the card that's unidentified.

Could be McGowan's but we don't have his blood—or DNA," Eddie said.

"Yeah, well, that proves nothing so far. It's his card so his prints are gonna be on it, maybe even his blood. But that could have happened at different times. It doesn't put them together at the scene. The card was lost, so nothing conclusive there," Krasnowsky replied. "I guess we need this guy's blood samples."

"Okay so let's get it," Eddie said.

"Just like that? We go and ask him for some of his blood?" Sitting in his office, Krasnowsky turned up his palms and shook his head. "No chance. We'd have to arrest him and then get a judge to okay it. He'll lawyer up right away. I'm not sure we'd even get it, and we'd lose our advantage right away."

"Advantage . . . what fuckin' advantage do we have? We're sitting here like a couple of assholes while he's out enjoying himself. Ah, come on, he's fucking dirty. You know it. Let's collar this motherfucker," Eddie said. "We'll shake it out of him."

"Not so fast. Our advantage is he doesn't know we're on his ass. It's easier to get something on him now than if we gotta fight through a bunch of high-priced shysters. Maybe he'll get careless and do something stupid—ya never know. Anyway, right now all we got is a jittery hedge-fund asshole who lost his card in a drunken stupor in the Bronx which was later found by a bad guy who was probably involved in a shooting in a gypsy cab. We can't place this guy in the cab. It just ain't enough—not yet."

"He was bullshitting and uptight when we talked to him. This guy was involved, no doubt," says Eddie.

"Yeah, maybe, but how do we prove that?" Krasnowsky scratched his head, dusting his shoulders with crusty flakes as he walked in tight circles in the cramped room. "We need his DNA," he said, staring into space. "I got an idea. Give me a little time to figure this out."

New Year's Eve was cold and clear. Joey and Larisia decided to go to the party that Morgan was having at the enclosed rooftop lounge at the W Hotel in Times Square, near their offices. It was a great venue to watch the ball drop. Joey thought it might also be a good opportunity to talk to Michael in an informal social setting. They had not spoken about personal matters since Michael came back from his honeymoon.

Joey donned a formal midnight-blue tux, black silk bow tie, and patent leather shoes. Larisia commented on how handsome he looked. She wore a simple black dress with an open neck and long sleeves. She was in her last trimester and her now ample breasts and bulging belly filled out the high-waisted dress. The flawless olive skin across her chest shimmered and her face glowed with late pregnancy contentment.

"You look so beautiful, honey . . . and sexy," Joey said.

"Even with my big belly?" she laughed as he nodded.

"Well, thank you, sir. You look great too . . . very James Bond."

Michael wanted to go to the party, too, and have a conversation with Joey. It was the perfect opportunity, and he mentioned it to Courtney, but she was not feeling well.

"Michael, I know you need to show your face at the party for business reasons, but I don't want to go. I'm not feeling great," she said, leaning back and stretching her long legs on the couch. "Why don't you stop by, say hello to whoever you need to see, and leave early. Get back to me so we can have a midnight glass of champagne together."

"That's a great idea, baby, but no champagne for you. Only apple juice. This will give me a chance to see some of the guys from upstairs and get them up to speed on the Sandoval deal. I'll do the rounds and get out of there," he said with a wink.

"Okay honey, but please keep the drinking to a minimum. One or two and say goodbye."

Her soft blonde hair curled down the side of her face as she smiled at him.

"Don't worry. I'll be good and I'll be back to you and our baby." He leaned over and gave her a kiss. "You look so beautiful. Pregnancy agrees with you. See you soon."

Michael showed up a little after eight and went right to it, shaking hands working the crowd as the lights of the city glistened all around. Just after nine, as the space began to fill up, Joey and Larisia arrived. Seeing them come in, Michael was stunned at how beautiful Larisia looked. Her long dark hair shined in the low light. Her smile was a beacon. He thought about the baby she was carrying and his heart sank.

"Wow, the beautiful couple. You both look great," he said, hugging them both. "I think pregnancy agrees with you." He kept his arm around her.

"Thank you, Michael," she replied. "You look wonderful too. And congratulations on the new baby coming."

"Thanks, exciting, huh . . .with new babies coming all around." He smiled at her and inappropriately stroked her belly. He couldn't help but feel a bit of macho potency having impregnated two beautiful women. Larisia subtly pulled away and stared at him, stone-faced.

"Is your wife here?"

"Ah, no she's at home not feeling well. Nothing serious —just pregnancy. I came by just to make an appearance and keep the higher-ups in the loop on the Sandoval deal. Ya know, politics. I'll be gone in a half-hour."

"Yes. good. You need to be with your new bride on this special night," Joey chimed in.

Michael turned to Larisia. "Joey told me what happened at your apartment, with Carlos. I admit I was shocked. I'm so sorry you had to go through that."

"Michael, it was the most terrifying thing I've ever had to go through in my life. Joey came and saved me. If I didn't have him to help . . . I . . . I just don't know." She looked down and quietly gasped.

Michael reached out and held her.

She gathered herself and looked up at him. "Thank God it's over . . . all of it. It's time to move on in our lives."

He got her message, releasing her as she stepped back and reached for Joey's hand.

"I'm glad it's over too. And that you're okay," he said. "You're an incredible woman, and brave too—so brave. Let's make a pact never to talk about it again, any of it."

They all hugged and nodded quietly. Michael, sensing her coolness, decided to leave. As he did, he glanced back one more time to look at Larisia as the couple headed off into the crowd. Once again, he felt that immutable attraction for her that he couldn't shake.

14

NO MORE SLAVERY

After their meeting at the party, Michael couldn't get Larisia out of his head, despite his love for Courtney. As he sat at his desk two days later, his phone rang. He recognized Joey's number.

"Mike, you free?"

"Yeah, what's happening?" Michael asked.

"I gotta come over and talk to you. Ya know . . . about Larisia and the baby," Joey said.

Five minutes later Joey walked in and dropped down in a chair. Michael, sitting behind his desk, ran his fingers through his hair and put up his feet.

"Okay, so talk to me," Mike said.

"Look, you know I love Larisia. I'd do anything for her. We're closer than ever," Joey started slowly. "She thinks, and I agree, that I be named the baby's father on the birth certificate."

Michael frowned. He sat up. "You mean I'm out

completely with my own child? You want me to give up on my baby, act like it's not mine?"

"Mike, it's for everyone's good. You need to make the right decision here. It may be your biological child, but I'm not sure about your rights here. We are married and I'm told that it may be her choice. I'm the father in everyone's eyes. Let's just keep it that way. We'll keep it to ourselves."

Michael found himself hurt and infuriated at the same time. "So I'm nobody? Just a friend of the family?"

"Mike, we're making plans for our future. You can't hang on to this baby. You need to let us start new, as a whole family—a clean slate. You can come over and be with the baby whenever you like as she grows up. But if you make your paternity public, shit, you'll destroy everything. And really, think about Courtney. Have you told her yet? Is she going to tolerate this now with her own baby coming? If she finds out she'll blow her stack. It'll destroy your marriage. She'll never forgive you. Larisia will never forgive you—I'll never forgive you." Joey got up and paced the room. "Come on, man, don't ruin everything. We could never be friends again. I don't want you hurt. You've been my buddy forever. I love you. But don't do this— don't make it a fight. Let's stay friends."

Mike whistled low. "You're really that far gone with her?"

"You know I am," Joey replied.

Mike grinned. "Who had to twist your arm to get you to marry her in the first place?"

"And I'll always be indebted to you for that. It was the best decision I was ever forced to make. But don't pull that now, it's old news. Everything has changed; let's all go forward in a good way. Please."

Michael closed his eyes and lowered his head into his hands. "Joey let me think about this. It's a lot, and I'm a little fucked up at the moment. Give me some time to sort all this out. With this deal percolating, my new marriage, the new baby—two new babies—it's a lot."

"Yeah, I got it, man. My head's spinning too. I threw a body into the river. That's a first. I mean, fuck, this shit's getting serious," Joey said with an ironic half-laugh.

Three days later Larisia was called down to the administrative office of the hospital. Despite her advanced state of pregnancy, she chose to continue to work every day. When she arrived, she was met by a state official who explained that she was being photographed and fingerprinted and she was required to sign certain forms that would be notarized for her nursing license. She found herself both excited about the prospect of finally becoming a full-fledged nurse like her mother and frightened that something might go terribly wrong. Now, for the first time in her life, she had her full personal documentation on file with both the state and the federal government.

On a cold night in late February, Larisia reached over and shook her husband awake.

"Okay, honey. My water just broke. The baby is coming."

"What? Now? Can't she just wait till the morning? I need my sleep." He laughed.

She turned on the light and stared at him. "No time for jokes. Get up."

He smiled and hugged her. "Okay, baby. Let's start the rest of our lives," he said, hopping out of bed.

On the way to the hospital Joey called Michael, leaving numerous messages. Larisia, barely holding on, practiced her deep breathing exercises in the passenger seat. Within hours their baby girl was delivered. At her side, Joey cried with Larisia as the swaddled pink infant was placed in her arms for the first time. The new family hugged each other as tears of joy flowed down their cheeks.

"I will always love you and protect you and our family, no matter what," said Joey, almost choking through the tears. "We're one now and this is our life."

She beamed at him. "This is all I've ever wanted."

"Me too," he replied. "I just didn't know it till now."

Later that morning Michael showed up at the hospital. He sat next to Joey in the waiting room.

"Mike, have you figured out how this is going to go?"

"I wish I could say yes, but I can't . . . maybe I'll tell Court about the whole thing. Just get it over with. She'll understand, I think. What is she gonna do? So she gets pissed. I can handle it. And with the new baby coming we can put it all back together," said Mike, slightly slurring his words.

"Mike, you've been drinking?"

"No … well, I had a shot and a beer. Maybe a couple —but it's me talking, not the booze. I really don't want to let her go … the baby that is."

"Oh fuck, dude. You really gonna do this? Turn every-one's life upside down. Juggle fatherhood with two new babies. Disrupt everything." Joey got up and paced the small room.

"Look, it's my kid—" Michael said.

"Oh, fuck you. You really want to do this the hard way?" Joey asked, steaming. "I'm not sure you have legal rights here. Especially if she fights you. We just may move to another part of the country. You want that? Really? What a shit show."

"Let me talk to Larisa. See the baby." Michael sounded quiet, almost resigned.

"What? Fuck you," said Joey, heated.

"I tell you what, let me hear it from her. I just want to talk to her about it. I want to be clear about her feelings," Michael replied.

"Okay but just this once—this is the only time," Joey said. "It's up to her. I'll talk to Larisia to see if she's willing to talk. Okay?"

After Joey checked with Larisia, Michael got the okay. He came into her room while she was nursing the baby. He still felt for her, he couldn't deny it. And with the baby, it was even more overwhelming. He began to cry, not fully aware of why.

She looked up, holding the suckling infant and motioned him to come over. She smiled.

"She looks like you, Larisia," he said.

"She does, I know, but you are there too. You always will be," she replied, turning the baby toward him and covering up.

"I want to be part of her life. Watch her grow up," Mike said, wiping away his tears.

"You can ... but I don't want you to have legal ties to her. You know what Joey and I want to do. Please let us have our life. I want him to be her father. You can share her life but not more than that, like an uncle. You should have that, but I want him to be her father," she said.

"Really?" He moved closer to her unconsciously, feeling drawn to her magnetically.

She put her hand up to stop him. "Yes, really. But please, Michael, I'm not the same girl you met last year, frightened and struggling alone, on the edge of American life. I was in the shadows. I don't want what has happened to me to be who I am, to define my life. I won't accept that anymore. I'm different now." She stared down at the brand-new life she gently held in her arms.

"I don't know, she continued, "I gave birth and I was reborn. It didn't happen the last time, but it did now. I won't allow you to hold on to her. No, no more. Please understand. You've gotta let go and let me, us, have a new life. You have yours. Embrace it. I gotta have mine—our new life. We'll always respect you and keep you in her life, that is, if you want that. But let me and her go, now. Don't try to hold on to me by holding on to her. It's the only way." She looked down at the sleeping child as though she'd found her strength, her wholeness.

Michael's eyes swept the floor as her words sank in. He began to sweat and his head was spinning. He swiped at the tears that continued to flow, said nothing, got up, and walked out of the room slowly on unsteady legs with her words ringing in his ears.

———

A week later, on a sunny winter morning, Joey bought a dozen long-stemmed roses for Larisia, and they spent an intimate family Valentine's Day together with their new baby at the Botanical Garden.

"We need to get you out of the Bronx. Let's get a new apartment in Manhattan, something bigger than my one-bedroom," Joey said as they sat on a bench rocking the carriage in the warm sun.

"You mean you don't like my second-floor walk-up?" she giggled.

"Honey, we need more—an elevator, maybe a door-man, and a view."

"Are you asking me to move in with you?" She smiled.

"Yes . . . yes I am. Forever and ever," he replied with a wide grin.

"Carmelita too?"

"All of us," he said with a wide smile.

"I want to, but I need to be close to my school, the hospital, and my aunt so she can take care of the baby during the day. We need to hold off till I graduate. I just need a little more time," she explained. "But I can't wait for us all to be together."

"Me too." He sighed with happiness as he hugged her.

A few weeks later, in March, an early morning crab trapper standing on the City Island bridge snagged a heavy object in the murky waters below. He pulled hard on the trap rope and a badly decomposed body wrapped in a shower curtain gently bobbed to the surface.

"Hey, chief," Eddie Johnson said, strolling over to Krasnowsky's cluttered desk. "We finally got our man."

"Who's that?" Krasnowsky asked.

"Estrada," Eddie responded.

"Carlos? Great," Krasnowsky said. "Where is he?"

"The morgue. They fished him out of the channel on City Island. Not much left of him. Been dead a while."

"Shit, you kidding me? That lowlife bastard gets himself killed. Our last hot lead. What the fuck do we do now?" Krasnowsky shook his head in frustration at the endless absurdity of it all.

"Beats me," Eddie said with a shrug.

"Any details yet? Time, place, shooting, stabbing, what?" Krasnowsky was annoyed.

"Found him wrapped up in a shower curtain, not much left of him, but you gotta talk to the medical examiner. They're working on the body now."

"Looks like he's been in the water a while. Probably died in late November or early December," said the medical examiner, when Krasnowsky called.

"Dr. Lee, can you give me some details on how he died?"

"Well, it was clearly foul play," came the reply.

"Yeah, thanks for that, doc. How many suicides wrap themselves up in a shower curtain and jump into the river?" Krasnowsky rolled his eyes and shook his head.

"Well, yes." Dr. Lee managed a high-pitched laugh. "But he didn't drown. He was dead when he went into the water. We found a shard of glass lodged in the right side of his neck. He probably bled to death. There was little to no blood left in the body ... what was left of it, that is."

"So you're saying somebody stabbed him in the throat and let him bleed out?" Krasnowsky asked.

"Well, it's not that simple. He also had a fractured skull, most likely knocked him out. It's not easy to determine right now. Probably would have survived the blow to the skull, but the glass looks like it completely severed the carotid artery. No chance," Dr. Lee said.

"A shard of glass? What kind of glass?" Krasnowsky asked.

"Actually, it was a shard of a broken mirror. Not a good mirror like you'd have on the wall. Thin glass, no structural strength."

"You mean thin glass, like those cheesy Home Depot ones made in China? Ah, no offense, doc."

"None taken . . . but yeah, like that. It had a partial print on it according to Forensics. Probably still there because it was stuck in the guy's neck. You should call them about that," Dr. Lee said.

"Yeah, I will. What else? Clothing?"

"Yes, jeans, shirt, belt, everything ordinary, even if it was all starting to disintegrate. Still had his wallet, cell phone, and his watch. It certainly wasn't robbery," the pathologist said.

"Well, thanks for your insightful crime analysis again, doc, but I'd say stick to your dead bodies, leave the motives and the rest to us," Krasnowsky said with a snide laugh. "Anything else?"

"Yeah, sure, detective. Just an odd thing stood out. When we unwrapped him, we found his pants were down around his ankles."

"Pants down? What the hell was he doing—having sex?"

"Well, I don't know, but his underwear was still on, just his pants were down."

"Pants down, mirror in the neck, fractured skull. Hmmm. I don't get it," the detective said, scratching and shedding flakes. "Let me ask you, doc, you think he was hit first or stabbed first?"

"Well, I can't tell for sure, but the head injury is consistent with someone getting hit in the back of the head or falling over backward and hitting a hard surface. My guess is he was stabbed first and then fell backward, fracturing the cranium—could have gotten his feet tangled in his pants," Dr. Lee said.

"Yeah, maybe. That's good, doc—really good. Any other stab or defensive wounds on the body, like on the hands or arms?"

"None as far as we could tell, which wasn't easy considering the condition of the body."

"Why would a guy stab his victim in the neck with a shard of glass—a lucky stab at that, with glass, not a shiv or a blade?" Krasnowsky held the phone to his ear hands free with a scrunched shoulder and stared at the scalp crust now lodged under his fingernails. "Not your usual weapon."

"Maybe it wasn't a guy," the doctor said.

"What? Oh, yeah, a woman. Hmmm. That's interesting," the detective said. "Why do you say that?"

"Well, it seems like an opportunistic attack, not a purposeful assassination. Pants down, strange weapon. No pro would use glass. I don't know, I'll bet he was caught by surprise rather than by force. That fits the profile of a woman."

"And, if you ask me," the doctor continued. "I'd say the killing took place in a bathroom."

"A bathroom? Okay, why a bathroom," Krasnowsky said, now rummaging through his desk for a nail clipper.

"Why? It's obvious, detective. You must be losing your edge." The doctor let out a shrill and annoying giggle. "The weapon could have been a cheap bathroom mirror. And for the head injury, the hard floor of a bathroom, like tile or marble, would fit the bill. It's also a good surface for containing bodily fluids from leaking through the floor or absorbing into a rug. There must have been significant bleeding. And, most obviously, he was wrapped in a shower curtain. Hello!"

"Ah, yeah, yeah. Ya know, doc, I take all it back. Maybe you should have my job and I should spend more time hanging out with the stiffs you got down there."

They both laughed before Krasnowsky hung up.

The corpulent detective leaned back in his tattered green vinyl office chair and sat silently for a long moment; the thought of losing his edge got to him. Maybe he wouldn't have missed that at another time.

"Fucking Chinamen," he grumbled.

"What'd the ME say?" Eddie asked.

"He was good. Said our boy was a piece of shit and got what he deserved. Stabbed in the neck with a broken mirror," Krasnowsky said. "Also, they found a partial print on the glass. You gotta check that out with Forensics."

"Okay," Eddie said. "Mirror? That's fucking weird. Any ideas on who did it?"

"Well, that he didn't know," said the detective, now

turning serious. "But he gave me some interesting points to think about."

"Such as?"

"Well, his theory is that he was killed by a woman, in a bathroom. My guess, her apartment since he didn't seem to have an address. Obviously, it wasn't a professional hit. Sounds like it was his girlfriend, or at least a girl he knew. He escaped from prison in Mexico and made his way up here to her place. Surprise!" said the detective. "Looks like she wasn't too happy to see him."

"Yeah, with that guy, who would be?"

They went through the box of belongings sent over by Forensics. Burner phone destroyed by salt water. Wallet with basic Mexican ID and about three hundred in US dollars. Rolex Submariner, stainless steel. Assorted clothes and a pair of sneakers.

"Eddie, track down the details on the watch. Probably stolen," Krasnowsky said.

"Okay, you got it," Eddie replied.

"Look at this." Krasnowsky held up a small plastic bag containing a crumbling business card. The name Michael McGowan, Morgan Stanley, was barely legible in faint print on the front.

"Well, there you go—guilty as charged," Eddie said. "I knew that bastard was dirty. Let's drag him in; he'll give it up."

"Yeah, maybe, but what does it mean? This lowlife could have picked up this card when he found the credit card on the street," the lieutenant said.

"What? Now it sounds like you're looking for excuses to cut him loose. I say put that hedge-fund bastard in cuffs and squeeze it out of him," said a heated-up Eddie.

"Look it doesn't look good for this guy, true, but in itself it doesn't make him a part of this killing," Krasnowsky replied. "It's not like McGowan was going to leave his card on the body just to make it easy for us."

"Well then what the fuck is his card doing in Carlos's pocket?" Eddie had his arms folded, head cocked to one side.

"Good question," Krasnowsky said, taking a minute to think. "Maybe our boy Carlos held on to it and was coming up from Mexico to settle a score. Or maybe McGowan had something he wanted and he came up to get it. Unfortunately, he ran into an angry girlfriend first. You know how mean women can be."

"Yes, I do," Eddie said, raising an eyebrow.

"Take a look at the back of this." Krasnowsky held the card under the light of his desk lamp and peered through an oversized magnifying glass.

"Whaddya got, Sherlock?" Eddie cracked.

"Is that some writing on the back? Could that be an 'L' and an 'A'? A name? And look, some numbers underneath." Phil adjusted the lamp. "Like a '7' maybe and a '1'? Can't make out the rest."

"Could be a Bronx number. Maybe some business associate," said Eddie.

"Yeah, maybe, but when was the last time you wrote your number down for some guy?" Kranowsky asked.

"Maybe this was a broad, some woman he just met or was picking up and she wrote her number on his card—ya know, the old-fashioned way."

"Huh, could be. Not bad," Eddie said. "But what is this card with this number doing in Carlos's pocket? Did he bring it with him all the way back from Mexico? Why?"

"Good question. If it's a 'she,' she may know both of them somehow," Krasnowsky said, wheels turning. "But shit, we're just guessing here. Maybe the lab can come up with more on this. Let's have them look at this."

Later that evening Eddie dialed a number from a graffiti-covered pay phone on the corner of Jerome Avenue and 168th, one of the last in the Bronx. He watched impassively as people lined up on the sidewalk to buy drugs. A dealer in a black hoodie stood in a doorway and did business openly, unfazed by a passing patrol car.

"Hola," said the voice on the line.

"Pablo, we found Carlos. He's dead. Fished him out of the river yesterday. Been dead a while," Eddie said.

"Yeah, figured that . . . gone too long," came the heavily accented reply. "Anything else."

"We got some prints. I'll let you know more once we run a check," Eddie said.

"Okay." They both hung up—no goodbyes.

15

KILL YOUR DARLINGS

"I'm shoveling shit against the tide," Krasnowsky said with a grimace, on the phone to his friend Jimmy Gronkowsky in Internal Affairs. "The bad guys are winning, and I feel like I'm losing my edge."

"Philly, I don't like what I'm hearing from you," Gronkowsky replied. "You're the sharpest guy I know."

"Well, I've felt this way before Jimmy, you know—especially after the loss of Anna. But now it's worse. We're wasting our time. Nothing gets solved, people keep showing up dead, the drugs are more deadly than ever, and now it's fentanyl, it's everywhere." Krasnowsky swiveled in his decrepit chair and propped his oversized, worn brown wingtips on his desk with a loud clump.

"Yeah, I know, it's not getting any better. And just between us, the department is a mess too. Never thought I'd live to see it. Can't mention any names, but we just collared a sergeant who was literally dealing drugs out of the precinct. A sergeant. It's the money, it's just too much for these guys to turn down. They're selling their souls," Gronkowsky said.

"Holy shit, a guy looking at a lifetime retirement check and he blows it. I can't believe what's happening," Krasnowsky said.

"Yeah, it's crazy."

"Yeah. Something is definitely happening on the inside. I got a shooting case and I can't help feeling someone is clocking my moves. I got a leak here somewhere. Too many witnesses showing up dead. How the fuck do they know what we're doing?" Krasnowsky was rubbing his head and gesticulating with his free hand. "And with these fucking judges and that asshole of a mayor, don't get me started. No bail, and now no more stop and frisk? How the fuck do we get guns off the streets?"

"Philly, it's not like it was. We all know that, but I'm worried about you," said his friend with deep concern.

"Jimmy, I'm fine, but the system is working against us now." Krasnowsky dropped his feet to the floor. "I can't make a collar stick. Gotta catch them red-handed or the courts throw it out—they walk. The perps are on the street before we are."

"I know, making a case is worse than ever and there's no question there are real leaks in the department. I told you, you gotta watch your back. It's why I'm leaving. But before I go, I'd love to help you," Gronkowsky said. "Tell me, who knows what you're doing on these investigations?"

"I keep it tight. It's only me, Eddie, and the captain with any real information. I don't talk much to any of the new guys."

"Captain Shanahan?"

"Yeah."

"Well, he's the best. No problem there. He'll go down with the ship, that fucking mick," Gronkowsky said. "That leaves your boy Eddie? How's he doing?"

"Ah, okay, I guess. He's no Einstein. But he does what I tell him. You know, he's been with me for six years now. Knows my whole family and you know, his brother was a hero. His Mom too. Great lady. I think I can trust him; don't think I'm missing anything."

"Yeah, well I hear he's drinking a little too much and his wife has a restraining order on him. Not good signs," Gronkowsky said. "I'd watch him. I'll see what I can find on him, but watch your back. You know what I learned after thirty years of this shit? It's always the guy who's the closest, the one you never suspect."

"Yeah, okay, Jimmy. Keep me in the loop," said Krasnowsky hanging up. The conversation left him with a deeply uncomfortable feeling. *What am I missing here.*

"Hey Phil, you're gonna love this," Eddie said, sliding half his unwelcomed ass onto Phil's messy desk. "It's about our buddy Carlos."

"Whaddaya got?" Krasnowsky asked. "He didn't come back from the dead to tell us his tale, did he?"

"No, but almost as good. I just got a call from Forensics. They got a match on a partial print on the duct tape that was on the shower curtain. It's a guy named Joseph D'Antonio. He's in finance, had a DUI a few years ago," Eddie said. "And get this, where do you think he works?"

"I give up . . . McDonald's, where all these bullshit financial geniuses should be working." Krasnowsky made air quotes with his fingers as he spoke. "Same bunch of fucking bums who nearly broke this country a dozen years ago."

"Yeah, you're right about that but no, not McDonald's. He's working at Morgan Stanley. The same firm where our buddy McGowan is working. In fact, they may be working in the same department," Eddie said.

"Really . . . now that is interesting." Krasnowsky leaned back and rubbed his chin.

"Hmm. How do you think we should handle this?"

Surprised to be asked his opinion, Eddie stood up from his half-seat on Krasnowsky's desk. "Fuck, you kidding? Let's bust him. No question. Prints on a murder victim. Cuff him and read him his rights. He'll be crying like a baby in a half-hour, probably give up his buddy too. Case closed."

"Yeah, but the prints are on the curtain, not the body.

Actually, not even on the curtain but on the tape on the curtain that wrapped the body. Isn't that what you said?"

"Yeah, so? What are you saying?" Eddie asked, shrugging his shoulders.

"Any prints or DNA on the body?"

"Not that I know of," Eddie replied.

"Well, I might be being overly cautious here, but it gives him or a lawyer a little wiggle room. I can see one of these fucking high-priced mouthpieces turning that into a reasonable doubt. Maybe he lent his roll of tape to someone . . . maybe the tape was stolen from him at some point. Maybe it was in his car and turned up missing one day," Krasnowsky said. "We can't put him at the scene, can we? We don't even have a scene, do we?"

"What? No." Eddie, pacing. "That's bullshit. We got enough. His prints are there."

"Have we got anything else on him? Any priors?"

"No, no other prints, and only the DUI five years ago. He got off light there 'cause he had Seymore Wolf representing him."

"Yeah, see, that's what I mean. We need a little more to nail a guy like this. He'll lawyer up right away," Krasnowsky said.

"Ah, shit, Phil. You starting to lose it? I remember when you used to take a piece of shit like this guy and slap cuffs on him right in the middle of his office. Drag 'em right out," Eddie said.

"Yeah, okay. That was then. We gotta get more now," Krasnowsky said. "And, let me ask you, what would this guy be doing with the likes of a Carlos, anyway? What's the connection? They don't exactly run in the same circles."

"Drugs? Or maybe Carlos tried to rob him?"

"Yeah sure, okay, so this stockbroker somehow, in a fight or something, grabbed a piece of broken glass, somehow, somewhere and managed to stab Carlos—a hardened gangster—in the neck with it, in one clean shot. Then wrapped the body in a shower curtain and threw it into the river, without leaving his print on the glass, and only a partial print on a piece of tape but nowhere else? Does any of that make sense to you?" Krasnowsky asked.

"No." Eddie shook his head.

"Me either. And it won't make any sense to a jury, either. Something's off. There's another unidentified print on the glass. Who's that? And what's with the Morgan Stanley connection? It doesn't hang together. There's something else going on here."

"Like?" Eddie asked.

"Like . . . I don't know what. But before we start dragging anybody down here, we should try to get some idea of what's going on." Krasnowsky thought quietly for a moment. "We don't want him to know what we know. I say let's spook him. Maybe he'll do something stupid. Tip his hand."

"Yeah, let's just yell at him, really loud, and maybe he'll get so scared he'll run in here and confess," Eddie laughed.

"Great idea," Krasnowsky said, not missing a beat.

"Here's a better idea. How about we call him and ask him some questions about his activities in the Bronx in late November. We'll tell him we picked up his plate number from some highway cameras. No mention of a body or anything else. Keep it light and informal. See what he says."

"Okay. It's a start, I guess," said Eddie, shaking his head at what he viewed as his partner's colossal lack of balls at using old-fashioned police interrogation techniques. Eddie's frustration was palpable. He gave up on arguing with Krasnowsky—wasn't worth it. His only thought was about the money.

Joey's assistant buzzed him as he sat in his office. "Mr. D'Antonio, I have a Detective Krasnowsky on the line. He says he needs to talk to you. Should I put him through?"

"Detective? What's he calling about?" Joey's heart pounded and his voice rose an octave.

"He wouldn't give me any details. Said it's just some routine questions about your car."

"My car?" Joey said, now annoyed. "I guess so, put him through."

"Hi, Mr. D'Antonio, this is Detective Phillip Krasnowsky, Bronx Homicide. How are you?"

"How am I? Really? I'm fine. What can I do for you, detective?"

"Well, we've been reviewing some highway camera footage and we see you were in the Bronx in late November. Can you tell me what you were doing there at that time?"

"What? The Bronx? November? I'm sure I have no idea, detective. Why do you ask? Is this some traffic infraction inquiry?" Joey's legs went numb.

"Well, not exactly. We've been reaching out to drivers and we wanted to ask if you saw anything unusual when you were in the area at that time?" Krasnowsky used his most innocuous tone.

"Unusual? Well, no, not that I can recall," Joey said, his mind racing.

"Oh, so you were on the Bruckner, by City Island at that time, is that right?"

Joey trembled with panic. "Ah, I'm not sure. At what time? I don't think so ... ah maybe."

"Well, we have your license plate number recorded. Did somebody borrow your car?" asked the detective.

"Ah, I don't know ... not sure."

"You're not sure if someone borrowed your car? Is that right?" the detective said.

Joey tried to recover. "No, no one has borrowed my car, sir, ever. Let me ask you, detective, what is this about? Is this about a killing?"

"Why do you ask?"

"Well, you said Bronx Homicide, so naturally I thought ...." Joey said, feeling slightly better.

"If it was, do you know anything about that?" Krasnowsky asked.

"Well, no. Ah . . . ." Joey said, now sweating. "I'm sorry, sir, but I don't know anything about any of this; I'm just too busy right now. I have to go. Good luck with your inquiry." Joey hung up.

"Well, shit, there's something there with this motherfucker," Eddie said after listening on the other line.

"Yeah, something. Wish I knew what," the detective said, staring at the ceiling.

"Are you serious? We should bust this bastard right now. He's as dirty as shit. He knows something and you know it."

"Look, Eddie, I think the same things about this guy as you do, but we gotta build a case here and not on thoughts or hunches. With just a partial print on the tape and nothing else we're weak. No motive, no clear connection to the victim, no other prints. We need more. It just doesn't hang together. Something . . . somebody . . . is missing here," Krasnowsky said.

"Phil, I don't know what else you need or what's missing. This guy is dirty. His print is there and we should bust him. Now. Period." Eddie stomped out, pissed off.

Eddie hopped into his car and drove to Hempstead. All the way on the LIE he steamed about this D'Antonio and

Phil and the whole fucked-up case. He walked into Duke's and ordered a beer and a ball. After a second round he went outside and dialed a number he had memorized.

"Hola," said a voice.

"I got a name for you. Write it down. Joseph D'Antonio, works at Morgan Stanley in Manhattan. We got a print on him, on Carlos's body. He's your guy."

"You sure?"

"This is the guy you want," Eddie said. "I want to pick up my package tomorrow—same place, same time?"

"You know, we pay afterward," said the voice.

"Don't bullshit me. I did my part. I need the money now." He hung up, went inside Duke's, and had two more rounds.

Joey, in a panic, breathlessly called Michael. "You're not going to believe this, but I just got a call from the cops about something that happened in late November in the Bronx."

"What the fuck? What thing?" asked Mike, looking to help.

"They were playing it cute. They didn't actually say, but it was a detective from Bronx Homicide." Joey's voice was high and stressed.

"Why you? How'd they find you?"

"I don't know. Just said they were checking cameras for

plate numbers of cars that were in the area at that time. Wanted to know if I had noticed anything . . . he was vague about it all."

"What? Sounds like bullshit. They're calling every car that drove on the Bruckner in late November? And how'd they get your number? Shit. That's got to be thousands of cars. And they call you? I don't know, man. This is fucked up, way too close to be a coincidence. Did they mention any names?"

"No, just if I had seen anything," Joey said.

"Whad'ya say?"

"Nothing really. Told them I don't remember being there at that time. Don't know anything," said Joey. "But, Mike, I might have fucked up. I asked them if it was about a killing?"

"What? Why'd you say that?" Mike said.

Joey thought he heard a catch in Mike's voice. "It just came out. He said homicide so I just threw it out," Joey said.

"Ah, no, that's not good," Mike said. "What'd he say?"

"He said, if it was, did I know anything about that," Joey replied.

"Ah, shit. You know what this means?" Mike said. "My guess is they found Carlos's body. That's what this is about, they found him. City Island? Late November? But why you? Could they actually be checking cameras and calling all these fucking people, and they get you randomly? Unlikely. It's a stretch."

"So shit, what do I do now?"

"Nothing. Don't do anything. Who knows, they may be watching you. Keep your regular routine. Stay frosty. Let's see if there's anything that shows up in the papers about a body found in the channel," Mike said.

"Yeah, I'll stay cool. On the 'lowdown,'" Joey said, trying to disguise his profound sense of fear.

"Ah, that's the 'down-low,' and yeah, do that."

"Mike, should I mention any of this to Larisia?"

"Ah, I wouldn't. No point right now. She'll just worry, and she's got enough to handle as it is. Let's see what happens. Just forget about it for now. Go about your regular day, and don't talk to any more cops. Okay?"

"Yeah, Mike. I'll put it out of my mind for now. See ya later." Joey hung up, but his panic gave him no peace. He reflected on his inability to handle this kind of stress. He realized it was part of the reason he vicariously leaned on Michael's seeming strength in tight spots. It had been this way between them since they were kids.

Two weeks later, Joey was at Murray's counter on 47th Street.

"Your friend Michael bought a beauty of a stone from me. Made him a great deal too. Maybe you've seen it? Are you looking for something similar?" asked Murray.

"Well, Murray, he told me you're the best so, yes, I want a good deal too," Joey replied, playing with the old man.

"Please," Murray replied with a shrug. "I always give good deals to my top customers, but I was referring to the type of stone. Top quality or budget?"

"Well, I'm not as extravagant as Michael, but something close. Just a little smaller," Joey said.

"Ah, you mean less expensive, right?" Murray asked, tilting his head and seeing an opportunity to give another life lesson, despite his wife's advice to not be so personal with his customers.

"Well, yes. But I also want quality."

"If I may, let me give you a little advice about stones and women: their sparkle, their beauty, entices us but their quality keeps us," Murray said, feeling full of himself. "Only get the best—don't bother with the rest. Years from now you'll forget the price. The quality will still speak to you and she'll know the difference—which is why you chose her and vice versa."

"That's good, Murray, very good, and true. Thank you. Please give me something that has both and is a good deal too."

"Oh, I see I'm dealing with a very smart man, like your friend, very smart," Murray said. He unwrapped a two-carat round-cut and placed it on a black velvet pad under the bright light. "You're not gonna get more sparkle than that."

Joey stared. "Beautiful. How much?"

"You're not impressed? It's top quality."

"No, I am ... very nice," Joey said. "How much?"

"You guys are all alike. Money. I'm offering beauty

here. Price is secondary. There's only one like this in the whole world—there are similar stones but none exactly like it. It's unique, that's the beauty. It's like her, the one and only. Am I right?" a smiling Murray said, using some of his time-tested lines.

"Yeah, you're right. Price?" Joey said, smiling too.

"Let me ask you, when are you planning to get married?"

"Eh, well, we already are," Joey said. "We had a small ceremony with a small ring but now I want to give her the real thing."

"Good, great, she deserves that. Mazel tov," Murray said. "How about kids? They're the real blessing. I got eight."

"Terrific for you," Joey's mind began to spin. "We have a newborn," he found himself saying.

"What? You're a fast worker, but good, make her an honest woman."

"Well—" Joey stopped for a long moment and thought about the situation he found himself in: the baby, Michael, Carlos, all of it. There's certainly no way he could explain it all to Murray, even if he wanted to. "Price?"

"Okay, okay, I'm too nosy. My wife tells me this all the time," said Murray. "For you, thirty-two thousand. And I'll set it, too."

"Sold," Joey said. "You've convinced me, she deserves only the best. She's one of a kind."

"Ah, and no schnorring. Good, you really are a smart man," Murray said reaching for a tray of settings.

Larisia was reluctantly staying in her apartment, despite its terrifying memories, till they could find the right apartment for all of them. And it helped for now that her aunt was close and happy to take care of her little Angelina while she went to school and studied for her finals. Larisia knew it was only temporary and looked forward to the promise of her future. "Soon we'll be all together in a new house—a new life," she whispered to herself.

When she picked up Joey's call, he barely gave her time to say hello. "Honey, I got some great news—great news! Let's go out for dinner tonight and I'll tell you all about it."

She took a deep breath. "Joey, honey, I'm just so busy. I got a load of studying to do, big exams coming, and later I got to pick up the baby."

"Babe, please, just this once. It's a special night. We'll go anywhere you like. After this, I promise, I'll give you plenty of time to study. I'll take the baby this weekend, give you and your aunt a break—weekend Dad. Come on," Joey said.

"Can you give me a hint about the great news?"

"Hint? No, I'm sorry, no hints, but I promise you will be happy. I'll pick you up at seven-thirty," Joey said. "I love you."

"Okay, I guess. If you insist. Love you too."

Joey picked her up right on time with a toot of the horn in front of her building. The warm air smelled of spring. She glanced out the window with a little wave and came down within a minute. As she strode down the front steps in a black dress that hugged her curves, a gray silk scarf, and silver heels, Joey was stunned. He got out of the car, handed her a single red rose, and opened the door for her.

"Could you look any more beautiful?" He grinned. "Wow."

"Ah, how romantic. Thank you, honey. And yeah, I lost some baby weight—feel good too. Wanted to look good for my hubby." She smiled, then leaned over and kissed him. "Do you like the dress?"

He was immediately aroused as he inhaled her fragrance. "Do I like the dress? Ah, yeah, I love the dress, but without you it's just a dress."

She saw the bulge in his pants and placed her hand on his crotch. "Looks like you're happy to see me."

"What makes you think that?" he laughed as they headed off to the restaurant.

She gave him a little squeeze and then slowly slid her hand away. "Horny? Me too. It's amazing how hot you get studying about human anatomy. It might be time for some 'hands on' lab experience, as they say." She giggled.

"Hey, babe, we really don't even have to go to dinner at all. Let's just go back to the apartment—right now."

"Ah, hold on, Romeo, let's give it some time. Besides, I'm hungry." She smiled and turned on the radio.

"Okay, babe, I'll sing to you. Maybe that will help," he said as a love song came on the radio. They looked at each other with a sly smile.

The host at Mario's on Arthur Avenue sat them at a quiet table in the back, away from the street. Joey was excited. She looked at him. "So, what's the big news?"

"Hold on, let's take it slow here," he said as the waiter brought a bottle of champagne. "Let's drink first."

He raised a flute of champagne to her; they clinked glasses. "Honey, the big news is very simple. I love you with all my heart. I can't imagine my life without you. So I'd like to propose to you again—um, for the first time, actually. This time, forever." He got down on his knee, reached into his pocket, took out the ring.

Larisia, wide-eyed and tearing up, looked stunned.

"Will you please marry me—again? This time we'll have a big celebration—the whole family. Let's get them all up here. All together, the babies, the grandparents, everyone. I can't live without you."

She began to cry but managed to get out, "Yes, of course, I love you," before a full cry of joy. He gently took her hand, slid off the small ring she was wearing, and slid the diamond ring onto her hand. She stared at it, dazzling even in the low light.

Joey stood up and kissed her. The host, waitress, and several patrons clapped as the happy couple hugged and smiled.

The waitress smiled and said, "You two, oh my God, you're just too beautiful. Congratulations." She hugged them both. They spent the rest of the meal, which they could barely eat, giggling and holding hands.

At one point, Joey looked around, smiling at some admiring patrons. "They should only know what we've been through to get here."

"They wouldn't believe it. But you know what, it was worth it—all of it. And I believe God meant for us to go through this and find each other. He has a plan for us. I know that in my heart. It was a test for our love." She pressed her ring to her heart.

"Well, if he brought you to me then it's all for the good. We'll make a beautiful family. We'll pull them all together around us."

"My little Carmelita too?" she asked.

"Of course. She'll be with us soon. I promise."

Her eyes lit up with joy.

At the end of the meal, after handshakes from patrons, he took her home. On the drive back they talked excitedly about wedding sites and who to invite. They parked the car on the street and headed upstairs.

Once in the apartment, they couldn't keep their hands off each other. They kissed deeply and she slowly stripped for him, unzipping her dress and letting it drop to the floor. In the soft light he unhitched her bra, caressed her full breasts, and inhaled her body and soul. She peeled off her skimpy panties and fell backward onto the bed, reaching up for him. Naked and wet she spread her legs.

Undressed, he slid onto the bed and entered her with a deep thrust. She climaxed almost immediately and moaned. He struggled not to release but within minutes he surrendered to her body and was overcome by a wave of ecstasy. As he came, she came again. They held onto each other gently and lost all sense of who or where they were. God's plan was working. They fell asleep in an embrace as the warm night enveloped them.

Several hours later he woke up. He looked over at her and kissed her. She opened her eyes.

"Honey, I've got to get back," he whispered. Can't leave the car where it is and I'm in early to the office."

She put her fingers to his lips. "Joey, you don't have to make any excuses to me. This is not just another one-nighter. I know you love me—got the ring to prove it." She smiled and flashed the stone. "I know, we're both busy. I've got to get going early too. Finals next week. Wish me luck."

"Good luck baby. Get some sleep. Honey, I do love you," he said as he kissed her and she pulled the covers close.

He slid out of bed, got dressed, and tiptoed out the door toward the car parked down the street. As he stepped out of the building, a black SUV moved forward with the back window rolled down. A burst of muzzle fire sparked from the darkness. Three rounds tore into his torso and he crumpled onto the concrete steps. The car sped up and screeched off into the night.

Larisia heard the ominous pop-pop-pop, ran to the

window in terror, and saw Joey lying face down on the steps, his blood flowing onto the sidewalk. She ran down in her nightgown and, in the amber light of a lamppost, held his head in her lap as he died without saying a word. She sat there sobbing and bloodsoaked, holding him close as neighbors looked on from behind curtained windows. It took the police almost thirty minutes to arrive.

16

FORGIVENESS

Joey's dad, his two brothers, and Michael carried Joey's casket up the stairs, into St. Anthony's Church and to the altar. Once inside, the silence was broken only by muffled sobs and a mournful organ dirge. The entire neighborhood had gathered. After prayers by Father McMullen, Michael ascended the pulpit to give the eulogy. His eyes were red and swollen. Tears welled, and he inhaled deeply to steady himself from an almost uncontrollable trembling. He was barely in his body.

He strained to look out into the pews. The church, in shadows, was dimly lit by a shaft of pale-yellow light that shone through a pane of stained glass. He looked up at the glowing window depicting a scene from the Bible where Jesus's limp body is taken down from the cross, bloodied and pale, his eyes closed. A crown of thorns had wrought rivulets of blood down his face and in his side, a bleeding wound from a Roman spear. A mournful Mary, kneeling, wiped his face with a bloodstained cloth as soldiers held back the sobbing crowd. Michael could barely take his eyes from it. The images nearly buckled his legs and he held onto the heavy marble lectern as he prepared to speak.

Michael cleared his throat. "They say you die twice in this world: once when you pass and one final time when the last person you knew on this earth says your name for the last time. Then your living memory passes into the true realm of spirituality. We all face that fate—for better or worse. It's a reminder that we only have now. Our living task here on this earth is to keep the memory of our loved one alive. To celebrate them by living our own lives in the best possible way and honoring them for all they meant in our lives." He took a deep breath and began to calm down.

"I've known my good and great friend Joey since the first days of grammar school. We lived on the same block. We knew each other's family. We shared everything as we grew up, everything from dreams to girlfriends, but especially—especially—secrets. And as kids, your secrets were important and they could not be shared with everyone. They were held deep within, in a very vulnerable place, a place of trust. It was our pact, it was sacred, and Joey was completely trustworthy. He was my best friend, and I know I was his."

Michael stopped for a brief drink. His hand trembled as he held the glass.

"We stood by each other, too, like brothers. He once got accused by one of the nuns of something he did not do. I did it. We were kids, it was nothing serious. But he never said a word to anyone about it and took his punishment. I should have stepped forward; I didn't, and I'll always regret that. We both knew the truth. He never brought it up to me; we never spoke about it." Guilty tears streamed down his reddened cheeks.

Michael continued. "As I look back there were times I should have been a better friend to him. In so many ways he was a better friend to me." Michael had to stop to compose himself. He looked again at the glowing stained glass window. "We have to say goodbye now, Joey. I'll see you again in our next life. I'll be a better friend next time."

Joey's dad, tears running down his face, saw Michael's unsteady gait as he stepped away from the pulpit. He got up, gave Michael a bear hug, and helped him sit down. The irony of the moment was not lost on Michael. He knew he was responsible for Joey's death. He had put his friend in the middle of all this. The consequences of his actions and the impact of those actions on all those he saw around him—Joey's family, Larisia, his child and family—were nearly unbearable. He wanted to confess publicly to all that had happened, all he was responsible for. But he could not. He simply wept, deeply, quietly.

Larisia sat in the back of the church, unnoticed. Her role in Joey's life had not been revealed to anyone. She and Michael had agreed that this was not the right time to do that to the family. There would be a better time for that later, they thought.

In the dim light she looked at the religious scenes of suffering and pain.

She stared at the crucifix that hung on the wall above her. The thin body of Jesus almost alive with writhing pain. As she cried, she implicitly knew about Michael's pain, and his guilt. She also felt a new anger toward him that seemed now to be boiling to the surface. Why had she sinned with him? Why did she invite this into her life?

She also struggled with her own guilt. What she had done to bring this all about, and the terrible price those around her would pay for her actions. She cried for her daughter in Mexico who had to live her life without her mother or a father—the man she had murdered. And her infant Angelina—the angel child—what would her life be like? How would she suffer from all this? And she cried for herself, for her sins, for Joey, and for Carlos. And she prayed for forgiveness.

After prayers and a blessing from Father McMullen, people said their goodbyes with a genuflect, a gentle touch of the coffin, and muffled sobs. They began to stream out of the church. Larisia stood outside the church on the sidewalk. The sunlight felt warm and life affirming after the chilling darkness. A small crowd of family and friends began to gather. Larisia, alone again and unnoticed, stood to the side. She stared into the blackness of uncertainty that confronted her now, and tried to come to terms with the inner storm of emotions that had overtaken her.

Sandoval approached Michael standing outside in the bright sun, gathering himself.

"Michael, that was a moving speech you gave. I know it was from your heart. I felt it. I'm so sorry all this has happened. This wave of crime in New York is tragic. Has there been any word from the police about this?"

"It just seems to be a random shooting. I haven't heard anything from them. I personally don't have any confidence they'll come up with anything. They're clueless," Michael replied.

"Tell me," Sandoval said. "What was Joey doing in the Bronx that late at night?"

Michael hesitated. Contemplating the words he had just spoken about his friend, he decided it was time to reveal the truth as much as he could.

"He was there with his new wife. She lived in that building. They had secretly married and had a baby, but he was reluctant to tell the family for a variety of personal reasons. They still don't know everything. At some point I'll have to tell them the whole thing, but now is not the time. If you like, I can introduce you to her. She's a lovely Mexican woman. Her name is Larisia and she's standing right over there."

"Mexican woman? I had no idea," Sandoval said.

"He had just given her a beautiful ring and they were making plans to have another wedding—a big family affair this time," Michael said. "It's so tragic. Her heart is broken, as you can imagine."

The pair walked over to Larisia as she stood alone by the side door of the church as mourners filed out the front and headed to the funeral cars. "Señora, my deepest condolences. I have just heard the details from Michael and I am so very sorry for your loss."

Larisia smiled at the elegant Sandoval. "Thank you, señor. I appreciate your thoughts. It's been very hard."

"Your husband was a wonderful person and a trustworthy partner in our business dealings. I liked him very much." Sandoval reached into his pocket. "If there's anything I can do for you and the baby, please do not hesitate to ask. Our people must help one another. It would be my pleasure to help you in any way I can. This card has my personal cell number." He handed her the card with a smile and a gentlemanly handshake.

Larisia, surprised by his warmth and gallantry, smiled back. "Again, thank you, señor. Right now, I'm at a complete loss—but I may take you up on that."

"Please feel free to do so," he replied with a slight nod as he took his leave. He turned to Michael, shook hands, and got into his waiting limo.

Michael approached Larisia. She stiffened as he put his arm around her and she tried to remain stoic. But in the face of all she had lost, she surrendered to her overwhelming grief and fear. Larisia buried her head into his shoulder and began to sob. "Michael, what do I do now? I'm so afraid."

"I know you are. I promise you I will help you in any way I can. I'll cover your expenses. Don't worry." He reached for his pocket square and dabbed her face gently. "Have you heard anything from the police?"

"No, they don't even seem concerned. They told me

they're investigating it, but that there has been a spate of drive-by shootings lately in the area. I think they suspect drugs were involved. I think they look at me like I'm involved, somehow. I don't really feel they'll do anything," she said as she tried to calm her galloping emotions.

"Yeah, they're at a loss. Too many killings," he replied.

"Do you think this had anything to do with—with the Carlos thing?" she asked.

"Oh, shit, I hope not. How would anyone know anything?"

"I don't know, but why would they just shoot him down in cold blood like that? Why him?" she said, tears flowing again. "Oh, God, what do I do now?"

Michael hugged her close. His body was warm but when she felt his bulge, she stepped away from him and her anger came to the surface. Anger for all that had happened since the fateful night they met, for the disaster that was now her life.

"Look, Michael, I just need your help to get me through this. I don't need anything else. Just please help me . . . as a friend." Her eyes were steely as she folded her arms across her chest defensively.

Michael, emotionally vulnerable from plumbing the depths of his sadness, was barely able to accept culpability for his actions that had so deeply hurt the people he loved. He reached his hand to her face and brushed away a tear. "I'm sorry, Larisia. I promise I'm there for you, one hundred percent. I'll be a total gentleman, scout's honor," he said to her with deep sincerity.

She looked at him with a half-smile. "Please don't say that. I remember the last time I heard those words."

"Okay. Okay. I'm sorry. But believe me, I'll take care of you." He stepped away from her. "I've got to go to Courtney now. Call you later."

"Michael," she said, reaching for his hand. "I didn't say it before, but your eulogy really touched me. It was beautiful. It brought me to tears. I know, now, how much you loved him ... maybe as much as I did." She smiled and let go of his hand, trying to let go of her anger too.

"Thanks," he said. "I meant every word. And I mean every word to you. I'll be there for you. Don't worry."

With that he turned and walked over to a very pregnant and teary Courtney.

"Who was that woman? You seemed to know her very well," Courtney said.

Michael, still in a swirl of grief and guilt and sorrow, struggled to give her as much truth as he could muster.

"That woman is named Larisia and she's Joey's wife. They have a new baby together. He's kept it a secret from his family, don't ask me why, and for now she doesn't want to say anything to them. She's heartbroken keeping it all to herself and trying to deal with her life now."

"What? Oh my God ... the poor thing. I had no idea. Why didn't you tell me about all this?"

"Honey, I know, I'm sorry. But he swore me to secrecy. It's a little of what I was talking about inside. She's Mexican and with the baby he just wasn't sure how they would take it. I guess he was embarrassed, with his strict

Catholic parents and all. I just don't really know," Michael said, uncomfortable with his half-truths.

"What? What, is he twelve years old? Embarrassed? He's a grown man. How do you hide something like that from everyone?" Courtney looked visibly distraught.

"He was actually about to announce the whole thing to them this week. They were planning another wedding. A whole family affair. But he made me promise not to say a word to anyone till he had a chance to talk to them and work it all out. It was complicated," Michael said, trying to ignore his abiding guilt and a torrent of conflicting emotion as he spoke.

"Even to me, your wife? You couldn't tell me? I know Joey all this time and he didn't trust me? I thought he was still seeing Melissa. When did all this happen?"

"Over the last several months," he replied. "They broke up a while ago."

"Well, it's got to be at least nine months. How old is the baby?"

"Ah, two months or so," he replied, the conversation beginning to feel like falling off a cliff.

"So you've been keeping all this from me for almost a year?"

"Well . . . yeah. I guess so. I'm sorry, honey. I had to honor his wishes. I'm really sorry," he pleaded.

She turned from him, shaking her head. "A year . . . how the hell can I trust you? You're too good a liar." She walked away with her eyes reddening, putting a white hanky to her face.

Michael followed her. "Honey, please—"

She stopped and turned to him. "Michael, this is all just too much for me. We're having a baby, and I feel so uncertain of us. I'm terrified. You just lied to me for over a year and you don't think that has any effect? I don't know what to believe anymore."

"Baby, please, try to understand. I had to honor his wishes. It wasn't against you. Please believe me. I've never lied to you, ever. Believe me," he said, tears welling.

She gently took his face in her hand and searched his eyes. "Michael, look at me. Is there anything else going on here? On the life of our baby, are you telling me the truth?"

Without hesitation he reached for her, holding her by the shoulders, staring back. "On the life of our baby, I swear to you this is the truth. There's nothing else going on here. I would never lie to you. I just had to keep my word to my friend. I love you."

He pulled her in and they embraced, both sobbing and quivering. As he held her, he looked back over her shoulder and saw that Larisia was already gone. The conflict of emotion in his soul refused to relent but, as was his talent, he managed to show no sign of it as he walked Courtney back to the car.

Gladys Krasnowsky took one last drag on the Marlboro as she sat on the peeling wooden back steps of her modest row house in Brooklyn. She wore tattered pink peaky-toe slippers on her swollen feet. Her ample girth strained the buttons on her faded housecoat. She stubbed out the butt in her secret ashtray, tucked it under the stairs, and dialed her husband.

"Phillip, Dr. Rosenberg wants us to meet him at his office next week, Monday or Tuesday. What do you think?"

"Okay. Let's meet him," the detective said, pacing and distracted about the investigation.

"No, I mean which day," she replied.

"Oh, well, either day. Whatever you want, honey. I'll be there. Maybe he has some good news for us."

"Well, yes, I hope so," Gladys said. "I can't take these treatments anymore. I'm at the end of my rope with all of it."

"Now, Gladys, you know what he said. It's a tough road but he's had some success with this kind of cancer. Don't give up on it. I know it's a battle."

"All right let's do Tuesday. I'll let you know what time."

"Anytime Tuesday's fine, honey. Don't worry, we'll get through this. You've been so brave. I love you," said the burly detective.

"I love you too, Phillip," she said as she hung up. She sat for a long moment surveying the weed-strewn backyard before she reached under the steps again for the hidden red-and-white box and took out the matches.

Eddie walked into Krasnowsky's disheveled office just as he hung up from the call with his wife. Now red-faced and trying to contain his emotions, Krasnowsky bellowed at him. "What the fuck is going on in this case? By some weird coincidence you want me to believe our only suspect in this fucking Carlos thing gets gunned down in a drive-by? For no reason, this guy—our guy—gets shot, just out of the blue? What the fuck was he doing in the Bronx anyway?"

"Looks like he was visiting his girlfriend. Uniformed cops said she was some Mexican chick. They checked her out. No drugs or anything. He just walked out and got blasted. Why, I don't know," Eddie said, staring at some notes he had scribbled on a yellow pad.

"There's got to be a reason. This white guy, blown away for no reason? Random? I don't buy it. A fucking bloodbath. This whole thing, too many dead bodies," said Krasnowsky. "Any witnesses?"

"No, none so far," said Eddie. "Ya know, this is not the first fucking innocent white guy to get shot in the Bronx. And it's the third drive-by we've had this year so far."

"Yeah, but they weren't our prime suspect in a murder," said Krasnowsky. "No, this fucking case is getting to me. Some shit is going on and somebody knows what the hell we're doing. Too many coincidences. Doesn't smell right."

"You think he knew something?" Eddie asked.

"Maybe, who knows, and now we'll never find out, but his fingerprint was found at the scene of a murdered

Mexican drug dealer. How it got there and what he knew, I'm not sure. But those bloodthirsty bastards don't let murders of their people go, and my guess is that's what this is all about—revenge. But, for what? How was he connected?" A visibly enraged Krasnowsky stared at Eddie. "What? You really think that this was just a random shooting? Really?"

"It's possible," Eddie replied, blankly.

Krasnowsky turned away, looked down at his messy desk, scratching his crusty scalp in resignation. "Possible? Yes, but do you really believe that?"

"Well, Phil, I know this—we'll probably never be sure. And worse, I doubt we'll ever catch the guys that did it, either. I think you know that as well as I do."

Krasnowsky felt the blood rush to his head. He tried to hold his temper. "Fuck ... fuck you. I don't believe that—and if I did, I might as well hang it up. What the hell do you think we're doing here?"

Both men were standing up. Eddie stabbed his finger in Krasnowsky's chest. "Phil, you're the one that doesn't want to collar these shitbirds. Every fucking time I say 'go' you have some reason to hold off. I ask you the same question—what the fuck are we doing here?"

"Look, Eddie, there's a big difference between making a collar and making it stick. Any fucking cowboy can bust people—that's for amateurs. We make cases—good cases, that's what we do." Krasnowsky turned away and kicked his office chair across the room, slamming it into the wall.

"Okay, Phil, I get that. But I hope we're not just keeping

our finger in the dike over here with this wait bullshit. Sure feels that way sometimes." Eddie turned and headed for the door.

As Krasnowsky watched Eddie stomp out, Gronkowsky's words rang in his head.

17

PUZZLE PIECES

E ddie, after downing his second vodka of the morning, went outside Duke's to dial. He stood in the parking lot, sweating in the shade, his back against the wall. His perspiration traced a damp imprint in the gray cinder block. Holding the phone to his ear, he folded his other arm across his chest defensively, ready for battle.

"Hello, Milstein and Hersch, can I help you?"

"Can I talk with Mr. Milstein, please."

"Ah, yes, who shall I say is calling?"

Eddie pulled the phone away from his face, and with a cocked head, yelled at the receiver as if it were a person. "You know who it is . . . it's me . . . Eddie Johnson."

"Ah, yes, Mr. Johnson. Let me see if he's available. Please hold on," said the secretary in a neutral, all-business voice. Eddie steamed as he listened to the firm's ad for their exceptional legal skills and extensive experience in divorce and foreclosures.

"Oh, hi, Eddie," Seymore Milstein said after a long wait. "What can I do for you?"

"You know what you can do for me. Start fighting this fucking thing. She's getting everything she wants and I can't get shit," Eddie said.

"Well, that's not exactly true—"

"Don't give me that bullshit," Eddie interrupted. "Last time you sent a fucking intern to court who didn't know her ass from a hole in the ground. She didn't do shit. I was there."

"Well, Eddie, it was only a procedural hearing and we're trying to save you money. Full-fledged lawyers are easily twice as expensive," Milstein said.

"Fuck you. They're going after my pension now and I can't get that restraining order lifted either. I can't see my daughter ... what the fuck?"

"Eddie, you have shown some violent behavior toward your wife and the court knows it," Milstein said. "They have to err on the side of caution there. Can't blame them."

"That little tussle? Complete bullshit. She swung at me first. I was defending myself—"

"Just a second," Milstein said, interrupting. "Your 'defense' landed her on the floor with a black eye. She had to call the cops."

"Fuck you, I'm a cop. It was bullshit."

"And another thing, Eddie," Milstein said. "My office tells me you're behind on your payments to her and to us. Now I'm sorry but you need to bring your account—"

"Fuck you . . . fuck you. All you lawyers want is money. You don't give two shits what I'm going through." Eddie hung up. For a moment he was going to smash his phone against the wall but thought better of it. He couldn't afford another.

At that moment his phone rang. He looked at the screen. "Mom." He thought about not answering but clicked in instead. "Hi, Ma, how ya doing?"

"I'm not good, Eddie. You know that. I need groceries but my check hasn't arrived yet and you know I have no savings. What am I supposed to do?" she asked. Her raspy voice was like fingernails on a blackboard to him.

"Okay, Mom, I'll get you some food. I'll drop off some things for you a little later. Don't worry," he said.

"Don't worry? That's all I do. My medicine is running out too. I can't live like this . . . if only your brother was still alive. He'd never leave me like this," she cried.

"Mom, Mom, please. I can only do so much. I'm trying. Just hang on, I'll get you what you need," he said raising his voice.

"Hang on? Oh, Eddie—"

He cut her off. "Mom, I promise I'll get you some groceries. I gotta go. Call you later."

"But, Eddie—" he heard her say as he hung up.

He went back into Duke's, ordered another vodka, and washed it down with a Heineken. His hands were still shaking as he drove in the slow lane into the Bronx. Beads of perspiration formed on his forehead as he pulled into the precinct house parking lot. He reached into the glove compartment for his last nip bottle of vodka, drained it, and flipped the plastic empty under the seat along with the others.

"Eddie, where the fuck have you been? You look like shit," a still steaming Krasnowsky said as he walked in.

"Yeah, been a rough morning," he replied, feeling the alcohol circulate in his bloodstream.

"Morning? It's afternoon, in case you haven't noticed," Krasnowsky said.

"Ah, okay, so? I got a lot of shit going on," Eddie said. "What's up?"

An angry Krasnowsky stared at Eddie, trying to contain himself. He took a breath to refocus, not sure exactly why he was losing it, but it all landed at that moment on Eddie. "Look, about this case, we gotta start at the beginning of this whole thing. It all starts with the shooting in the cab. We know there were three people in there, two are now dead. Who is that third person? That's the key. And my guess, that shooting is somehow connected to why Carlos ends up dead and why Joey D'Antonio was shot. With his print on the tape, it's clear Joey was involved somehow with the Carlos murder."

"Yeah, so?" Eddie replied with a shrug.

Krasnowsky looked at him, beginning to steam up, but he continued. "Forensics confirms there's no trace of Joey's DNA in the cab. So, Joey is not that third person. The only other person of possible interest, then, is McGowan. We don't have his prints or DNA and that's not going to be easy to get without an arrest. He'll lawyer up, so we'll have to figure that out." Krasnowsky paced in circles. "But right now he becomes our prime target."

"Yeah, McGowan, like I said. How do we get that lying fuck, who I know is dirty here, and tie his lily-white ass into this?"

"Well, whadda we got? To me the Rolex found on Carlos is a start. He doesn't strike me as a high-end watch buyer, how about you?"

Eddie shook his head.

"If it's real, where did he get it? First guess, it's stolen . . . but from who? Why don't you go and talk to the Rolex people. They got records, maybe they can give us some answers." Krasnowsky handed Eddie a plastic evidence bag with the watch in it. "See what you can get, okay?"

"Yes. Good idea. On it," said a suddenly energized Eddie. "What are you gonna do?"

"You mean aside from sitting on my ass?" replied Krasnowsky with a side glance.

"Yeah, like you do all day, every day."

"Well, I'll be busy getting legal to get us an ATM tape of the last transaction on McGowan's credit card," Krasnowsky said.

"Oh, shit, another good idea. Let's get this motherfucker," Eddie said.

"This is what we do," Krasnowsky replied, shaking his head. "Solve crimes, in case you haven't noticed."

"So far I ain't seen no crimes solved," said a defiant Eddie.

Eddie walked into the Rolex watch company's 5th Avenue retail store and approached a smiling, skinny young clerk with an off-kilter haircut and undersized suit. The plush carpet and glowing white marble walls made Eddie feel self-conscious about his street sneakers and worn Members Only jacket. "Hi, I'm Detective Johnson," he said, holding up his gold shield enclosed in a worn leather fob. "I need some information on this watch."

He placed the watch in the plastic bag on the sparkling glass counter. "Can you help me?"

The clerk lost his smile and backed off. "I'll get the manager."

"How can I help you, sir?" said an imperious voice. "I'm Dieter Schneider, manager here."

"Well, sir," Eddie said. "We found this watch on a murder victim fished out of the river. We have reason to believe it was stolen and need to find out if you have records on the name of the original purchaser?"

"Well, sir, we don't give this sort of information out as a general rule." Deiter's smile was dismissive.

Eddie tried to hold his temper but the manager's arrogance struck a deep chord. He leaned into Schneider's face. "I don't give a fuck about your rules. This is a murder investigation. You now have a fucking choice: I can take your smart ass downtown to headquarters for a long conversation about this whole thing—and I'll get my answers—or you can help me now without a whole lot of bullshit. Your choice." As he spoke, droplets of Eddie's spittle landed on Schneider's face and stained his sky-blue silk tie.

The manager blinked and stood back in disbelief. "Ah, just a minute, sir. I'll have to call upstairs." He picked up the bag with a shaking hand. "I'll need to give them the serial numbers."

"You got five minutes, that's all," Eddie said, grim-faced and breathing hard.

A re-collected Schneider returned in minutes with the watch and some handwritten notes. "It just so happens that that watch was sold from this store last year. It was purchased and picked up by a woman—a Courtney McAllister. She paid $9,750 plus tax with an American Express card. Here's her phone number and address. That's all we have. Will that be adequate, sir?"

"Yes. That's all I need," said Eddie, grabbing the watch. "Thank you."

As Eddie headed toward the door, the clerk nodded to Eddie, leaned over the counter, and spoke quietly. "Detective, I have a little background that might help you. I was the one that sold it to her. I remember her well. She was very nice, well dressed—really lovely. She said she bought it for her boyfriend—Mark, or something like that. He was in finance. It's a difficult watch to get, huge demand. She waited two months for us to finally get one for her. Talked to her several times."

"What? For that kind of money you can't just buy them?" Eddie asked.

"Are you kidding? People wait to buy them here at retail and can turn around and sell them for double the next day. They put them right on eBay. It's a very hot market at the moment," said the clerk. "She wasn't that kind of person, though. I certainly hope it wasn't her boyfriend that was killed."

"No. It was someone else. Probably stolen from her guy." Eddie smiled and extended his hand. "Thanks for the heads up. You just gave me some very valuable information that might help track down a killer."

The clerk seemed thrilled. He reached back and shook Eddie's hand. "No, thank you for all you do for us."

Eddie, feeling good, left his unmarked car parked on a side street and headed for the subway with a special mission in mind. Getting off at the Canal Street station, Eddie climbed the grimy stairs to the street. He shaded his eyes from the glaring sun to pick off a target. Scanning the storefronts, he spotted a Chinese guy with darting eyes in a doorway, anxiously shifting his weight from side to side in his red-and-white Air Jordans.

As Eddie approached the budding Asian entrepreneur smiled at him.

"You got watches?" Eddie asked.

"Depends, man. What are you looking for?" he said in perfect English.

"Rolex," Eddie replied.

"Everybody wants a Rolex. Might be able to help you. What model?"

"Submariner. Stainless. Black face. Automatic."

"You know your shit. Great watch. Got cash?"

"I didn't expect you to take credit cards." Eddie flashed a half-grin.

"Got it on ya? Let's see," the Chinese guy said.

"Hey, buddy, you think I'm a fucking idiot? I don't flash money. Let's see what you got."

"Okay, okay. You stay here, I'll be right back." The Chinese guy quickly disappeared around the corner.

In five minutes he was back with his hands in his pockets. "Take a look at this," he said as he stepped into the shadowy doorway and opened his palm. "It's the best you can find. Real Swiss movement—not Chinese. Brand new. Never worn. Got all the factory stickers on it too."

Eddie looked at the watch. Seemed identical to the one he had in the evidence bag. "Can I hold it? Wanna see the weight."

"You got money? Five hundred dollars, you can hold it."

"Hey, man, don't be like that. I got the money. It's no problem for me. I just want to see if it feels real," Eddie said.

The Chinese guy handed it over.

With that Eddie stepped back, pulled open his jacket, and showed the badge and gun on his belt. The Chinese guy froze.

"Look, you fucking crook. You know this is illegal. I could drag you to jail right now. And don't think about running. I got two guys across the street just waiting for you to resist. They're watching us now."

"Man, I don't want trouble. Give me a break. You keep the watch. I'll just walk away. You keep the watch," the Chinese guy said, suddenly fearful.

Eddie stopped for a minute and stared at his prey. He nodded. "Okay, okay. I'll cut you a break. How much you got on ya?"

"Ah, shit, I gotta feed my kids. Maybe two hundred bucks."

"Okay, keep fifty, give me the rest. I'll keep the watch as evidence—just in case," Eddie said. "You, nice and easy, just turn around and walk the fuck outta here. I'll give them the sign to leave you alone. And don't say a word to anyone. I know where you live, motherfucker. You got that?"

"Yeah, I got it. Here." He handed Eddie the money, turned and walked out into the sunshine. Eddie smiled, shoved the money into his pocket, waited a minute or two, and headed toward the subway. On the way back uptown, he switched the fake Rolex for the real one, put the counterfeit watch in the evidence bag for return to the property clerk. Two days later he put the real one on eBay and got $17,500 from a buyer in Ohio. He paid his lawyer, his child support, and dropped off some groceries at his mom's apartment.

"What took you so long," his mom asked with a grimace as he helped her put away the groceries.

"Hi, Courtney McAllister?" Eddie said on the phone.

"Well, yes. Who's this?"

"This is detective Eddie Johnson from Bronx Homicide. I need to ask you a few questions about a Rolex that you bought last year."

"A Rolex . . . you mean a watch?" Courtney said, sounding confused.

"Yes, did you purchase a Rolex watch last year?"

"Ah, yes, I did. Why?"

"Well, that watch has been connected to a murder investigation we are conducting here in the Bronx. It was found on the body of a man who was killed. Was it stolen?" Eddie said.

"What?" Courtney said. "Who are you again? Is this a joke?"

"No, this is not a joke, lady. The Rolex you bought last year at the 5th Avenue store was found on the body of a murder victim here in the Bronx. I have the serial numbers and full details of the purchase in front of me. I spoke to the clerk at the store who sold it to you. He remembers you well. Said you were giving it to your boyfriend—Mark, was it? You talked to him several times. Do you remember that?"

"Yes, of course. But the watch is not missing—my husband has it. It wasn't stolen. I just spoke to him," Courtney said, her tone now indignant. "This must be some kind of mix-up. And his name is not Mark, it's Michael."

"Oh, okay, Michael," Eddie said. "In any case, there's

no doubt the watch you bought for him was found on a dead body in the Bronx. Do you know anything about that?"

Eddie heard her stunned silence.

"What . . . me? Do I know anything about it? No, nothing at all," said Courtney.

"What about your husband, Michael, would he know anything about it?" Eddie said, reaching.

"Detective, I haven't the vaguest idea about any of this and I can't speak for my husband, but I'm sure you've got the wrong people. You haven't even gotten my name right," said a shaken Courtney.

"I apologize, what is your name?" Eddie said.

"McGowan. Courtney McGowan, and I'm sorry but I have nothing further to say to you. Thank you." She clicked off.

The name echoed in Eddie's head as he stood motionless, holding the phone to his ear.

After a few minutes he dialed Krasnowsky. "Another nail in his coffin," Eddie said.

"What, who?" replied the detective.

"Your boy, McGowan. It's his watch. Given to him by his now wife. Just got off with her. Rolex gave me all the details," Eddie said. "Had to get 'street' with them but they gave it up."

"No shit, this guy just keeps coming up, doesn't he?"

"Yeah, he must be lying to her, too, 'cause she was totally surprised—said he still had it," Eddie said. "He must have replaced it. Sneaky fuck."

"Well good work. I'm getting the ATM tape. Legal is moving on it for us. Let's see what that shows," said Krasnowsky. "And Eddie, really good work."

"Thanks, Phil," Eddie said as he clicked off.

Mike came home after a long day.

"Hi, honey. How did the nursery painting go?" he called out from the apartment hallway as he hung up his jacket in the closet.

Courtney walked in, visibly upset. "Michael, I got a very disturbing call today—from a detective. He wanted to know about the watch I gave you. Are you wearing it?"

A rush of adrenaline hit his bloodstream. Unwavering, he smiled and pulled up his sleeve. "You mean this watch?"

She walked over to him and turned his wrist to examine it. "Yes. That one." She inhaled in relief then shook her head. "He said it was found on a dead body . . . in the Bronx."

"What? How could that be? Here it is. And I'm still alive . . . as far as I know."

"He was sure the watch I bought you was found on a body in the Bronx. Do you know anything about that?" she asked, agitated.

"Are you serious? What the hell would I know?" he replied, looking at her in disbelief. "You think this guy had his facts straight?"

"Well, no. He actually had your name wrong and kept calling me by my maiden name." She stopped and thought for a moment, seeming to settle down. "I guess he could be mistaken, somehow. That's what I thought at first, but he seemed very certain—had full details. He even interviewed the people at the watch store where I bought it. Crazy."

"How'd he get our number?" He felt his breath racing and hoped she wouldn't notice.

"I guess from them," she replied.

"Well, honey," he said. "This sounds like a mix-up to me. Maybe they gave him the wrong information. If you give me his number, I can call him and try to straighten the whole thing out."

"Okay, yeah, do that. I don't want to deal with him. With the baby coming I've got enough to worry about." Courtney's eyebrows knitted. "You know, this whole thing really spooked me. A dead body in the Bronx; Joey just getting shot in the Bronx? What the hell is going on?"

"Honey, I got it. It's just a weird coincidence. It's nothing, let me handle it." Michael leaned in and hugged her. They stood in the center of the room as he held onto her for a long time. She seemed to release all her tension in his arms.

After a while she stepped back and looked into his eyes. "Michael, it's too much for me. Are you hiding anything? I'm just so scared lately. Something just doesn't feel right."

Michael had been stunned to hear the news of the

watch. Seeing her growing discomfort with all of it, he immediately went into damage control. "Honey, please, trust me. I'm not keeping anything from you, I swear on our baby," he said, reaching for her again. He struggled to keep his expression calm as his mind spun with what now seemed like certainty that the police had in fact recovered Carlos's body.

"This is just another freak, random thing—seems worse than it is. Nothing to do with us. It's a mistake. I'll straighten it out."

His assurances came across flat and she closed her eyes.

"Come on, we've got a lot to deal with right now and I don't want you to worry. We'll get through this. Let's just concentrate on having a healthy and happy baby. Okay?"

She pulled away slightly. "You smell like you've been drinking again?"

"Well, I stopped by McHale's with Frank Murdock and had two beers. He's so excited about the Sandoval thing. This is going to be huge. But that's it, just two beers."

"Michael, you said you weren't going to drink during the week. You promised," she said, tearing up.

"Baby, please, two beers with my boss. It's nothing." He kissed her and smiled.

She stared at him and struggled to smile back.

"Let's see that nursery—I can't wait. Do you like the color?" He tried to distract her and perhaps himself from a tension within him that felt bottomless and malignant.

Courtney inhaled and with some reluctance went with

it. "Absolutely, you're gonna love it," she said, the tremble in her voice betraying her fear.

Michael was on the phone with Larisia early the next morning. "I don't want to worry you, but I'm pretty sure the cops have found Carlos's body."

She inhaled sharply. "How do you know that?"

"An insane connection, cops traced the watch he had on—which he stole from me—to Courtney. A detective called her asking if she knew anything about a dead body found in the Bronx," he replied.

"Oh, shit, Michael, that's not good. What does it mean?" Her voice rose in concern.

"I don't know exactly. I replaced the watch already. Don't worry. In any case, it has no connection to you. I wouldn't be concerned," Michael said.

"But finding the body is not good news, Michael. I'm terrified, especially with Joey's death. The police have told me nothing. Can barely return my calls," she said in resignation. "They can find out about a watch on Carlos but they can't do anything about Joey's death?"

"That's cops. They don't give out anything. Suspect everybody," Michael replied.

"I mean, how did anybody know where Joey was? It wasn't random," she continued with growing anxiety. "This had something to do with the Carlos thing—I just know it. It's scaring the hell outta me—feel like things are closing in." She was losing patience with Michael and his breezy answers.

"Larisia, just calm down. I'll get you through this. You're covered. I'm with you." Michael paused. "You wouldn't want a little company tonight, would you?"

"How can you say that to me? Please, Michael, I'm frightened to death, I don't need you making things more difficult for me. I need a friend, but don't play with me. That's not what I need right now," she said, with a flash of anger.

"Okay, okay. I'm sorry. I just meant it as a friend," he said.

"I wish I could believe that." She hung up without another word.

Krasnowsky and Johnson stared at the blurry images on the office computer. The camera's fisheye lens distorted faces, making them almost zombie-like, and an unnatural blue-gray light only heightened the effect.

"If you ask me, these two are in it together. Looks like a drug deal," Eddie said.

"Well, in the middle of the night pulling out thousands of dollars in cash from an ATM, it's either a drug deal or a shakedown. McGowan doesn't look too happy to me. Almost looks like Carlos is holding something in his hand . . . is it a gun?" Krasnowsky said, pausing the images and leaning into the screen.

"Can't really make it out. Could be the drugs," Eddie said.

Krasnowsky squinted. "That looks like blood on McGowan's shirt."

"Could be . . . or steak sauce," Eddie said.

"Well, either way we know now that McGowan was with Carlos that night and money was involved—some shit was up," Krasnowsky said. "And this is only an hour or two before Carlos is found on the street with a bullet hole in his face."

"Yeah, like I said, a fucking drug deal gone wrong," Eddie said.

"Maybe, but it doesn't help us with the shooting in the cab, and it doesn't put McGowan in there. We got to connect him to the scene," Krasnowsky said.

"Okay, but it sure makes him look suspicious. And there's no doubt he was bullshittin' us. Let's run him down and collar him. He'll give it right up. If that lying fuck sees this, he'll cry like a little girl. I'm telling ya—grab 'em, case closed."

"Yeah, it's strong, but I wanna put him in that cab. We gotta get his prints and DNA without tipping our hand," Krasnowsky said. "I got an idea."

Krasnowsky's phone buzzed.

"Hi, Phil, it's Mary," said Jimmy Gronkowsky's wife with tension in her voice.

"Hey, Mary, getting ready for retirement?" he said.

"Oh, no, Phil . . .it's about Jimmy. He's on his way to the hospital." She began to cry. "I think it's his heart. He's been having some chest pains lately, and shortness of breath. The doctor said it was angina. But today he couldn't get out of bed and couldn't breathe. They just took him in the ambulance. Just before he got in, he told me to call you. Said it was something really important about Eddie. He wants to talk to you about it."

"Where are they taking him?" he said, turning away from Eddie.

"Kings County. Phil, please get there as soon as possible."

"I'm leaving now, Mary, don't worry," he said, walking toward the door.

"I gotta go to the hospital," he called out to Eddie, voice echoing as he headed down the hall.

Krasnowsky hopped into his unmarked Ford, stuck the cherry top onto the roof, and took off through the crush of midday traffic. A half-hour later, sweating profusely, he jogged into the chaotic Kings County Medical Center and found his way to the reception desk. He went up to the young attendant, flushed, wiping his brow.

"I'm looking for Jim Gronkowsky. He was just brought in. Can I see him? It's an emergency," he barked.

"Ah, are you a blood relative?" she asked, barely looking up from her computer.

"No, just a close friend. We worked together—"

She cut him off. "Sorry, sir, but I can't give you any information unless you're related."

"Look, I'm a detective. We're working on a case together." He flashed his gold shield.

"I'm sorry, sir, but—"

"Goddamn it! Who's in charge here? This is life or death."

She flinched, but got up, came around the desk, and pulled him aside. "Sir, I'm not supposed to tell you anything—it could be my job—but my father's a police officer too. So I understand." She hesitated. "I'm sorry, but from what I was told he didn't make it. They couldn't resuscitate him. He died in the ambulance."

"Are you sure?" he asked, stunned.

She looked down. "Yes . . . yes, I am. They brought his body to the morgue."

———

At Gronkowsky's funeral in Saint Stanislaus Kostka Church in Greenpoint, Krasnowsky approached Mary in the pews. Police bagpipes played a mournful dirge that echoed through the modest chapel. When she saw him, she reached out her arms and hugged him. They both cried.

"Oh, Phil, we lost him," she sobbed with her arms wrapped around him.

He embraced her, tears tracing down his cheeks. He held her there for a long, quiet moment in that sacred place where he'd held the heart-wrenching funeral for his murdered daughter. Where, as a youngster, he recited his first Hail Mary, received his first Holy Communion, and reluctantly confessed his sins through a screened window to a seemingly indifferent priest in a cramped and airless confessional. The smell of the burning votive candles, the purposeful dimness and lack of fresh air brought it all back from another time, making him feel out of body and dizzy.

It all washed over him in a rare moment of deep and abiding emotion, for a man who had spent his whole life avoiding it. The poignancy of life sunk into him and resonated in his very soul. It changed him. Right there, right then. He was being baptized in the church of everlasting sorrow and regret.

"Mary, Mary, I'm so sorry, I never got to say goodbye to him." He stumbled for words. "He was—you both were—my very best friends. He was my brother. I'll never have another like him. It all went too fast."

"Phil, he loved you," she said, gathering herself. "You two were a pair to beat a full house, that's for sure. The department will never see the likes of you guys again. That's sad too."

"Yeah, we had a great run. Now it's all changing," he replied. "Mary, tell me, did he ever say anything about that Eddie thing you mentioned?"

"Ah, no, Phil. Nothing. You know how he was about that. Everything about the department was confidential. He never talked about it."

"Yeah, I know. He was trying to protect you and the

family. I hope you know that. It's the toughest job, investigating cops."

"Yes, loyal to us, always, and the department. That's what mattered to him," she said. "What about you, Phil, now, with Gladys sick?"

"Oh, God, she's not doing well," he said. "But I haven't really thought about what's next—maybe I'm in denial. Got too many things I'm working on. You know me, I need to stay busy. And the department needs me."

"Yeah, you're like Jim. It's always the department, another investigation." She smiled and put her hand to his cheek as she stared at him. "Phil, if there's a lesson here, I'd say, don't stay too long at the party."

He smiled. Her words struck a chord with him. He took a moment and then changed the subject. "I'll see you again, maybe in North Carolina where the living is easy."

"I'd love that, Phil. You're a brave and good man and I know where you heart lies. But please, mark my words," she said as tears began to well.

They hugged. And they both knew they'd never see each other again.

18

THE GYPSY SWITCH—PART 2

C ourtney, dreaming about floating in a warm pool, woke up to wet bedsheets. Slightly panicked, she shook her husband awake. "Michael, I think it's time. My water just broke."

Still groggy he leaned over and kissed her. "Okay, baby, here we go. Nothing's gonna be the same after this."

They got up quickly and followed a pre-planned protocol. Her bags had been packed for more than a week. He got dressed and called for an Uber as she put on clothes that she'd already laid out. He helped her walk gingerly to the elevator and they were off to New York Hospital in minutes. On the way, while she practiced her breathing, he called their doctor from the cab, who said he'd meet them there.

Five hours later the baby was born. "Courtney, you're made to have children," said a smiling Dr. Steinberg, in their private room. "A great delivery, and she's beautiful and healthy. Eight pounds, six ounces. Perfect."

Courtney glowed as they placed the napping pink infant on her chest. She and Michael beamed at their little princess. "Nothing beats this, honey. Everything's gonna be just fine," he said as they kissed her. Courtney smiled back and wrapped her arms around his neck. The three of them stayed there quietly holding each other for a long moment. They both felt it, a deep love and connection that went beyond anything they'd ever experienced before. Tears of joy ran down their faces as they both held on tightly to their new family.

Soon the MacAllisters walked in, hugged their daughter, and giggled at the newborn. Courtney's dad, beaming with pride and affection, grabbed Michael in a bear hug. "She's just beautiful, Michael. Really. Ya done good, son."

"Thanks, but clearly Courtney did the heavy lifting— or should I say pushing. I was just an assistant," said a smiling Michael.

Michael was ebullient as he made calls to friends and relatives. "Mom, she looks just like you. Really. Blonde, fair, and a little rowdy. You're just gonna love her. The doctor said she's perfect. And she is."

Within hours the room began to fill up with flowers. Top management from Morgan sent a bouquet of thirty-six long stem roses in a crystal vase with a congratulatory note. Sandoval had delivered a basket of flowers so large it took up a whole corner of the room. Michael's coworkers sent an oversized arrangement of pink peonies with pink and silver balloons. More flowers and friends showed up. The "ohs" and "ahs" filled the room.

In the midst of it all, Michael's phone rang again. It was Sandoval. He stepped into the hallway to take it. "Michael, it's Miguel. Congratulations to you and your lovely wife. How is everyone?"

"Ah, yes, thanks. They're doing great. Courtney and the baby are resting now. Both happy and healthy. Imagine my luck, now I've got two beautiful girls in my life," said Michael. "And your flowers are amazing."

"My pleasure. You are a lucky man," Sandoval responded. "I have more good news. We got a shot at the World Cup coming back to Mexico—provided we build a new stadium. I'm proposing the idea of building it just down from the casino on land we already have under option. I'm flying back to Mexico City tonight to discuss it with the president. If this works, we'll be talking about a major bond issue. I hope you can handle it."

"Handle it? We'll kill it. No doubt. That's great news—unbelievable really. You know we're with you all the way," Michael said, fist bumping the air. "Whatever you need."

Michael's phone buzzed with another call. "I got Frank calling right now. Should I mention it to him?"

"Yes, sure. Tell him to get ready. We'll talk in a few days. For now, enjoy your beauties," Sandoval said as he clicked off.

Michael clicked into Frank's call. He tried to contain himself. "Frank, hi, we just got your flowers. They're beautiful, thanks so much."

"Well, I just wanted you to know how much we appreciate you and what you're doing. Tom McAdams, the senior VP, told me to get you the best flowers they had. He's all over this deal too and very impressed," Frank said.

"Thanks. Please tell him I'm so grateful," Michael said. "But Frank, you're not going to believe what I just heard. FIFA wants to bring the World Cup to Mexico if they can build a new stadium. Sandoval's pushing the idea to build it right near the casino. A perfect match—gambling and soccer. They've got an option on the land already. This could be gigantic."

"You're not kidding. This whole project could double in size. Just tremendous work, Mike."

"Thanks, Frank. He said for us to get ready. I'm sure they're gonna go with us on this one too." Michael was tingling with excitement.

"You're the man, Michael. You've certainly impressed them. Stay with it and let's get it over the finish line. Okay? I gotta go but, most importantly, congratulations again on the baby and love to Court," said Frank as he hung up.

Michael stood alone in the hallway as happy as he'd ever been in his life. Joyful images of where his life was going mixed in his mind with the sounds of his excited family giggling and talking in the room with Courtney and the baby. *It doesn't get much better than this.* He closed his eyes and basked in the feeling of contentment, so rare for him.

At that moment Lara, Michael's assistant, called in. He let it go to voicemail. A minute later she called again and he knew it was urgent. Mike picked up Lara's call and instantly heard the distress in her voice.

"Michael, I'm in the office and those two detectives are here again, same as last time. They say they must talk to you, now. I know this is not a good time. I told them you were at the hospital but they're insistent—won't leave. Said they'll wait for you here or would come over to the hospital. What should I do?"

"What? Ah, shit. I don't want them here. I'll have to come over there and talk to them. Just tell them I'm coming in; ask them to go out and get a cup of coffee. I'll be there in twenty minutes," he said. "Don't worry, it's nothing, probably a follow-up about Joey's shooting."

"Oh, okay, sorry. I'll tell them and, ah, congratulations," she said as she hung up.

Michael felt the blood rising in his face as he walked inside and whispered to Courtney. "Honey, I've got to go over to the office. Lara has a problem."

"Oh, Michael, what's more important than this? Can't you put it off?" she said. "Are you okay?'

"Yes, I'm fine—in fact fabulous." He took her hand. "Court, you know there's nothing more important than you and her," he said as he caressed the baby's head. "I'll be an hour or two, the most. Promise. With Joey gone, I have to take the lead on some of these things. They just need me now."

"Oh, okay. I know you've got a lot going on," she said.

"Yes, I do, but it's all good. I love you, honey. Be back

soon." He leaned over and hugged her and said his good-byes to the family.

In the cab on his way over Michael thought about calling his lawyer but decided not to. *If it gets sticky, I can always bail on these dopes.*

Sweating and impatient from a long night, Michael marched into the conference room just as the two detectives were taking their seats.

"Oh, you guys again. What the fuck now?" Michael said.

"Hello, Mr. McGowan. I'm Detective Krasnowsky and this is Detective—"

"I know who you are," Michael said. "Look, my close friend got shot and killed in your backyard and I'd like to know what the fuck you guys are doing about it?"

"We're well aware," Krasnowsky replied.

"Well, why the fuck aren't you out catching these bastards?"

"Huh? Maybe we are," said an irate Eddie. "What do you know about it?"

"Me? What? You're the fucking detective. Do your job. What have you done so far?" Michael shouted.

"Fuck you," Eddie shouted back as he stood up. "We're working on it."

"Working on it? Bullshit, you've got nothing." Michael leaned forward with both hands on the table.

Krasnowsky intervened. "Hey, fellas, let's just settle down here. We need to talk to you, but this ain't gonna get us anywhere." The grieving detective looked on as they both slowly sat down, staring at each other across the walnut table.

"Let's just take a breath here and start over," Krasnowsky said. "Could we get some water?"

Michael picked up the phone and asked Lara to bring in some bottles of Fiji Water. They all took short sips and put the bottles on the table.

Krasnowsky turned to Michael. "What we're doing here is part of our investigation. We need to ask you some questions about that night—the night Joseph D'Antonio was shot. Maybe you can help us get these bastards, as you say. Believe me, we all have the same goal in mind."

"Yeah, okay," Michael said. "But what kind of answers can I give you?"

"Well, for one thing, as you said you and Joey were friends, right?" asked the detective.

"Yes," Michael said. "He was a great friend. I've known him since childhood. We grew up in the same neighborhood."

"Good. Then maybe you know what he was doing in the Bronx that night?" Krasnowsky asked.

"He was with his wife and their new baby. He wasn't committing a crime, I can tell you that."

"Now relax, I wasn't implying that. But I don't get the whole thing with the wife and new baby in the Bronx and him living in Manhattan," the detective said.

"Yeah. What was it, some kind of shack-up job—second family? Didn't want anyone to know?" Eddie asked.

"Hey, fuck you." Michael stared at Eddie and took another sip of water. "They were getting ready to move in together in a new place. They were good—great, actually. It was all working out. But what does any of that have to do with the shooting anyway?"

"Well, you tell us. Any relatives who didn't want it to happen? Or a drug involvement? Anything like that?" Krasnowsky asked. "Maybe somebody was pissed off at them."

"No nothing like that. They have good families and she's a great girl," Michael said. "I introduced them."

"Oh, nice hookup job. Maybe you guys shared her," Eddie said.

"Again, detective, fuck you," said Michael looking at Eddie. "And let me ask you, are you the guy that called my wife and asked about a Rolex she gave me?"

"Yeah, that was me," Eddie replied.

"Well, here's the watch." An emboldened Michael pulled up his sleeve. "I still have it. It's not stolen and if you have any further questions about it, just call me. Leave my wife outta this. Okay?"

Eddie nodded and smiled. "Nice watch. Can I take a closer look at that?"

"Fuck no. Go talk to my lawyer," said a heated Michael.

At that moment Lara knocked on the door, stuck her

head in, and asked Michael to step outside for a minute. He got up to talk with her in the hallway out of earshot, holding the door half-open with his foot.

Krasnowsky saw his chance and switched his water bottle with Michael's.

In a minute Michael was back. "Well, where were we?"

"We were talking about anyone you think might have had a grudge against them."

"Oh, yeah, and no, I don't know anyone like that. They were a great couple," Michael replied. "No enemies I know of."

"How about her? Drugs?" Eddie asked. "Ya know, Mexican and all?"

Michael, shaking his head, turned to him. "What the fuck does that mean? I already told you. She was a very good person, working hard and taking care of their baby."

"What was her name again?" pressed Eddie.

"Larisia," Michael said. "Larisia Diaz. Don't you guys have that in your report?"

"I'll check," Eddie said with a half-grin.

"Well, I guess we got what we needed for now. We'll get back to you," Krasnowsky said, getting out of his chair, water bottle in hand.

Michael stood up with a start. "What? That's it?" he shouted. "This is what you dragged me across town to talk about—ten minutes of fucking bullshit?"

"Yeah, that's it," Eddie replied. "You'll be hearing from us soon. Don't worry."

"Jesus Christ, my wife's in the hospital with our new

baby and you waste my time with this shit? No wonder you don't get anything done," Michael said.

"We appreciate your cooperation, Mr. McGowan." Krasnowsky shook Michael's hand with a meaty grip. "We're working hard on this case. We'll let you know."

They left and an aggravated Michael went back to his office.

Lara knocked on his office door just as he was back and trying to calm down. She stepped in and closed the door behind her. "Michael, I have to tell you something strange."

"What?"

"I saw that detective switch water bottles with you while we were talking in the hallway. He carried that bottle out with him when he left. He wrapped it with a tissue," she said. "Why would he do that, take your water bottle?"

"Are you sure?" he said. "I didn't notice any of that." He felt a cold chill of fear creep up his spine.

"Yes. Absolutely. He walked out with it. I think you were caught up with being angry at them," she said.

"Yeah, I sure was. I think they're a pair of assholes. I just want them to catch those rat bastards that shot Joey," Michael said, masking his distress that was now even more intense. "They're clueless. Total assholes. I'll take care of it."

Sweating despite the air-conditioned office, Michael dialed his attorney as soon as she left.

"Shell, how ya doing?" Michael said.

"Oh, Michael. I'm doing fine, thanks. I guess the real question is how you are doing. I heard you and Courtney just had a new baby. Congratulations," Shelly said. "Is everyone good?"

"Yeah. Healthy and happy. I just left them at the hospital. Our new girl's a beauty and Court is on cloud nine with her, both doing well. I'm very lucky."

"Yes, you are, so what can I do for you?"

"Listen, I've got a possible problem . . . not sure," Michael said.

"What is it?" Shelly asked.

"Well, I had two detectives here asking questions about Joey's shooting but when they left, one of them switched water bottles with me when I wasn't looking and then wrapped it in tissue and took it with him. What the hell would that be about?"

"Oh, shit. Are you a target in that investigation?" Shelly asked.

"No, I don't think so. I had nothing to do with it, of course. It was a random drive-by. That's what the cops think. Why the hell would I be a target?" Michael said.

"Yeah, strange, but it sounds like they're trying to get your prints or something. Did you give them any permission to do that?'

"No, of course not. Didn't know they were doing it," Michael said.

"Well, it's illegal then. Not admissible. But why are they on you? Is there anything else I should know about? Like your 'friend' that had that problem?"

"No, no, that's old news now," Michael said.

"And what the hell are you doing talking to detectives without me? I am here to protect you from anything like this. You don't know what they have in mind. Don't talk to police alone," the attorney said.

"I know, Shelly, but believe me, these two are lost. They don't know what the hell they're doing with this shooting. We need somebody with brains looking into this," Michael said.

"Don't be so sure," replied Shelly.

Michael's phone beeped with Larisia calling in.

"Shell, I gotta take this. I'll call you back." He clicked over.

"Hi, Larisia," he said. "You okay?'

"Oh, I guess, okay. How's your new baby?" she asked.

"Oh, she's beautiful. Court's good too," Michael said, feeling awkward. "How's my little Angelina?"

"She's fine. My aunt is taking care of her now while I'm studying," she replied. She sounded like she was about to cry.

"Look, these are both my children. I love them both . . . equally. I'm the father," Michael said. "Maybe I can come up and see you both at some point?"

"Michael, you don't have to do that. I know you love her, and you can see her soon, but I know you've got your hands full." The fear and tension in her voice betrayed her placating words.

"Larisia, I know you're afraid but I'm there for you—and her too. I'm gonna get us through this. Don't worry," he said.

"I wish I could really believe that, but I can't." She began to cry. "I'm terrified all the time, Michael. I just have this feeling someone is after me like they went after Joey. I'm scared of what's going to happen."

"Nothing, nothing is gonna happen. You'll be fine," Michael said. "Baby, you got to get hold of yourself. Calm down. No one is coming after you. I'll get you outta there—get you a new place downtown as soon as I have a chance—just a little difficult to do right now."

"It's just this eerie feeling since Joey got shot. Can't seem to shake it. I just know there's more to this," she said.

"Larisia, I promise. I'm gonna fix this. You'll be safe. I'll help you both. I swear to God," Michael pleaded.

"Thank you, Michael. I, we, need you now more than ever," she said.

Michael felt aroused talking to her. "I'd really love to see you," he said.

Larisia let out a frustrated gasp. "What? How can you keep saying that? Michael, please, just help us. We need your help. That's all. I just need you to be my friend. Nothing else, nothing, just be my friend." After a moment she realized it was hopeless. "Look, this is not what I need. I've gotta go." She hung up, put her hands to her face, and sobbed as she sat in her apartment, terrified and alone.

19

IN THE WIND

E ddie walked into the precinct house as the sun was setting.

"What the hell are you doing here at this hour?" Krasnowsky cracked, looking at his watch. "Day's almost over."

"I was in family court this morning. Don't ask," Eddie grimaced. "What's going on?"

"A lot, as it turns out, and oddly you got perfect timing. I just got a call from Forensics. They got a print match on the glass shard found in Carlos's neck." Krasnowsky turned away dismissively.

"Okay, so who?" Eddie impatient with the game.

"It's a Larisia Diaz. Picked up her print from a state nursing license application. She lives in the Bronx and works part-time at Lincoln Hospital," Krasnowsky said.

"Isn't that the name of the girlfriend of our victim Joey D'Antonio?" said Eddie.

"Shit, yeah, Eddie. That's your best contribution to this case so far," cracked Krasnowsky.

"Great, let's pick her up," Eddie replied.

"Okay, but hold it just a minute, I wanna see one thing I was just thinking about." Krasnowsky went over to his desk and took out a plastic bag with the crumbling remains of Michael's business card found on Carlos's body. He held it up to the buzzing fluorescent light.

"Is that an L and an A? Maybe an R? Can't read the rest, but Larisia fits." Krasnowsky squinted at the faded lettering. He walked over to his unwashed window and raised the yellowed shade. He scratched his head and dandruff floated through the shaft of receding afternoon sunlight as he stared at the card. "And that's definitely a seven and a one, and maybe an eight. A Bronx exchange maybe?"

Krasnowsky stopped for a minute. "Sure enough, that fits, and son of a bitch—that fucking Dr. Lee. He said it was probably a woman who stabbed him. Bet this is her."

"And this is why D'Antonio was shot in that drive-by," said Krasnowsky with the sudden feeling of clouds parting in his mind. "They were working together. Could be drugs."

"Yeah, and that fucking McGowan knows her too," said Eddie.

"Hmmm. Maybe this thing is coming together. Let's pick her up and see what she's got to say," said the lieutenant.

In his unmarked car blocks away from the precinct house, Eddie pulled over to the curb to make a call on a street pay phone.

"Hola," said a voice he had become familiar with.

"Got a woman's name. Larisia Diaz. She was part of the Carlos thing. She's a nurse at Lincoln Hospital."

"Bueno," came the reply.

"Let me know where I can pick up my money," said Eddie as he heard an abrupt click off.

Larisia sat in the school library staring at an open anatomy book, but her mind couldn't absorb any of the information on the printed pages before her. Her only thoughts of anatomy were on her last night with Joey, just a few short months ago, when her world was so different. They shared a love like nothing she'd ever experienced before and now that world had disappeared.

Joey's death proved the police were of no help. All their conclusions about the shooting seemed like half-baked assumptions to cover their incompetence. The department offered her no information about the investigation and certainly no protection. She couldn't shake the feeling that someone had come for Joey. And they were coming for her too.

Her thoughts and emotions collided in her mind and

heart and set off an abiding feeling of panic. Nothing made sense to her. With Joey gone, she was alone. Her sense of trust and confidence in Michael had waned, and clashed with her belief that he truly cared. But his obnoxious overtures undercut everything and chafed their every interaction.

All of it set her on a razor's edge. No one could help her and her precious Angelina. There was also an aching part of her that felt retribution was coming for her, and that she deserved that inevitable punishment for her transgressions. Was there any chance for redemption? Who would save her?

She was startled out of her dark reverie when her phone buzzed. She saw it was her nurse supervisor at the hospital and stepped outside to answer it.

"Hola, Dominga," she said.

"Larisia, there were two men here looking for you. Said they were detectives. Wanted to talk to you," Dominga replied.

Her heart was suddenly pounding, "What? For me? What did they want?"

"They wouldn't say. I told them today was your day off but you'll be here tomorrow. Was that okay? I didn't want to get you in trouble."

"No. No. That's fine," said a trembling Larisia. "There's no trouble. It's probably something to do with my license application."

"Do you want their number? They left their card."

"Ah, no, not right now." Her mind was racing. "I'll pick it up when I get there tomorrow. Don't worry, it's fine."

"Okay, bueno. See you tomorrow."

Larisia didn't bother to close her books. She left them on the table, right where they were, and hurried out of the building. With a quick sprint she caught the Fordham Road bus as it pulled up to the corner. Overwrought and sweating in the humidity, her damp skin stuck to the worn plastic seats. She stared out of the unwashed windows with her mind in turmoil, and a wave of desperation came over her as the evening darkness began to engulf the busy Bronx streets.

The bus lurched to a stop at the corner of Jerome. She jumped off and turned the corner of her block. As she did, she saw a black sedan parked in the shadows across from her apartment. She could see the outline of two figures inside and the glow of their cigarettes. She stopped dead in her tracks then side-stepped into an alley, hoping they hadn't seen her. Her heart pounded. At that moment her cell phone vibrated, and a chill went up her spine.

"Larisia, are you okay?" her aunt asked.

"Yes, Tía. Why? Is the baby okay?" Larisia cupped the phone to muffle her voice.

"Sí, sí, she's fine. I just fed her. But two men came by the restaurant—two detectives. They wanted to talk to you. Are you in trouble?"

"What? No. What did you tell them?" Larisia asked.

"I told them that you were studying for your tests. You were probably at school."

"Good." In that moment, Larisia made a life-changing decision. "Listen, I have to leave. I need to get Angelina and take her with me. Can you get her and meet me around the corner from the restaurant? Just pack a bag with some clothes and diapers. I can't explain now, but I've got to go. Don't worry, it's gonna be okay."

"Don't worry? I worry about you and her every day, my bebé. What happened?" her aunt pleaded.

"I can't talk right now. Meet me in thirty minutes," said a crying Larisia. "Please do what I say."

"But, but—"

Larisia hung up.

As darkness descended, Larisia went through the alley, down through trash-strewn backyards, and hopped a sagging fence like she used to as a kid. She came to the back door of her building, went in, and cautiously padded up the worn marble stairs to her door. She slipped silently into her apartment.

Blood pounded in her ears as she gathered a small bag of belongings in shadows. With trembling hands, she peeled back the edge of the worn shade ever so slightly and peered out the window to check the street. She could see the dark silhouettes of the two figures still sitting inside the unmarked car. Cigarette smoke wafted out of the partially opened window. Terrified, she pulled back and leaned against the wall for a long minute. Dizzy, she looked around with sorrow and regret, knowing there was no way she could stay. This life she had known was now over. As she headed for the door, she noticed Sandoval's card on the end table. She picked it up and put it in her pocket. Quickly she retraced her steps out through the backyards. In minutes, she was walking away on River Avenue.

Larisia's aunt stood in the dim corner of an alley behind the restaurant, holding a small bag and the infant Angelina in a pink blanket. Larisia came around the corner cautiously and let out a slight sigh as she saw them. Silently she hugged them both. Tears traced down her cheeks.

"My sweet Tia. It's going to be all right. I can't be around here. You've helped me so much; I love you for that but right now I've got to go. I don't have the time to explain but I will soon as I can. I promise," she said, sobbing. "Thank you for everything."

"My bebé, you and Angelina are all we have in this country—really, in this world. You're our life. We'll do anything for you and we won't ask questions. Please protect yourself and our little angel." She handed Larisia a roll of bills in a rubber band. "This is for you. It's all we got. Call me as soon as you can."

"I will." Larisia took the baby, hugged her aunt, and stuffed the roll in her pocket.

"God will help you, my love. Ask God. He's always there for you," she urged. "I will pray for you both."

"I love you," Larisia said as she turned and walked off into the darkness with her baby.

Despite her assurances to her aunt, Larisia had no plan. Terror gripped her and tears flowed down her face as she walked aimlessly through the shadowy streets of the Bronx carrying her dozing child. She wandered for nearly an hour and, by chance, found herself in front of St. Thomas Aquinas Church.

Exhausted, she entered the empty basilica, sat down, and placed the child on the wooden pew next to her. She looked up and stared at the statue of the Blessed Mother in a blue gown holding the baby Jesus. Lost in fear and sadness, Larisia got on her knees, closed her eyes, and prayed.

"Please forgive me for what I have done. Help me protect my child. Guide me. She is innocent and pure and has committed no sin. I have. I am the sinner, and I know I must pay for my sins. I would give my life for her, but she needs me now. Please help me protect her." She cried with her face in her hands. Tears flowed between her fingers and down her arms.

She reached into her pocket for a tissue and Sandoval's card fell to the floor. She picked it up and thought for a moment, then stepped to the back of the church, leaving her sleeping infant in view in the pew. She dialed his number.

"Hola," the gentlemanly Sandoval said.

"Señor Sandoval, this is Larisia, Joey D'Antonio's wife," she said haltingly.

"Oh my God. Nice to hear from you. How are you?" he said with great surprise.

"I'm in trouble and I really need your help, señor. I have no one to turn to and I'm so frightened, for me and my baby. I need to leave here ... to leave America. My life is in danger here."

"Danger? Can you call the police?" he asked.

"They can't help me, and I don't know if I can trust them. I'm sure Joey was killed by gangsters, and I believe his killers are after me too." She sobbed.

"But why? Why would they want to kill you?"

"It's very complicated, but you must believe me. I know they want revenge for something I did, something I had to do, but it wasn't my—"

"Larisia, stop. Don't tell me. I don't want to know. I can't know," he said. "Just tell me how I can help you."

"Can you get me to Mexico?" she asked. "I was born there but I have no papers. No passport. I have my baby here with me. I'm in a church and I have nowhere to go. I need to get back to my parents."

"You mean now? Tonight?"

"Yes, señor. I'm packed and ready to go. I must leave this all behind."

"It's that bad, eh?"

"Yes, it is. I have nothing left here for me. I only want to protect her. At least I know she'll be safe there with my family."

"Please, hold on for a moment." He covered the phone but she could hear muffled conversation in the background. "Can you get to Teterboro Airport in New Jersey?"

"I'll get there—just where exactly?"

"Meet me at hangar seven, in the back. Can you make it in an hour or so?"

"Yes, I'll be there."

"Look, Larisia, I'm not going to ask you any questions, especially if I shouldn't know the answers. But I'm doing this because I know you're a good person and I'm for helping good Mexican people with their lives. We have to help each other in this world," he said.

"Muchas gracias, señor. You are saving our lives."

"Bueno. See you there."

Before she gathered up the baby, Larisia looked up at the statue of the Madonna, made the sign of the cross and put her hands together in prayer, and sobbed, "Thank you, su madre. Please forgive me."

Holding her baby, she stepped outside into the warm summer evening and dialed an Uber.

A grim and disheveled Eddie walked into Krasnowky's office, finishing off a taco. He smelled of cigarettes and Cholula.

Krasnowsky looked up. "You get her?"

"No, nothing. She's in the wind. I just spent the last twelve hours in front of her apartment. No sign of her. Left another guy there. Neighbors haven't seen her. Not at the hospital, school, or restaurant. Just gone. Incidentally, she's got her baby with her."

"A baby? Shit. How far can she go with a baby? Put out an APB, and an Amber Alert too. I'll call the Port Authority to cover the trains, buses, and planes. We'll get her."

"Did you get anything back on McGowan from Forensics yet?" Eddie asked, changing the subject and now wedging his wide ass on the corner of Krasnowsky's desk.

"Yeah, but right now I have to meet my wife at the doctor's office. So I gotta go," said an aggravated Krasnowsky, getting up to leave.

"So you're not going to tell me?"

Krasnowsky, inhaling Eddie's alcoholic breath, looked at him. "Eddie, do you really give a shit about this job or are you just interested in going after a guy you don't like?"

"Both," said a defiant Eddie.

"Well, you just may get what you want," Krasnowsky said, shaking his head. "We got a match on his prints and DNA in the cab. We also got a DNA match with his blood under the handle of the gun. We got him cold. No question."

"Fuck yes. I knew that piece of shit was lying to us all along. Since we can't get her, let's put the cuffs on him right now."

"Well, now, you're just gonna have to sit on this one, a little, 'cause I gotta go. My wife needs me."

"What? I wanna lock this motherfucker up to-*day*," Eddie said.

"No can do, son. He ain't going nowhere. You waited

this long, you can wait a little longer. And don't pull a cowboy on me and try to bust him yourself. Just sit tight," Krasnowsky warned." We'll get him."

As he headed to the door he stopped and stabbed his finger at Eddie's chest. "And remember, don't say a word about how we got those prints—you could blow this whole case."

Eddie put up his hand to do a high-five but Krasnowsky ignored him and headed out.

At the door he turned around. "And Eddie, taking a fucking shower and brush your teeth. You stink."

Twenty minutes later, Eddie was at a pay phone making a call to a familiar number.

"Hola."

"I got your man. The name's McGowan."

"Bueno," came the reply.

Krasnowsky's phone buzzed as he walked out of the precinct.

"Phil, it's Dr. Morton. You need to get down to Woodhull Hospital as soon as possible. Meet me there. I had to admit Gladys today."

Phil ran to his car, took off with screeching tires and, sweating, arrived at the hospital in twenty minutes. He was directed to the ICU on the third floor of the grim city hospital and saw Dr. Morton standing in the hall outside the unit when he got there. Phil reached out his hand to the doctor, who struggled to smile and return the handshake.

"It's not good," Dr. Morton said as he shook his head. "We've had to do a lot of intervention."

The doctor turned and peered through the windows of the double doors. Phil looked in with him to see Gladys in a bed with tubes protruding, surrounded by video screens, eyes closed.

"Phil, has she been smoking?" the physician asked.

"Not that I know of," Krasnowsky replied. "She wouldn't do that—would she?"

"Some people just can't stop, no matter what. It's a terrible addiction. I've seen it before."

"I can't believe she'd do that," Phil said. "I've told her."

"Well, her lung function and oxygen levels have dropped dramatically. The cancer has progressed. We had to intubate her, so she won't be able to talk to you," he said. "There's not much for me to say, Phil. This is your time to be with her." He put his hand on Phil's shoulder, nodded, and walked away.

Phil pushed through the double doors, pulled up an aluminum chair, and sat down next to his wife of forty-three years. A ventilator inhaled and exhaled for her with a mechanical pumping sound. Tubes sprouted from both arms; her forefinger had a metal clip on it. She seemed semi-conscious. An electronic heart monitor beeped with each precious beat.

He took her hand, bent his head down, and began to cry. He cried for all the years they had and all the years they would never have. For everything in his life that meant anything to him and all that he had sacrificed—that they both sacrificed. He thought for the first time about her selfless love and that, maybe, just maybe, she had sacrificed more than he had. And she had done it with no demand, no complaint, no anger.

She had let him have his way all these years. The danger, the all-night stakeouts, the interrupted holiday dinners, and skipped vacations. She tolerated the life of a detective and his dedication to the department and righting wrongs, to justice. If not him, who will do it, she would always say. The medals and accommodations all faded memories now, gone forever. After Anna's death, which they rarely talked about—too painful—all they had was each other.

"Honey, I can't lose you now. I need you . . . probably more than you ever needed me. We lost our little girl—our light. You were so strong then. You got me through that. I'm still haunted by all of it. Please stay here . . . stay with me," he said through tears.

He looked up and she seemed to blink. She knew he was there. She let him know. Was that a half-smile? He squeezed her hand and he felt her squeeze back and hold on. Then, a minute later, she abruptly let go and the heart monitor stopped beeping.

Alarms went off, a call for epinephrine, and suddenly a rush of nurses surrounded the bed. He was pushed aside as they worked on her feverishly. He stood up, hands to his mouth, and backed away.

They asked him to leave as a tech rushed in with the paddles. The last word that rang in his ears was "clear" and then he heard a brief electronic pulse, and then another. He stood in the hallway, with his face against the wall, sobbing.

20

CIGARETTES AND SHADOWS

A week after Gladys's funeral, Krasnowsky had some unfinished business. He called Eddie into his office.

"Hey, Phil." Eddie reached out his hand. "I'm really sorry for your loss."

"Thanks, Eddie," he said, as he shook his hand. "I got a lot on my mind but I've got to finish this case. Let's collar this fucking McGowan and see what else we can get out of him."

"Yeah, that's what I'm talking about," replied Eddie.

Michael was sitting in his office dialing Larisia's number for the tenth time. He hadn't heard from her in days. Her phone only went to voicemail. He was struggling with an uncomfortable feeling about her disappearance when

Lara called in on the intercom to say he was wanted up front in reception.

"Lara, I'm busy right now. Who wants me out there?" he barked.

"Those two detectives are here again. They said they want you out here right now." Her voice was strained.

"What? Who the fuck do they think they are?" he replied with impatience. "I'm coming out, and I think you oughta call security. These guys have no right to pull this shit."

Michael barged into the reception area, red-faced. "What the hell? You guys have no right to just keep showing up here and harassing—"

"Michael McGowan," the burly detective said, cutting him off. "You are hereby under arrest in the killing of Juan 'Paco' Acivedo. Please turn around and put your hands behind your back."

"What? Who? I don't know who you're talking about. What is this?" Michael said, stepping back, heart suddenly pounding. His body went numb but his first instinct was to fight.

"Hold it right there, motherfucker," Eddie warned. "Turn around now and put your hands behind your back or I'm gonna drop your ass right where you stand."

Michael saw the look in his eyes and turned around, shaking his head. "I don't think you guys know what the fuck you're doing. I don't know any Juan, whatever his name is. You got this wrong."

Eddie grabbed him, pulled his hands behind him, and tightly squeezed closed a pair of cold handcuffs.

Michael winced. "This is wrong," he said, looking around at his coworkers who stood gobsmacked amid the plush mahogany setting. Lara, hands covering her mouth, began to cry.

"These guys are wrong," Michael insisted to everyone, his eyes wild, scanning the crowd of colleagues with their mouths agape.

Krasnowsky turned him around, leaned in, and spoke close to his face. "You are under arrest. You have the right to remain silent. Anything you say can and will be held against you in a court of law. You have a right to an attorney. If you can't afford one, a court-appointed attorney will be provided. Do you understand?"

The words echoed in his ears. Michael, stunned, nodded his head.

"I need you to say yes or no," Krasnowsky said. "I need to hear it."

"Yes," Michael replied. He felt the blood rushing to his head as beads of sweat began to form across his brow.

"Okay, motherfucker," Eddie said. "Your ass is ours now."

As Eddie began to lead him away, Michael stopped him by yanking his arms away from Eddie's grip. A risky move that got him a rough grab from Eddie.

"I need my coat and phone. I gotta call my wife." With that Lara ran off to retrieve them from his office. She came back with tears flowing down her face, and gently draped his suit jacket on his shoulders, covering the cuffs. Krasnowsky stepped forward, put out his hand, and took the phone from her. They led him away to a cacophony of ringing telephones and the muffled voices of his stunned coworkers.

Michael was booked, photographed, fingerprinted, and processed in grimy Manhattan criminal court at Center Street. The place stank of a noxious mix of industrial strength Pine-Sol, body odor, and urine. Every sound echoed in the halls and in Michael's head. Dirty fingerprints and years of unwashed grime shaded every corner of the ancient, pale-green walls.

After an invasive body search, he relinquished his clothes for a detainee's orange jumpsuit and a pair of white flip-flops. Sitting in the corner of a holding cell, a correctional officer came in and announced he could make a call to his attorney.

"Shelly, I got arrested," he shouted into the receiver of a jailhouse wall phone in a noisy and smelly hallway.

"What? For what?" replied the attorney.

"They said I murdered some guy in the Bronx but it's bullshit. I didn't do it. It was self-defense. I can explain the whole thing to you but first you gotta get me outta here."

"Where are you?"

"I'm in the Tombs."

"Oh, shit. Did you have a bail hearing yet?"

"No, not yet," Michael said.

"Okay, fuck, I gotta make a couple of calls for you and then I'll get down there. Michael, make sure you don't talk to anyone about anything. Just hold tight. And definitely don't talk to any cops. I'm on it. Be there as soon as I can," said the attorney as he hung up.

The gray metal door squeaked as it swung open in the sparse private meeting room. Shelly walked in with his expensive leather briefcase, silk suit, and a grim look.

"Mike, how you doing?"

"I've been better. What's the story?" Michael sat at a metal table looking pale and forlorn in his orange jumpsuit in the center of the windowless room. His mind was spinning, unable to comprehend his current situation. His first thought was it was a simple legal maneuver and he'd be out.

"The DA tells me they have a very solid case against you. Your DNA and prints are all over a murder scene. Some guy named Paco, a gypsy driver from the Bronx, who was shot in his cab. They're calling it a drug deal gone bad. They even got your DNA on the gun." The attorney placed his briefcase on top of the table to avoid the ever-present roaches and brushed off the seat before he sat down. "What the fuck happened?"

Michael's mind reflexively spun different scenarios, but he knew the only way was to come clean. "Shelly, it was self-defense. I swear. They were mugging me. Robbed money and my watch and threatened to kill me and throw me into the river. What the fuck was I gonna do? At one point, I saw my chance and grabbed the gun and shot both of them."

"Wait, hold it. There were two of them?" the attorney asked.

"Yeah, there was another guy there—a Carlos, bad motherfucker. He was the one who really did this shit," Michael said. "This guy Paco was kind of innocent, but he got shot in the struggle for the gun—it just went off. His brains were all over the windshield."

The lawyer shuddered. "What about the other guy— this Carlos?" the attorney probed.

"That fuck. I shot him too, up close, right in the face. But somehow he survived, I guess. I heard the cops found him bleeding and passed out on the street a couple of hours later. After I shot him I jumped out of the car and ran, just ran. Went back to my apartment. Didn't tell anyone about it— well, except—"

"Except ... yeah? Except who?"

"Ah, my friend Joey. I told him the next day. But as you know he was shot and killed in what the cops are calling a random drive-by," Michael said, pausing. "I know, it's getting complicated."

"What happened to this Carlos? He could be a valuable witness," said the attorney, staying on point.

"They sent him back to Mexico. Had an outstanding warrant, but then he showed up dead in the Bronx River a few months ago," Michael said with a shrug, trying to convince a now suspicious attorney that he had no involvement in it. "Ya know, drug gang shit."

"Wow, there's a lot here. Is there more to this shit? You know I gotta know everything, Michael, you're facing a serious charge here. The whole story."

"Look, Shell, take my word for it. I'm innocent. This was self-defense, but the story gets more complicated from here. I'll give you everything I can, but please get me the fuck outta here first? What kind of bail are they asking for?"

"More complicated? How much more complicated?" Shelly's eyes narrowed.

"A lot more. It involves a girl and some other shit that happened. There's a lot. Okay?" Michael stood up and walked around the table. "What kind of bail?"

"A girl, of course. There's always a girl." The attorney let out a deep breath and a crooked smile. "Well, they're playing hardball. The best I could get the DA's office to agree to was $750,000. Can you swing that?"

"I'll have to put up my stock portfolio, but yeah, maybe. Just spring me from this shithole. We can straighten the whole thing out later. Okay?" Michael turned and ran his figures through his scraggly hair as he paced the tight room.

"Look, Mike, I'll get you out. But if you want me to help you, you gotta give me the whole story, not just pieces. Okay? Your word? Everything? No surprises and no use in hiding anything." The attorney stared at him. "You can't finesse your way out of this one. The best way is the truth. And, incidentally, if I may, as your friend, I don't mean just to me but to everyone in your life. Especially your wife. She deserves it. The whole truth—nothing but."

"Shell, you got it. You're right. I promise. I'll explain everything. But please, just please, get me outta here."

"I'll do everything I can for you—you know that. But it'll take a little time. Don't talk to anyone—especially cops," said the dapper attorney as he headed out.

Michael spent the rest of that late afternoon in an anxious daze in the corner of the holding cell, accompanied by a variety of petty crooks and a sick junkie who vomited on his feet, soaking his socks and state-issued rubber slides. Michael peeled off his rancid argyles and tossed them. He shivered through the night, sitting upright with the lights on full and the incessant racket of the jailhouse ringing in his ears as he waited for his paperwork to be processed.

By morning he was startled awake from a fitful doze by the duty officer calling his name. "McGowan, let's go. Your bail's posted, we're processing you out."

He walked out into the warm sunshine a little after noon, reeking, sockless, and disheveled. His first thought was Courtney. He called her twice, no answer, then hailed a cab and headed to the apartment.

She was in the bedroom packing a suitcase. She turned to him, tears streaming. "Michael, how could you?"

"Where are you going?"

"I'm taking the baby and going to my parents' house till I sort all this out," she replied.

"Honey, I'm innocent," he pleaded. "It was self-defense—"

She put up her hand to cut him off. "Michael, I don't care what you say. It's all lies. I can't trust you. I can't trust anything you say." She broke down in sobs.

"But, honey—I know you hate me but please, listen to me, please," he said. "Sit down. I've got to tell you everything ... the God's honest truth."

"I don't want to hear your story. I'm done. Just tell me, did you shoot that man? Yes or no." She crossed her arms, and stared, waiting for an answer.

He hesitated.

"You see, you can't just say the simple truth. Can you?" She turned to leave the room.

"I can." He walked over to her. "Baby, it's true ... I shot him ... but it was in self-defense. It was four in the morning, there was no help, they were robbing me. I thought they were going to kill me. I had to." He opened his arms to plead his case.

"Well then why didn't you tell me what happened?" she said, holding back tears. "You lied to me about the whole thing—about the whole night. And kept it all from me like you didn't trust me—just like you lied to me about the Joey thing. You had no trust in me and you treated me like you treat everyone else. You lie and finesse and spin. I can't live with that. Our family can't be a family unless we are honest and trusting. How can we teach our daughter about honesty if we can't be honest with each other?" she shouted as tears flowed down her pink cheeks. "You can't just manage me. I don't want to be managed. I'm your partner. You have to let me in. That's what a marriage is. Don't you get that?"

"Honey, I was trying to save you from—"

"Stop! Just stop it! You're not getting it. I don't want to be saved. I just want to believe in my husband . . . in what he says. I need that. I can handle anything, but I must have that—or we've got nothing." She covered her face with her hands and sobbed.

"Babe, I'm sorry, please, I know I was wrong." He shook his head. "But I just thought I could make it all just go away. I swear, I'll be completely honest with you. I'll tell you everything. Just ask me. Anything. Honey, I want what you want. Hand to God. I only want us to be okay. I can't live unless we're okay."

She wiped away the tears with her palms and crossed her arms across her chest.

"I'm so, so sorry." He reached for her and tried to pull her close.

She pulled back, paused, and stared at him. "But . . . what were you doing in the Bronx so late that night? Were you that drunk? In a fight? Doing drugs? What the fuck were you doing that you had to lie to me about it?"

Michael listened to her. His first thought, as usual, was to lie his way out of it. Tell her he had passed out, fell asleep on the train or in a doorway somewhere. But his own words at Joey's funeral echoed in his head. He couldn't take that route anymore. He dreaded what he knew he had to say, but he was committed to telling the whole truth. To change his life forever against all his deepest instincts—a new path. He took a deep breath as he plunged himself into the raw, cold truth, into a new world.

"I was with a woman," he said without flinching.

"A woman? What? What woman?" she shouted and turned away from him.

"Joey's wife, Larisia. I slept with her that night," he said, eyes down.

"What the fuck?" she screamed. "You slept with his wife that night?" She stormed out of the room.

"No, it's not like that. She wasn't his wife at that time. I met her first," he shouted, following her. "She was a waitress in a bar. I met her first—that night."

"You . . . you what?" she said, incredulous. "You met her first? Are you kidding me? That woman we saw at the funeral? Her?" She spun around and raised her hands in disbelief. "What the fuck am I talking to you about? Do I know you, you fuck, you lying fuck? My dad told me you were no good . . . he told me." She shook her head, stormed back into the bedroom, and started to pack her bags again.

"Honey, please, it was a fling. I love you with all my heart. I was drinking and it just . . . it just happened." He heard his own words as if they were coming from someone else.

"It just happened and you weren't gonna say a thing to

me about it, were you?" She grimaced and jammed more clothes into the bag.

"No, I was. And I've got more to say." He lowered his voice as he turned to the wall and put his hands to his head. The dread of the moment literally shook his body. Everything in him recoiled at his determination to reveal his truths. He turned around.

She stood before him, hands on her hips, eyes red, tears flowing, and leaned toward him. "More? There's more—you fuck!" she shouted in disbelief.

"Her baby . . . that baby is mine . . . from that night. I was going to tell you but then you got—"

She screamed as she grabbed a water glass from the bedtable and threw it at him. It shattered against the wall as she kicked over the bedtable and fell into a sobbing heap on the bed. "Get the fuck out . . . get out now before I kill you, you lying bastard. I'll divorce you, you'll never see your daughter again. Get the fuck out."

"Honey, please—"

"Get the fuck out—now," she screamed.

He sprinted to the closet, grabbed an overnight bag, stuffed it with some clothes still in plastic cleaner bags, and headed out the door, leaving her heaving into the pillows. He could hear her sobs in the hallway as he pressed the down button. Her cries resonated as the doors closed.

Michael hailed a cab and headed uptown to his office on West 47th Street with tears streaming down his face. Getting out on a bustling Broadway he was completely disoriented. His ears were ringing and the city's constant roar registered as a distant echo. His head throbbed. Nothing looked the same to him as he walked into the familiar lobby of his office building. He could barely focus. He swiped his ID card, but the glass barrier remained closed. He did it again. Nothing. Grumbling, he walked over to the security desk.

"I'm sorry, Mr. McGowan. Your entry has been flagged. You need to call upstairs. I can't help you," the guard said.

Michael, inhaled and tried to calm down as he dialed his boss. "Frank, it's Michael, what's going on?"

"Michael, I think it's better if you stay away from the office. You've been fired. We'll clean out your desk and send your things over to your apartment. For now, there's really not much for me to say. You were one of my best, but we can't be associated with what's going on here," Murdock said.

"But Frank, you haven't given me a chance to explain," Michael said, shaking his head in disbelief.

"Mike, don't bother. This has gone right to the top, and everyone upstairs is in agreement. They won't listen to you at this point. You were on the front page of the fucking *Wall Street Journal* for Christ's sake!"

"But I'm innocent," Michael shouted. His voice echoed in the marble lobby and for a brief second the passing crowd of businessmen stopped to look.

"Mike, listen to me, it's over," a stern Frank said. "Sandoval pulled his account. Said he can't be involved . . .

suspects there was something more to Joey's shooting too. He's gone. Too many problems."

"No, no, he doesn't understand," Michael said, holding the phone away from his face and shouting.

"Look, Mike, you ruined our reputation with them. They're gone and the company is livid about it. I don't want to make this any worse, but the guys upstairs are talking to their lawyers about suing you for breach of your employment contract. They're on the warpath. Stay clear. They handed you a plum account and you ruined it. Your stink is all over this deal now. No legitimate source of funding will touch anything that whole Sandoval group is doing—now or ever. They're done in the financial world because of you. Believe me, no one will come near them. You really fucked up. It took us years to build that relationship and now you've not only wrecked our reputation with Mexico, but you've destroyed them too."

"But, Frank, it was self-defense—the shooting. Really. This is outrageous. It wasn't my fault." Mike felt he was in a bad dream. He kept telling the truth but nobody was listening.

"Mike, please, tell it to your lawyer and the judge. I hope it works out for you. I gotta go, sorry." He hung up.

"Frank, Frank—" he shouted into the phone. The guards at the desk, trying not to stare, turned their backs to him as he walked slowly out the door.

Mike walked out to the corner of 47th Street and Broadway on this warm summer afternoon with the whole world rushing by. Nothing seemed to make sense to him. The world seemed to turn upside down. The thought that the truth went nowhere and lies worked better flashed through his mind.

He was sweating in the hot sun and his head was swimming. Unable to focus his eyes, he felt unsteady on his feet and for no reason at all, he slowly walked east, made a left when he hit 5th Avenue, and headed uptown. At 55th Street he found himself in front of the St. Regis just as the after-work crowd was beginning to fill the King Cole bar. He went in, sat down on a corner stool of the clubby bar with its richly colored wall murals, and ordered a martini, very dry. He turned away from the painting of the jolly king and his merry courtesans. It only made him feel worse.

He thought about calling his parents or some friends but didn't know what to say. It was all too incomprehensible. He decided to try Larisia one more time. His call went immediately to voicemail but the sound of her voice stung him and made him want to talk to her even more. It wasn't about her well-being, it was about his pain. He skipped the message, clicked off then instantly regretted it. He wanted to leave her a message asking her to meet him at the St. Regis, but then he had a flash of insight about how outrageous that thought was.

He put his phone on the bar and it began to buzz immediately, a call from Shelly. He was going to ignore it and savor the moment of solitude as the alcohol ebbed into his bloodstream and anonymity prevailed, but, obsessively, he picked up. It also occurred to him at that moment that Shelly was probably the only friend he had left.

"Mike, how ya doing?"

The cool air and the martini dulled his pain. "I'm okay, I guess, other than getting divorced, getting fired, and facing prison time."

"Oh, shit. I hate to hear that, Mike. You don't deserve it," the attorney said.

"Yeah, well, tell that to the aggrieved parties. I'm sitting here in the King Cole bar drowning my sorrows." Michael's voice cracked. "I don't really know what the fuck to do right now, Shell. My whole world is coming apart."

"Well hold on, buddy. I may have some good news, or maybe some light at the end of the tunnel for you."

"Any good news you got I'll take," Michael said.

"Well, this may be a little premature, but from what I can tell those fucking cops might have made a serious mistake by getting your prints and probably DNA from that bottle without an arrest or your permission. We'll have to see how this goes, but I think I have a shot to suppress that evidence based on an illegal search. If that flies, we have a half a chance of knocking out the whole case," the attorney said.

"What the fu—"

"Look, don't get too excited yet, but we may have something here. I thought that that might help you on this shitty day," the attorney said.

"Shell, you son of a bitch, I love you. You're the best lawyer in this whole fucked-up town." Michael stood up and looked skyward like a man in a deep well, first seeing the sunlight. There was a brief moment where he wanted to thank God, but it passed as quickly as it came.

"Hold it, pal. We're not there yet—it's just a shot."

"For now, I'll take it," Michael said.

"And Mike, take my advice, hold off on the booze. Get yourself a room and get some sleep. That's what you need right now. Put all this shit out of your mind," the attorney said. "Let me handle the rest."

"You got it, man. Thanks, Shell. You're the best." They hung up and Michael ordered another martini.

As he drained his second see-through he thought about how the promise of the truth setting you free was just another lie. He'd tried the truth, and this is where it got him. When he went off his instinctive path of spin and obfuscation he was lost and helpless—the way he felt right now. His only lies were to protect others, people he loved. A lie wasn't always a bad thing. He also thought about a third martini but decided to take Shelly's advice, even if a little late.

Michael took a suite on the tenth floor with a small balcony overlooking 55th Street. The city was abuzz as usual. He stepped out onto the balcony and inhaled the thick, warm air of summer as he looked down at the people in the street, the frenetic midtown traffic, and the cacophony of humanity.

He stepped back inside, closed the doors, and surveyed his sumptuous surroundings. It didn't compute. Half-drunk, he struggled to comprehend how badly things had turned out and why. He was sick at the thought of losing his family but at the same time felt lucky to have survived the brutal night of the shooting. It was his first time really thinking about it. He'd always resisted the dark thoughts. Unable to hold off the terror, the images of that night overwhelmed him. The fear that gripped him, the intimate smell of his assassin's breath and the feel of his clammy flesh as they struggled for the gun. The nightmarish bloodbath that unfolded as he fought for his very life. *How did I survive? Where did it all go so wrong? Should I have gone to the police?*

"My moral compass must be way off. I was only trying to do right by everyone. I had to keep it quiet," he said to himself. At that rare moment of introspection, a wave of dizziness overcame him. He realized he hadn't eaten in almost twenty-four hours. He picked up the phone.

"Hello, room service. I'd like to order a ribeye steak, please. Medium rare. A Caesar salad, baked potato with sour cream, creamed spinach, and a good bottle of cabernet. And, ah, a creme brûlée, what the hell. Yes, room 1017. Thanks." He headed into the bathroom to take a hot shower, unconsciously hoping to wash away all the memories and guilt of that fateful night.

Barely out of the shower, he heard a knock on the door.

"Room service, señor," the voice said with a Spanish accent.

Michael threw on the hotel's sumptuous terry cloth robe, opened the door, and watched as the server rolled in a rattling food cart covered in a white tablecloth. "Wow, that was fast," he said.

"Yes, sir. Where would you like me to set it up?"

"Ah, the dining table is fine, facing the window, please. I'll be right back," Michael said as he walked into the bedroom to finish dressing. He closed the door and unpacked a pair of light linen slacks and a fresh white shirt. He slipped on his favorite Gucci loafers, no socks.

Michael stepped out of the bedroom and to his surprise saw the French doors to the balcony wide open and no food on the table. Before he could turn around he felt the first crushing blow to his skull, which drove him to his knees. His head exploded with electrifying pain; all circuits were jammed. Suddenly everything went into slow motion, but he managed to stay conscious and partially upright. Reflexively, from a crouching position, he lunged at his opponent, slamming him into the wall and mirror. The furniture and walls rattled from the force of the body slam. In seconds, Michael was turned around, pushed up against the wall, and took another powerful strike to the side of his head. He saw a flash of light from the blow, which wobbled and disoriented him. He tried to grapple with the stocky killer but his strength began to wane against the stronger man. Quickly, another heavy blow landed on the side of his face. The stunning force of the assault shattered his eye socket and cheekbone and instantly dropped him to the floor. At the edge of consciousness, his arms and legs were paralyzed.

Face down, helpless, he had a vague awareness of

being half-lifted and dragged, limp-limbed, across the room. He felt the cool iron balcony railing against the back of his legs as he was propped up and then pushed over the side of the balcony. He tumbled backward into the darkness, his last earthly sensation the dreamlike feeling of floating weightless through the warm air of a New York summer night.

The police had set up a taped-off perimeter around the street scene of the crushed limo and the dead bodies. Craven curiosity prevailed, as pedestrians had gathered at both ends of the block, craning their necks to get a glimpse of the carnage.

Eddie Johnson stood across the street in the shadows smoking a cigarette, talking to one of the cops at the scene. He kept his identity to himself.

"What the hell happened?" he asked.

"Yeah, a mess, that's what happened," the baby-faced officer said. "Looks like this guy took a swan dive to get away from his troubles. I heard he had just been released today from the Tombs on murder charges. I can see why he might wanna take the easy way out."

"Where'd you hear that?"

"Oh, ya know. Word gets around," the cop said, striving for a tone of law-enforcement nonchalance.

"I guess he did it then. Huh?" Eddie said.

"Sure looks like it," came the reply. "Too bad he killed some unfortunate limo driver in the process."

"Yeah, too bad." Eddie glanced down the street and saw a familiar face. He turned to the cop. "Nice talking to ya," he said as he walked away.

He headed toward Madison and stepped into a shadowed doorway stacked with oil-stained cardboard boxes and pungent trash cans. A stocky man in a light jacket came up to him and handed him an envelope. In dim light Eddie thumbed through the envelope of cash, nodded, then stuffed it in his back pocket. He pulled his shirt down to cover the thick packet and the bulky Glock-19 in his waistband. Sparks flew when he flicked his butt to the curb, pulled up his collar and, with hunched shoulders, vanished into the black night.

21

THE LAST STRAW

Krasnowsky arrived at room 1017 in the St. Regis the next day with a bad feeling and a worse attitude. Eddie was just finishing up a conversation with the Manhattan Homicide detectives, who nodded to Phil as they left. He smiled and looked around.

"Another one of our suspects ends up dead. What the fuck is going on? Somebody's clocking us?" Krasnowsky said, shaking his head. "So, what's their take?"

"Simple. No signs of forced entry. He was alone, depressed. Looks like he decided to take a dive. Case closed. He saved the city a lot of time and money," Eddie said.

"That's it? He jumped?" Krasnowsky asked. "Any note?"

"No, but it's obvious, isn't it? He figured he'd save himself from being someone's bitch for the next twenty years in the joint. I'd probably do the same," Eddie replied, with a cold indifference.

Krasnowsky stared at him then wandered into the bedroom. He looked at the empty dry-cleaner bags strewn across the bed. Glancing around the bathroom, he picked up the damp towels on the floor.

He walked back out and surveyed the sumptuous the living room. "Fancy place. You wouldn't think they'd leave this cracked mirror hanging up like this. They shouldn't. Not for the kind of money they charge."

Eddie shrugged.

"What's the cart full of food doing here?" Krasnowsky picked up the unopened bottle of cabernet.

"Oh, the room-service guy brought it. Said he delivered it and knocked but there was no answer, so he opened the door and brought it in. That's when he saw the window open and heard the commotion down on the street and called the front desk."

Krasnowsky walked around in silence for a while then turned to Eddie. "What about these black marks across the floor? What the hell is that about?"

"I don't know—didn't notice them. Maybe he was moving furniture around," Eddie said.

"Moving furniture? Really?" Krasnowsky asked. "Does this whole thing seem right to you?"

"Yeah, what's wrong with it? We had him dead to rights, and he knew it. A shit show. I can see it. Got half-drunk, according to the bartender downstairs, and figured, what's the point of going on?"

"Yeah, I got that. But I mean . . . this whole scene. I just didn't peg this guy for a jumper," Krasnowsky said. "And why would he take a shower, change into fresh clothes, order a meal—a good one at that—never touch it and then just decide to leap out the window? Just like that. No note or anything. Doesn't make sense."

"Makes sense to me," said Eddie.

Krasnowsky rubbed his stubbly chin and paused. He stared at Eddie again, holding off his impatience and suspicion. "Ya know, after thirty years of this shit, I still can't figure people out. No way of telling what they're really thinking or what they're gonna do, or why. They can lie right to your face, and you don't know. Sometimes you can tell, you almost learn to smell it in this business, but not always. Some people, ya just can't figure."

"Yeah, you never know," Eddie said, avoiding Phil's withering stare.

"I don't like what I see," Krasnowsky said. "Call Forensics and have them go over this room for blood and have them check out those marks on the floor. See if they match his shoes. And ask the clerk at the desk if anybody complained about disturbing noises last night, like in a struggle. Also find out the exact time this guy called for room service and the time the server made that food delivery. We gotta know that time frame. It had to have happened then."

"This is Manhattan's case. Why are we getting involved?" Eddie asked.

"Because this was our suspect. We arrested him. And somebody killed him. That's why."

"Killed him?" Eddie asked. "I thought he jumped."

"Just do it, okay?" barked Krasnowsky as he walked out in disgust.

"Okay, but they're not gonna like us butting in."

Days later, in Queens, the McGowan family held a quiet and private ceremony at their home to say goodbye to Michael. The shame surrounding his death nearly killed them. Michael's mother couldn't bear it and needed medication to get through the day. The MacAllisters were invited, but did not attend; neither did a thoroughly distraught Courtney. The McGowan family remained unaware they had another family member and had no contact with Larisia.

The following week, Krasnowsky was sitting in his office thinking about what Mary had said about staying too long at the party, when he got a call from Tom Fenton in Forensics.

"Phil, it looks like you were right about that hotel room," Fenton said.

"Oh, really. How right was I?"

"Well, looks like there was a struggle. We used the

black light and found blood splatter on the doorway by the bedroom, blood on the rug, and interestingly, blood on the iron railing on the balcony. Looks like somebody tried to wipe it all away, too," said the lab tech.

"Ah, I knew it," Krasnowsky said. "Anything else?"

"Yeah, those scuff marks across the floor were a match to the heels of his shoes," said Fenton.

"Hmm. So are you saying, unless he was doing a fucking moonwalk to the balcony before taking a dive, it looks like he was dragged?"

The straightlaced scientist suppressed a laugh. "Well, I'm not saying that, detective. That's your job. But yes, the marks are consistent with being dragged."

"I knew it. Send me the report, okay?" Krasnowsky said as he hung up.

"Hey, Phil, I'm sorry to hear about your loss. How ya doing?" a rotund Captain Shanahan asked as Krasnowsky walked into his office.

"I'm dealing with it, but it's rough," Krasnowsky said grimly.

"Well, please accept my condolences. I know you were married a long time, Phil," said the captain, getting up and putting his hand on Phil's shoulder for a moment. "Did you ever get that woman suspect you were looking for?"

"Well, no," Krasnowsky replied, sitting down in a chair across the desk from Shanahan. "She's gone so far. Traveling with a baby, so we'll catch up with her. We'll get her."

"Yeah, talk to the Port Authority police. They'll cover the bus station. That's the most likely place she'll go," Shanahan said.

"That's already covered. But, Captain, I got bigger problems: somebody's clocking my investigations. They know what I'm doing. All my witnesses are getting murdered or disappearing. She's gone and may be dead already. And this guy, McGowan, who was involved in that cab shooting, looks like he was tossed off the balcony of that hotel."

"I thought that was a suicide."

"No, I just got a call from Forensics, there are clear signs of a struggle. Looks like he was dragged to the balcony and thrown over the railing."

"Are you sure? What are the guys from Manhattan saying?"

"They're taking the easy way out, calling it suicide. They don't want to look any further—what's with them?" Krasnowsky said.

Shanahan grimaced and stood up. "Phil, let me explain something to you. Everybody's getting pressured to keep the numbers down. Headquarters is doing the same to us here. I get it, they don't need to have an open investigation that's going nowhere. If it looks like a suicide, good, leave it there."

"Bill ... what?" Krasnowsky stood up. "That's not the way we do things. This guy was murdered. They overpowered him and tossed him over. Homicide, plain and simple."

"Phil, I'm telling you to leave it alone. It's not even in our jurisdiction. It's on them."

Krasnowsky walked around the office shaking his head. "This was my case. This guy committed a felony in our backyard and you're accepting this bullshit? We can't do that. Is this what we've come to?"

"Phil, you're doing your job. You did it. Your case is closed. He's dead. Move on, work on locking up criminals that are still walking around," Shanahan said. "It's over."

"Yeah, well, it's not over. The perp that killed my guy is still walking around. That's my point. Somebody is tracking all this shit, I'm telling you. My guess is it's all drug-gang related. McGowan killed one of their guys in a mugging, so he was marked. That's it. They're settling a score and sending a message to anyone who fucks with them. No mercy. They track down everyone." Krasnowsky leaned on the captain's desk, knuckles down. "This is why we're here. It's our problem, we don't walk away from this kind of shit."

"Okay, okay," said Shanahan reluctantly. "Maybe you're right, but so what at this point?" asked Shanahan.

"So what? This is everything. This is what we do," Krasnowsky implored his friend of so many years, so many battles.

Shanahan stopped for a moment and looked down. He realized the truth of his duty, to the citizens, to himself. He looked up, nodding toward Krasnowsky.

"Fine, Phil. You're right. We can't accept that. The politics of this department is killing me. Got any idea who's tipping them?"

"Ah, I don't know for sure, but I have my suspicions," said a cagey Krasnowsky.

"Don't hand me that shit. Who?" Shanahan stood up.

"I think it's Eddie Johnson. He's the only guy that's been part of all this stuff all along. He knows everything," Krasnowsky said.

"Eddie? Your guy? Got any proof?" Shanahan asked.

"No, nothing solid. Wish I did. But I smell it, Bill. It all points to him," Krasnowsky said. "Gronk tried to get me a message about Eddie before he died. Probably had a hot tip for me but I never got to talk to him and no one in Internal Affairs is willing to tell me anything."

"Yeah, they're like that," Shanahan said. "Ya know, Eddie's brother was a firefighter. He died a hero in 9/11. I can't go after a guy like that without something solid. They'll crucify me. Call me when you have something solid. Okay? Right now, there's a lot of political pressure from City Hall to put minorities in management positions. It's all about diversity."

"All that's fine, Bill, but it's nothing but politics now. It's not the way it used to be."

"I know Phil, but it's the world we live in," Shanahan said. "Look, you put in your years. You can bail from this job right now with the full package. I've still got fourteen months to go. I'm just trying to keep my head down and do the job. Don't make life more difficult for me. Okay?"

"This shit is getting to me," Krasnowsky said. "I don't know if I can put it behind me."

"Oh, and one last thing while we're on this stuff, I wanna let you know I saved your ass with the Manhattan DA. They said you collected evidence improperly before you arrested McGowan—wanted to throw out the whole case. His lawyer was making a big deal out of it—especially now that he's dead. I shut them down. Told them you had probable cause, but I'm not so sure that lawyer is going away. It's another reason to leave that case alone. Get away from it as soon as possible."

"What the fuck? These fucking crooked lawyers. Always trying to beat the system. We don't stand a chance," Krasnowsky said. "I'm getting nowhere here."

"Don't do that, Phil. You're one of my best . . . but you can't catch 'em all and you can't save 'em all. Ya gotta drop it. Take a couple of days off."

"All I'm trying to do is get to the truth, make the bad guys pay. That's what we do here. Isn't it?" Phil said. "It's why I get up every morning and deal with all this shit. But I'm not sure that matters much anymore."

"It does. As long as I'm in this job, it does. But it's not as simple as that—not these days," Shanahan said to Krasnowsky as the burly detective walked out the door shaking his head in disgust.

Phil stood on the front stoop of the house he had shared for four decades with the only woman he had ever loved. With not much thought or regret, he dialed a local realtor and listed the house for sale. They said it would sell immediately. Vague images of North Carolina and low-country fishing floated in his head.

In the fading sun of the late summer afternoon, his footsteps echoed in the silence as he went to the back porch and sat down on the wooden steps. He remembered the day he taught Anna to ride her bike back there. He surveyed the overgrown backyard and the sagging laundry lines that stretched between a matching pair of now off-kilter posts that he had installed years ago. He remembered Gladys laughing at his amateurish attempts at home improvement. *They weren't pretty*, he thought, admiring his work. *But they did the job and, shit, they're still here.*

Sitting there in the afternoon heat, he looked down and discovered her secret hiding place beneath the stairs. He reached down and took out the hidden box of Marl-boros and a pack of matches sealed in a plastic bag. He stared at the familiar red-and-white box for a moment, then opened it and placed a cigarette in the corner of his mouth and struck a match. It was the first cigarette he had touched in thirty years. He inhaled deeply and thought about Gladys and all he had lost.

Within a few days, he called Shanahan to tell him he was taking his advice. It was over for him. Time to hang it up. He made a point of turning in his gun and gold shield to his friend, the captain. No one else. Shanahan shook Phil's thick hand at the end of a brief ceremony and embraced him in silence, then each stood back and saluted. Neither man allowed the emotion of the moment to show.

The following month, Eddie Johnson was promoted to Chief of Detectives of Bronx Homicide.

About the same time, the McAllisters held a luncheon at a waterside restaurant in Greenwich for the christening of their granddaughter. She was named Eloise Lucy McAllister in honor of her maternal grandmother. A half-dozen family members celebrated with the grandparents, Courtney, and the baby. Champagne, lobster, and fresh oysters were the order of the day.

John McAllister gave a champagne toast and a short speech honoring his brave daughter and their newest family member. There was no mention of Michael. The luncheon was quiet; a somber mood hung over everyone. Courtney soldiered on, but her eyes filled with tears as her dad spoke of the road ahead.

He ended his speech with the words, "No matter what challenges you face, my sweet, sweet daughter, we'll always be here for you and our beautiful Eloise." Everyone clinked crystal glasses and repeated, "We're all here for you, Court." She hugged the sleeping child as tears rolled down her face. Later they all took the short drive back to the family home and had drinks in the sun-drenched garden.

The entire afternoon Courtney could barely contain her emotions. She later went to her room and cried herself to sleep, leaving the child in the care of the new Mexican nanny they had just hired.

The McGowans, despondent and broken, never saw their grandchildren again.

The End

EPILOGUE

Word of Larissia's return to Mexico had traveled in her little town of Huatulco. Like in so many small communities, she was sometimes the subject of biting gossip. People speculated about the father of her children, why she was back from America, and the whereabouts of a husband. She and her mother ignored the petty sniping of the locals and stayed close together. Their only concern was that her return did not draw the attention of poppy farmers who illegally processed raw opium which they sold to the cartel. They were always suspicious of newcomers.

Several months after her arrival, her heart dropped in her chest when, during a walk through town, she saw the headline in a months-old copy of the *New York Post*.

Murder Suspect Commits Suicide in Midtown

She knew immediately it was not a suicide. Michael had been killed. By the same people who killed Joey, she had no doubt. All of this stemmed from the death of Carlos, at her hand. She was terrified by the thought that they might still be looking for her too.

It all came back to her in a nauseating wave that made her dizzy in the hot sun. She had to steady herself against the side of a building. The fear and rush of adrenaline reminded her of the world she had escaped. The one she had put behind her, here, in her new life. But now it was clear: She had to redouble her efforts to keep a low profile, be vigilant, and protect her family, somehow, some way. She needed help. She knew there was no way she could do it alone.

After that, she tried to put it all out of her mind again and put on a happy face for her family. They needed that; they deserved that, she thought, and they were certainly overjoyed to be reunited. Larisia's mother was thrilled with little Angelina. She doted over the infant who looked just like her mother. Carmelita, now eight, though upset at not being with her father, loved having her mother and now a little sister in her life. She relished her new role as big sister and often took on the task of feeding the baby and changing her diapers.

The family was deeply Catholic, so on a hot day only a few months after coming to Mexico, Larisia brought little Angelina to the Chapel de Santa Cruz to be christened. There in the airless baptismal, the elderly priest in a white tunic and flowing vestments poured water over the forehead of the squirming infant, who began to wail. Larisia, her mother, and several family members smiled over the child as the intimate ceremony proceeded. The baby was now brought into the community of church as a newly washed soul. Her original sin had been expunged; she was no longer tainted in the eyes of God and the church.

"By the mystery of your death and resurrection, bathe this child in light, give her the new life of baptism and welcome her into your Holy Church," said the priest.

"Oh, Lord, hear our prayer," was the response.

The enveloping veil of incense and the rapturous incantations wove a spell of tranquility and joy for the family, but in Larisia's mind the tragedy of Michael's death and the sorrow she felt for Angelina, who would never know her father, overwhelmed her with tears. *Why is God so cruel*? Why had God condemned her to a life with no one to love and protect her and her children?

She also thought about the sad irony that had befallen her life. *Had Michael not met me he'd be alive today, but then again I'd have no Angelina.* Tears rolled down her face as she prayed to God to help her understand. *Is my joy worth his life?*

She cried too for Joey, her true love. In him she had found the love she had searched for throughout her life. She sighed for her losses, and the losses for her children. Silently she prayed for absolution for her part in the death of Carmelita's father, and she prayed for her own redemption and forgiveness for her acts.

Carmelita, I had no choice, she inaudibly implored her daughter who stood next to her, eyes closed, hands folded in prayer. *I would have died. I did it for you. I had to protect your future.*

Her tears flowed down onto the infant she held in her arms as the priest dipped his thumb into the holy oil and traced the sign of the cross onto the child's pink forehead.

"Keep her and her family always in your love and light," the priest prayed aloud.

"Oh, Lord, hear our prayer," everyone replied.

Silently Larisia prayed for her children and pleaded for atonement from a God she felt she had abandoned, or perhaps, who had abandoned her.

"I baptize you in the Name of the Father, and of the Son, and of the Holy Spirit." Then with a smile he blessed the child and the family with a broad wave of his hand and the sign of the cross. "By water and the Holy Spirit, she is to receive the gift of a new life from God. Welcome to the new light of our loving church. Amen."

The family all smiled in return. "Amen," they said in unison.

"Thank you, Father," Larisia's mother said as they all filed out and down the steps of the old chapel, into the warm afternoon sunshine. Larisia held the child gently as the infant smiled faintly, closed her eyes in the brightness, and began to doze.

The family crossed the plaza toward a small cafe to celebrate the happy event. Everyone lifted by the joyous spirit of the ceremony was just settling into their chairs when a black limousine pulled up and a tall, handsome man stepped out and greeted Larisia.

"Buenos días, señorita," he said with a broad smile and white teeth.

"Buenos días, señor," replied an excited Larisia, who then turned to her mother. "Mom, I want you to meet my new, ah, friend—the man I was telling you about. His name is Miguel Sandoval."

Her mother smiled broadly.

"So nice to meet you, señora," said Sandoval. "I'm sorry to be interrupting this lovely family gathering but I have a surprise for you, Larisia. Can I please ask you to join me to see something special? It will take you away from your family celebration but for no more than an hour or so—I promise. I hope that will be okay."

Larisia excitedly turned to her mother. "Would you mind, Mama?" she asked, smiling now at her new friend.

"Ah, we'll be fine. The baby is already asleep in Carmelita's arms. We'll have a light lunch and meet you back at the house. Go and enjoy," said her smiling mother.

"Ah, thank you. See you at the house." Larisia grabbed Sandoval's hand and they headed off to the waiting car. He opened the door for her and they traveled to a clearing just ten minutes away where a helicopter waited.

"I hope you are not afraid of flying in one of these things," he said as he held her hand and helped her up into the aircraft.

"Not at all."

They flew for twenty-five minutes to a ridge just south of Cancún that overlooked the Caribbean Sea and a sprawling construction site that spread out for miles before them. The chopper landed in an open spot. They got out and walked over to the edge of the ridge. The blue sea glistened in the distance and reflected a blazing sun.

Sandoval swept his hand out in a grand gesture. "This is what I've been working to build for several years and now, finally, it is coming to life. It will change the world's view of Mexico. I hope it will be the springboard to my leadership. What do you think?"

"It's amazing."

Larisia shaded her eyes and looked out at the massive scene. She was stunned at the scope of the work that was taking shape. Sandoval held her hand gently.

"I'm so proud of what we're doing here. We're creating thousands of well-paying jobs for the people, and our economy will no doubt get a huge benefit too. I'm hoping this will bring Mexico to the forefront of the world stage. And I want to be the man who brings us into this new modern world. I want to leave the third world behind and become the center of a new first-world business economy. And the new Mexico is in the perfect place, geographically as well as economically, to bridge the gap between North and South America. We'll be a new world leader, and I want to take us there." His dazzling smile won her completely. "Oh, I wanted you to be the first to know, my divorce was finalized last week. We can officially date."

Larisia startled by the news, tried to calm herself. "Oh my God. That's great news for you." She hesitated. "For us . . . but you know with my new baby and in my new life, thanks to you, I need to go slow."

The gentlemanly Sandoval smiled, still holding her hand. "Señorita, I understand completely. There is no pressure. I only wanted you to know so you would be comfortable with me in public. I can assure you my intentions are only to respect you, your family, and your life."

She smiled and squeezed his hand as a black car drove up. Two burly men in suits got out and looked around, then the back door opened and Jorge Lederer, head of the Sinaloa Cartel, stepped out. He smiled and stepped forward to greet Sandoval and Larisia. The two men shook hands and Lederer courteously bowed to Larisia and offered his hand. She shook his hand with a smile. She didn't know who he was, but she found him charming yet gruff and somehow disturbing.

After brief introductions, Sandoval asked her if he might have a private conversation with his business associate. She nodded and the two men stepped away to survey the scene, with Sandoval's hand on Lederer's shoulder. She quietly stepped back, feeling slightly uncomfortable as she stood alone in the bright sunshine.

Larisia's mind lurched between the excitement of the moment and apprehension for the future. Was this man her future, her safety, or was she deluding herself, letting her heart get carried away, again? Was Sandoval real? Was he sincere? Certainly, she was dazzled by him and his world. What she had seen in the short time they had known each other was a universe she had never dreamed of; it overwhelmed her, enticed her, and frightened her all at once. The vision of what lay before her now also struck a deep note of anxiety in her, especially after all she had been through. But the draw of it all, the magic, the status, the money was nearly irresistible.

The two men walked toward the edge and surveyed a scene that looked like a small city being built all at once. Three thirty-story buildings were already completed along with numerous smaller buildings; some commercial, some residential apartments and condos, a massive retail shopping mall with some stores seemingly set to open. The whole complex was connected by covered and landscaped walkways to huge parking lots. Sleek electric golf carts and moving sidewalks would carry crowds to the sprawling, multi-level casino with a half-dozen oversized swimming pools complete with rock formations and towering waterfalls, all interwoven by a manmade river that snaked throughout the massive property. Farther on the distant horizon, the semicircular foundation of a soccer stadium surrounded by vast parking lots was taking shape. New roads were being cut through the thick jungle vegetation, connecting to a new eight-lane highway that featured a new engineering marvel and a first in Mexico: a raised monorail system with gleaming stainless steel railcars, all to accommodate the anticipated crowds.

"Señor, your investment here will bring more benefits to the people of Mexico than any business investment in the history of our country. Thank you for the help you have given to our people and to me. Your return will be enormous, no doubt, but your participation as we have agreed will remain confidential," Sandoval said. "And there's more to come, as you know."

"Anything I can do for my country, my friend, I will do," Lederer responded. "Also, anything I can do to help your upcoming campaign for president, it would be my pleasure." He paused for a moment, then leaned in. "I know you were reluctant to come to us with this opportunity but you have my word, sir, we are completely hands off. We will not be involved. We only want to help you and our country."

"Thank you, amigo. That's very important. After what happened in New York, frankly, you know I didn't have much choice. The money had dried up," said Sandoval, looking down. "But now I think maybe that was a blessing. This project is about Mexico, and everything involved has to come from Mexico. We do not need America to control us. We want to control our own fate. And in this imperfect world sometimes the best we can do is take the opportunity that supports that goal. This project is for our people. Mexico for Mexicans," Sandoval said with his fist raised above his head.

"Viva Mexico," came the reply.

The two men embraced and said their goodbyes. Lederer nodded to Larisia as he got into his car and drove off, trailing dust in his wake.

Sandoval came back to her, smiling, and she smiled back. "It's fantastic what you are doing. The people of

Mexico should know what a great leader you are and will be," she said.

"Thank you. I only want the best for my country," he said.

"Who was that man?" she asked.

"Oh, he is one of our main investors. He's a patriot too," he said as took her hand, touched her chestnut hair, and smiled at her in the warm sunshine. "You are a beautiful woman—inside and out."

She smiled back and gently kissed him on the cheek. "And you are beautiful too," she replied.

After a moment, he said, "Let's go back now to your family and celebrate." He guided her toward the chopper.

Larisia's emotions swirled as the prop blades began to spin with a massive roar. They formed a vortex of dust and sand as the vibrating aircraft lifted her off to what she cautiously hoped would be a new life, a new beginning.

ACKNOWLEDGMENTS

Thanks to my wife, Michelle, whose perspective and encouragement quietly guided this book's path.

Thanks as well to my editor, Stacey Donovan for her sage input and to Victoria Ross and Marc Greenwald for their design and layout.

ABOUT THE AUTHOR

Arthur Weigold is a New York City native whose lifelong connection to the Big Town inspires his writing. His work blends sharp observation with a deep appreciation for the city's contrasts, character, and complexity. *In the Cold Shadow* is his second novel. He splits his time between New York and Connecticut with his wife, Michelle, and their beloved dogs, Beatrice, Daisy, and Molly.

www.ingramcontent.com/pod-product-compliance
Lightning Source LLC
Chambersburg PA
CBHW070624260626
47161CB00007B/2576